GW00374590

This book is a work of fiction.

Special thanks to Ben Robertson who designed the cover.

Thanks to my family.

Published by Hamster Wheel.

This book wasn't written for any particular reason, perhaps just a way of keeping sane over a troubling year, but I hope it makes you smile, laugh, cry.

Stay positive and enjoy life.

Immersed

By James Loman

Chapter 1

Alive

There aren't many things I hoped for in life. Money wasn't one, nor was the latest fashion or technology. Social media disinterested me, driven by popularity and the feeling of self-importance. I can safely say I was never a westernised person. But what kept me going, throughout times of pain and anguish were the visions of freedom, somewhere I could be at peace, losing the spoilt, selfish nature of western society. The hubbub of a Monday-Friday job seemed pointless to me, a routine shaped like a ball that keeps on rolling.

So here we were, home. Laid up on a southern beach of the Thai island, Koh Kood. In this world you don't rise to the sound of an alarm but the sound of monkeys howling in the tree canopies above. The cries and joys of nature. The beach of Ban Ao Jak is one of the worlds rare natural beauties, a Robert Stevenson re-creation. Trees bent towards the sea from the forest verge, coconut and mango trees. Their leaves spanning wider than we can reach and their fruits growing larger than you can ever imagine. It was six-fifteen in the morning, so the sun was still rising behind the deep forest, giving a dappled effect through the trees and onto the sand below. Beautiful. The sand was slightly damp underfoot from the waves that had rolled over it during the night, leaving it crisp and cool, crunching when you moved and creating imprints like art strewn across the beach. There was one set of faint prints now, straight across the beach from the mouth of a narrow path through the forest towards a fisherman barge laid further down the beach. They broke into the day, stretching over the shadows of forest canopies a few feet from the shore. The sea was also soaked in sunlight, giving off a blinding glisten that seemed almost magical and completing what was a very picturesque scene. The barge was a bright white boat, clean as a whistle and basking in the sunlight seeping through holes in the forest foliage. It had one thick blue ring around the base, a recreation of the deep-sea blue It would be floating in within a few hours. The blue ring was home to the boats name, painted in that fancy writing that you see everywhere but never know how to do – *Jasper*. The sea was peaceful, and the waves didn't crash, they rolled. Colliding with the sandy beach fluidly and calmly. This is what people called paradise. It was only then that I notice the second path of prints in the white sand, from the boat down toward the sea. There was a singular figure breaking the waters solidarity across the horizon, waist height in the water no more than twenty metres from the shore. Hands in the air as they looked up to the sky, it wasn't a religious gesture by any means, more a sense of accomplishment. You could feel their aura across the beach, a free spirit. As the sea water spat at their face, they began to sing. A beautiful voice albeit more of a murmur, turning the atmosphere into something sacred. It reminded me of our time together back home, we'd drive my rustic VW Polo up to the heart of Scotland and camp on the shores of the great Lochs. We'd sing and dance, embracing the connection with nature. We tried to find the areas with no phone signal and considered anything less a failure, for the power of our relationship was so strong and we needed little else. I'd play the guitar whilst my friend would sing smoothly and respectfully as if trying not to wake the wildlife. A fire would be ablaze, sizzling and popping in tune to the song as the wood burned to ash. This moment on the beach and those fond memories both resembled the tranquillity I lusted for many years, far from the buzzing atmosphere of Mayfair, its big red buses were now thousands of miles away – oh boy, how far we'd come. The figure dimmed their singing until it was inaudible over the rolling of the waves. Then they began to laugh, a contagious chuckle I hadn't heard in years but recognised instantly. A laugh of liberation.

This was my best friend, a soul that has found peace. Civilization never suited them, they were trapped unsure of their place in the system. I felt a sense of pride in myself, this person was free, the caged spirit and suicidal temptations dispelled, the rollercoaster of life finished, or at least now it would be enjoyed – as they had rediscovered themselves. We didn't belong in an immersion of social media, politics and crime. This was where we belonged, we were home. Together.

*

Time passed by quickly as I continued to be immersed by the picture in front of me. As I cleansed my lungs with a deep inhalation of sea air, I closed my eyes, letting the darkness take me and drifted off to my friend's chuckle filling my world, as it always did.

I heard their voice as I was falling back. "We did it Jasper, we fucking did it."

Chapter 2

Stuck

2 years earlier

As I waited for the lift outside my apartment, I felt an all too familiar wave of deja-vu. Of course I did, the arms of my watch signalled the same time each and every morning, with the exception of Saturdays and Sundays. No wonder the latter was known as the Lord's day. A man that performed miracles hundreds of years ago. Sure, why not name a day after him, the Christian family along the corridor swore by him but I guess that's just freedom of speech for you. I never liked the family; the kids were rude and the parents arrogant, pretty sure the bible doesn't specify that as a way of life. How hypocritical. *The omnipresent being looking down on me hasn't helped me in the past twenty-two years, why should I believe in such a farce?*

The fucking lift finally arrived, and so did hell for the next three minutes. Sandy from two floors above was waiting in the lift, also heading towards her nine to five routine. The woman talked for England, usually about herself. Some days she'd make a snide remark about how young I was, or perhaps delve deeper into my life - how uninspiring I had become and how she was so different at her age? *Fuck off love.*

As I stepped into the lift, with my bogus smile and pleasant greeting, the wind seeped through the gap between the lift and the corridor, brushing my hair across my face and into my eyes. I was grateful, a second of respite from the sadistic, boring face of my fifty plus year old neighbour. I was adamant the gap between the lift and corridor was getting bigger, but I didn't mind it. I thought of it as a reminder I had to leave the apartment before I fell through, maybe I'd just fall through as soon as it got big enough. *I could bring Sandy with me, fuck it.* Sandy began bickering about how I needed a haircut, taking note of it across my face as the wind hit it. I smiled admitting she was true and suggesting her putting the clippers to it all so I could look like her. Sandy had just been through chemotherapy for bowel cancer, she was a strong woman and whilst I hated her, I almost admired her. Of course, this was met with a face screwed up and distorted, to which a barrage of screams and tears flooded her face and the lift. *Keep crying dear and if we're lucky we'll both drown in this pathetic lift.*

*

Sometimes I jumped on the train to work but this particular day I preceded to retrace my exact steps from the day before. Out the lift, left down the street, right towards the supermarket, pick up lunch, back the way I came, past the local pub. Glass of red wine for four quid in London isn't bad at all. Perhaps that's the only thing that kept me sane, god bless the Royal Oak. Or perhaps it wasn't, I have no idea. I followed the pavement for a further five minutes, passing the same Big Issue freak handing out the equally uninspiring magazine that I had passed for the previous year and a half. I stepped a couple of strides away from him, as the stream of people in front also did, almost like a show of the hierarchy of society nowadays, what the fuck is the world? As I began up the steps of Mayfair Journalism and strolled through the revolving door, I couldn't help but reflect the nature of the door to the spherical world we live in. Rise, work, sleep, repeat. Everything goes around in circles, the same routine day in day out. I'd gone through education, found myself a job, but for what? Where is the living in this way of life, people travel through eighty years without going beyond the supermarket twenty miles down the road, and here I was, doing the same - stuck.

*

I stepped into the reception area. It was brightly lit by two metal dish-shaped lights suspended halfway between the high ceiling and the posh tiled floor. I was greeted by the familiar faced receptionist, Claire. Friends since the age of fifteen we had joined Mayfair within a month of each other and were both considered newbies at the same time. Whilst I was a journalist, the staff were sincere and accommodated Claire into the family like myself. She was around five foot six, and summoned the shape of an Oompa Loompa, that made me laugh. It made her laugh, she was always chirpy, a smile constantly drawn across her face. Whilst I couldn't bear most people with their pretentious smiles and conversations that made me want to die, I liked Claire and so I went over to greet her. I spent the next twenty minutes of an eight hour shift talking about Sandy and the unpleasant aura she always addressed me with, I told her about my dark humour. I made it out as humour and twisted the story in my favour slightly, but it wasn't humour. I kept that to myself. Whilst Claire laughed it was clear she was also debating a path of conversation. I had seen that look around eighteen months before in my parents. I used to amble around moaning and fighting the hands of employment, desperate not to be caged by a manager or more experienced, better person.

In the end Claire did speak up. "You need to be more positive about life."

I shrugged. "What the hell is there to be positive about?"

She considered this, pondering on the words trying to escape her mouth, choosing to finally speak just before the silence got awkward. "You're still here, and though sometimes you may wish you weren't, there are many people that want you to stay here. I want you to stay here, you're one of my best friends."

I was never an emotional person in front of anyone and felt no desire to change here, so just shrugged it off.

So, she continued. "Your pessimistic nature isn't doing you a world of good you know, you've had a rough time, but the only thing anyone would want is you to get off your arse and get back living. This world is too great to miss." As she tailed off, the final sentence lingered in the reception. It was quiet so no-one noticed my moment of silence and consideration, apart from Claire. I knew she wasn't talking about the world of Mayfair Journalism, nor was she talking about the apartment block I lived at, she was dreaming big, not for her, but for me. But what? I nodded slowly, the minimal show of acceptance I could offer her, she was grateful nevertheless.

I span on my heels, making a squeaking sound against the polished black and white tiles to begin my illusive work on the latest news stories. 'You could do with getting off your fat arse,' I called back and began to climb the arching stairwell. She smiled, I could tell.

*

The day dragged. Terrorism, poverty, and crime covered the headlines of the latest newsreels. Again. *What a shit world we live in.* It had reached lunchtime, well more like eleven-thirty, but I sat down at my desk nevertheless with the meal deal I brought in the morning, mother nature shitting it down outside. The floor-to-ceiling windows helping to display my mood like a TV screen in 4K. *Fuck this.* The day continued to drag following lunch, and it's safe to say the tuna and sweetcorn sandwich was the highlight of it as I packed up my bag, half an hour before five. My bastard boss stood in the doorway as I rose from my chair without noticing him. He coughed to announce his presence and I looked up uninterestedly, the arrogance was like a fire in him. He beckoned me to sit in a way I can only consider Hitler acted towards the Jews. We know how that ended for them. I sat nevertheless, the doors locked and gas starting to seep slowly through the vents in the ceiling. Zyklon-B rained down on me in slow motion. Or not.

He was a wiry man, top-knot and thick Tom Ford glasses. Nice glasses to be fair, only nice thing about him. I didn't know his age, but I can only imagine mid-fifties, a wife and two kids, the usual. A tinted Aston Martin and a house with a pool, cinema, and tennis court. *Yeah, a pool in England, he's as stupid as he looks.* He was wearing one of those pathetic earpieces that connect to your phone in his left ear, singular strands of hair had resisted the grasp of the hairband and sat loosely over his forehead and down towards his ears. It was a mousey brown but signs of silver where beginning to appear and this continued in his fifties tache. I noticed he often stroked his moustache, perfecting the curl at either side by his cheeks, I bet that saw a lot of oil. The navy-blue waistcoat and trousers completed the out-dated look of a prime-minister slash scientist, somehow reiterating his arrogance and self-love. I smiled and asked what I could do for him. He suggested going for a drink one day which I politely declined. He continued to bicker though I didn't pose much interest, instead pretending as best I could to show I was listening. Something about the wife and something about a desire to get away? He then began to brag about his long, gratifying career - which he often did. Thirty-six successful years as a top journalist. *Well Sir, aren't you the fucking man.*

Once he had stopped gloating I dared to ask a question I had been considering for weeks. "Are you content with life?"

He was startled for I often did not input much to these conversations, he spluttered and splurred a bit before answering, arms outstretched as a symbol of power. "I have all the money I need."

I nodded satisfied and begun to leave the office, pulling back the thick wooden door, he called to me. "And you?"

I stopped as if to ponder my response, not that I needed too. "Nope." I replied swiftly and assured. "Money doesn't buy happiness, love or success, nor does It let you appreciate that around you. You're a perfect example." I could feel his eyes clutching onto my back as I began to walk away. *He's just as fucked off with life as I am*, I thought as I raced down the stairwell and out into the toilet of mother nature.

*

Pulling back the duvet, felt harder the longer the days became, it was ten forty-three at night, which was abnormally late, must have been the bottle of red wine. As I crawled in, I felt relieved. It was the only place I truly felt it was just me. No phone, no one contacting me over new work, old pathetic reunions or the foreign man calling about the accident I had been in earlier today, little to my knowledge of course. The wind outside was howling through the window, the storm continued to prevail and would do so throughout the night. I left the window slightly ajar to give myself a slight breeze, combatting the thick duvet I had covering me, dressing me up as if I was wearing a Burqa. I closed my eyes, preparing to doze off all alone. Except I wasn't. There was a map under the bed, a memoir of an old friend, my best friend. As I began to fade into a life I would much rather in my sleep I was blissfully unaware of the timer I had set off in my life, for within the next year I was going to rediscover the importance of life and tackle my mental health. But arguably the most important steps of my journey occurred within the weeks to follow, events that occurred and people that I met, the dreams I dreamt and the visions I saw. It was like a jigsaw perfectly falling into place, laying a foundation to conjure an idea so emphatic it would make Jasper proud. What were these events? Well, I'll tell you right after you hear about Jasper.

Chapter 3

Jasper

That spherical world was a component of the greedy, obnoxious first world Jasper had so commonly referred to. How he dreamed of travelling the world, leaving behind the selfish ways of civilisation. I scoffed. As I stirred my coffee, grown in Southern Africa, I knew Jasper would be laughing at me. Wherever possible Jasper had a desire to run, run away from his family and friends. Not because he hated them, he loved loving them and they brought him joy, dissimilar to mine, but Jasper was a free soul, he was made for adventure. He couldn't be caged, he was open, my job at the Mayfair would have him dying with laughter, but at least I'm here to live it. He was exciting, I was not. I was lucky, he was not.

*

I grew fond of Jasper in my early childhood, living just doors away from each other we'd often play in the local forests, building camps and fortresses that would make King Arthur proud. We'd fight hordes of creatures in our heads till the sun went down before pausing the game for a well-earned dinner back at home. As we got older the childish creativity grew distant, replaced by the ambience of tranquil jazz, fire, and booze. We'd head to the same woods and camp at fifteen before travelling up to Scotland, France, and Wales to seek something more picturesque than the local woods as we grew closer to adulthood. We'd pack our car with minimal equipment before setting of on our road trips away, we loved the fun of it, adapting our way of life to fit in tandem with the world. Sometimes we didn't even take a tent, sleeping on the natural bed of leaves and soil or attempting to make a tepee, posing as a more thrilling alternative in our minds. Whilst I had always been quite outgoing, I took a backseat with Jasper, his creativity and free spirit exploded with things like this, denying the easy way of life and opting to return to historic times with the complications of survival. Jasper was a loud character and made me look abundantly shy, he'd often speak to strangers in shops or on the streets for hours and his like-able personality often left us in precarious, yet fascinating situations.

We visited Edinburgh for a weekend of camping and ended up having dinner with a family of five through Jasper's charming and talkative character. Their faces forever imprinted in my mind, a reminder of a beautiful evening of discovery and recollection. The kids Sam, Frankie, and Lou all engrossed in the stories me and Jasper told about our camping adventures and sailing over great lakes that went on for miles and miles. The family became fascinated by Jaspers invigorating desire to unearth the hidden wonders of the world we live on and nodded continuously through Jaspers plans of a cultural immersion. The parents put the kids to bed but then returned, keen to continue their discovery into this young embodiment of energy and peace. I became a shadow as the night went on, but I didn't mind, he was my best friend. They became fascinated, both motionless as they listened to Jasper's beliefs and desires for his life. In their world that was so civilised, they listened to his attitudes to western culture as he almost spat on the world we were all so absorbed in, the bogus nature of social media and adverse energy of the internet as a whole. How these human creations have created the problems that haunt our existence today.

"Mental health has become a victim of social media," he called out, whilst continuing what seemed like an inspirational and spiritual rant about human life pressing on issues of greed, power and hegemony, whilst suggesting many people had forgotten about aspects of enjoyment, tranquillity and love. What life really stood for.

I remember stumbling out of their family home at round half one in the morning, arm round Jasper both crying with laughter. The dinner had been amazing, and the endless river of homemade cider and wine completed a brilliant evening, the family appeared truly grateful for our presence.

"Four people that didn't know each other when the sun rose this morning," Jasper said. "Each of us unique and beautiful in our own right, let's travel and meet so many other journeys."

He was damn right.

*

Jasper had always reflected on his need to travel the world, he'd often hint it to me after he had asked me to go with him at the end of sixth form, around four years ago. Whilst I would have loved to follow him through a pathway to peace, I was not as adverse to the culture we lived in as he was. I intended to settle down in a journalist job and work my way. I justified my career prospects with the consideration that I could write about all these problems of civilisation me and Jasper would list as teenagers. Deep down however, I just didn't enrich the same optimism as Jasper, hesitant that this adventurous nature we'd enhanced throughout our latter teens could last all our lives. "It's a magical dream," I would say to him, around the time I turned twenty-one, "but it's a child's dream. It's not a viable life to live."

He detested my pessimistic tone. "What is living? We can do whatever we want."

"Don't be so obnoxious," I scoffed, raising my voice. "You can't go living in a tent your whole life, staying clear of any problems you think exist. You just need to suck them up like everyone else, nothing is perfect."

We never argued, but throughout our friendship, this felt the closest to it. "How can you tell me what I can and can't do?" He said, quietly as if to signal the end of the conversation. He opened his mouth to continue but shook his head and signalled it was the end with a flash of the palm as he walked away. A figure that never leaves my mind, even now, hands in pockets, shoulders slumped, rejected. It had me feeling awful for weeks.

*

For the weeks that followed our conversation we spoke little, until the day he told me he was heading off to travel the world. "I'm doing what you think I can't," I remember him saying in his usual confident tone. I never knew how I felt when he told me. I was proud of him for sure, chasing his dream and pushing the boundaries as far as he could. He was doing what he did best – discovering and being free. Above all though I felt a failure. This wasn't his dream, it was ours. Since kids we'd tell people that we would travel the world and find cultures we didn't know existed, I had been institutionalised to the western world and I have never got over that decision. Jasper laughed at me, when I came sobbing to him, hours before his flight. "The world is going nowhere," he said, one hand on my shoulder in the middle of Heathrow's terminal. "Be patient and you'll find the right thing to do at the right time." He flicked my cap up off my head to see my face behind it.

I looked into his eyes, fruitful as ever and managed a smile. "Carpe Diem," I said.

He nodded but dared not to speak, a lump in his throat. He gave me a plain envelope as we began our goodbye, it was unsealed at the top, the contents thick enough to have broken the adherence of the thin sticky line on the lip. I held it in both hands looking down at it, and whilst I had no idea what it could be, I decided it could wait. We hugged, a show of our love and harmony and that was that. I watched him offer farewells to the rest of his family before saluting us all comically with a smile and swivelling on his heel. I followed him with my eyes, not daring to break my gaze as he faded into the plethora of other sightseers and travellers.

I'm adamant I saw him look back once and offer a singular hand of good-bye into the air, but I can't be sure. Maybe that's what I dreamt I saw. Maybe that's what I hoped.

*

The journey back from the airport was miserable, Jasper's family weren't quite the same nature as him and sometimes I wondered how they were all related. I sat in the back-middle seat of the Vauxhall

Insignia with his two sisters on either side, and his parents up front. We engaged in light chat about his adventures ahead, but they all seemed disinterested, either to talk to me or about their brother. Probably both. I receded to remain silent for the rest of the journey back, thinking about him wandering the terminals restaurants and shops. I imagined he'd used his communication skills to sneak into one of those fancy lounges, free of charge. *He's probably sitting behind a plate full of food now* I thought as I roared along the motorway. That made me smile, he'd be just fine I convinced myself.

Chapter 4

All just dreams

I got home around eight the night I said farewell to Jasper, I skipped dinner, as I wasn't much in the mood for food anyway. It seemed like the emotions had drained my appetite. For some reason I felt an anxiety to know the contents of the envelope, as if aware of its importance to my own life. I opened the front door to my family house and barged through, my family were erupting into a violent hurl of words and insults, no physical violence, yet. I ignored it as if it were commonplace, which it was quickly becoming. It tore me up inside, how can love be lost so easily over the most insignificant problems? Jasper had always tried to console me when he began to notice its effects on my wellbeing. I knew not having him there was going to make my life in this home a lot harder, *but at least he would always be at the end of the phone* I remember thinking. I didn't even bother to listen as I rushed in, instead focusing my efforts on racing up the stairs, missing two at a time. As I reached the landing and in turn my bedroom door at the end of the hallway, I had a sudden dread of the envelope and flung it onto my bed as I entered my room. A fairly dull room with cream walls, a desk on the left which housed my laptop, and a plethora of folders, my latest addition open on top of the laptop keys – job applications. I was fortunate enough to have a double bed, neatly made underneath the double window. The window looked out to the garden and I noticed two aeroplanes in the sheet of blue above the ostentatious flowers and trees at the back of the garden. I wondered if Jasper was on one of them.

I turned back to my bed, more specifically the envelope and pulled out its contents, a paperclip binding it all together. I took hold of the clip and slid it off, leaving me staring at a hand-written letter and a bunch of paper beneath that was flopping toward the ground. I bent the papers in that way where it all goes rigid and no longer sags to the ground like dying flowers. You know what I mean. I then preceded to flick past the opening page of writing to be greeted by a further two pages. Beyond these was a map of the world, with no country names or borders to distinguish what was what. I even had trouble finding the UK, impressive. The map would have been bare if it wasn't for the numbers scattered around the world, I managed to locate a few but my geographical knowledge largely escaped me. The map was followed by loads of pictures of me and Jasper, a memorial of the history we had, he loved me a lot more than I could ever have presumed. I just hope my love for him was displayed as much as I felt. I postponed flicking through the pictures knowing I probably had seen many of them anyway and laid them aside, opting to read the letter instead.

To my friend I have grown up with, laughed with, cried with, and lived with.

I don't see this as an end to our adventures, I can foresee the prequel already. I wish you to know how much I would love you to have been by my side as you read this, but know our paths are different as well. Don't feel ashamed that you denied coming with me for I do not, I'm proud you have found your own way and I would hate you to follow me into something you are not set on.

I felt apprehensive as I read that, have I found my own way? Oh boy it was hard to tell.

I want to thank you for everything. Without you I maybe would not be setting out on the ambition of my life. I want to find peace and you have helped me on that journey already.

I have enclosed a map of my travels, you are the first and only person I have told.

California, USA. I intend to start my travels in San Francisco. Heading along the West coast through the Big Sur and toward Los Angeles. Heading through LA and down to San Diego, on the border of Mexico.

Mexico, beginning my Mexican journey in Tijuana, I felt it only necessary to continue my venture along the West coast down through the Baja California peninsula, continuing to harness the pounding waves of the Pacific. Rumour is the coves along the coast are to die for. La Chorera, San Juanico and Cabo San Lucas? I'll jump on a ferry just south of La Paz to get across to mainland Mexico, from here I'll either head towards the cosmopolitan and distinguished culture of Mexico City or look to Oaxaca's mountain forests slightly further South, to hike and tent rurally. Maybe both - What would you do?

The Caribbean Sea, from Mexico I'll head east to explore the beauty of the Caribbean Sea and snorkel with the colours of the underworld, I hope I can grasp an insight into the mass of organisms we share our world with and feel the peace that they do, for the moment, protected in a special place. Cuba and Jamaica appeal to me within my adventures around the Caribbean Sea but the options are endless.

Whilst I hope to see much more of Central and Southern America, I want to keep my map brief, and therefore have not furthered my adventure here. Should I? Instead I will head to India, to find a sumptuous array of tradition, spirituality, landscape and respect. I would love to see the tropical shores of the south, but the northern mountains seem too tranquil to not pay my respects, I shall head there, likely taking me further into the Nepalese mountains.

I will go in search of a natural pathway to begin my island-hopping, whilst I can't imagine where I will end up, I picture a treasure island. Not an island full of gold or gems; an island undiscovered, untouched by the human world. That to me is a treasure island. I'll find my island my friend, be sure of that, and there I will find my peace and respect for life. Oh how blissful life will be.

I hope for the day that you join me, to transpire our past experiences into a new continent and culture. I will miss you my friend, but I will be waiting. See you soon.

He signed the letter with the same scribbly writing that he had adopted since a child, only this time signed it *Captain Jasper*. It was fitting, he was going on a voyage. For the majority, who knows where. But he was in charge and he would complete whatever he set out to do, which only he could truly understand. As I finally looked up from the roughly written letter, I no longer felt the anxiety I had previously, neither did I feel upset from my friend leaving. I was proud, as I beamed a smile, a single tear left the duct of my left eye. *Tear of happiness* I thought. *Yes, of course it was.*

*

It must have happened around the time I was reading about Jasper's expedition down through the Baja California peninsula. Envisioning him tearing up the waves on a board in the Pacific, before rendezvousing with the locals for Mexican margaritas as the sun fades behind the sea. A plane lost three hours ashore of the New York coastline, not crashed, lost. Missing, unknown.

Chapter 5

Dejected and Rejected

I woke the next morning, alarm set for half seven, and immediately felt the bottle of red wine from the night before rush to my head, I felt worse than I normally felt, and that's usually shit. The sun shone through the blinds, like daggers piercing my vision, so I pulled the duvet back up over my head and went back to sleep, *fuck off would you.*

*

I rose again at nine-thirty, work started half an hour ago, *bollocks.* I got out of bed sluggishly, disregarding the common desire to rush in and apologise profusely for my lateness. The sun had been replaced by the all too common black clouds and thunderstorms, which I preferred. They gave me something to relate too, mother nature's impersonation of me, a sort of pathetic fallacy if you will. Pathetic summed me up pretty nicely. I began to thumble around for my jeans strewn within the heap of clothes at the foot of the bed, before pulling them on. I didn't shower, couldn't be bothered, if I smelt so be it. *It might keep people away from me* I thought, that would be nice. It's safe to say a lack of self-motivation had got the better of me following the presumption of Jasper's death, broadcasted around the world. What's the point of living I wondered? It had been three years since. three years driven by grief. Well not really driven, more like a car without half its parts, choking and spluttering its way to a stop. I almost did the week before, I had tried to overdose on some prescripted tablets, but I couldn't even do that. *What a fucking loser.* I went into the toilet and got a glimpse of myself in the mirror, white like a zombie with the exception of the dark red rings around my eyes, hair all over my face giving an almost haunting look. Darkness with a torch illuminating my face would have scared myself. I decided to get the red wine out of me, not to make me feel better but so I could have more at eleven. I bent down to the toilet, knees by the base and propped my head over the bowl. Two fingers down the throat. As I paused there waiting, I strangely recalled Jasper's naïve adamance that the water at the bottom of the toilet was like the sea he one day wanted to visit. Still, only subtle waves from side to side and beautifully clear. I would laugh at him and offer to shove him in as a joke. I looked down at the water and for the first time in around ten years could almost see where he came from. But these waves were greater, and they continued to grow. Bigger and bigger. More and more aggressive, until it was like a storm, waves crashing left and right. I blinked adamant I was going insane. The waves continued to grow. Ferocity intensifying in the cauldron I was staring dumbly into. The waves crashed all around me like an amphitheatre around my head. A single drop reached the tip of my noise. Dead. The waves stopped. An incomparable, almost unnoticeable wave lay in its place, rocking from side to side. I pulled my fingers out my throat and got back up, a picture of Jasper's I didn't want to taint.

*

I swanned around the rest of the day, comatose and empty. The world passed me, blind to my unhealthy visions of suicide and discomfort. I was irrelevant, unimportant to everyone and unnecessary. *No-one looked forward to my company, so no-one would miss it.* That's what I thought. I drew a dejected figure at work, procrastinating for most the day. Hands in pockets behind my desk, shoulders slumped. Where had we seen that before? I passed the time by spamming the delete button on the keyboard. *Maybe it might transverse into deleting me, like some sort of magical shit?* No, the world wasn't that kind unfortunately and neither was that Christian family's god. I had two glasses of wine at eleven that day as I said I would, opting for an early lunch break in order to swerve the pressures from colleagues to go to lunch with them. *I'd rather slit my wrists than listen to Jason's stories of love or Amber's mounting social media dilemmas. Maybe I would soon.*

*

The same routine occurred for the days that followed during that week, until one evening beckoned a flicker of light in my dark, lifeless soul. The beginning of the resurgence to living, the beginning of a new me. The TV news was on but I paid little attention to it, my body slumped across the double sofa in my living room. The room was poorly lit, and at eight-fifty very few features of the room could be seen. There was a bookshelf in the darkness to the right of the TV, stacked from floor to ceiling with adventures. It had provided an escape to a more pleasant life for the past months, but reading fiction was becoming dull to me and I was beginning to detest the idea and the authors that came with it. There was a lamp on a coffee table by the side of the sofa, but it wasn't on, the journalist wage was so dire I made sure to minimalise the electrical bill wherever possible. That was as dense as the living room got apart from an old, mosaic rug linking the sofa to the TV stand. To say it was ugly was kind, but it kept the warmth in to a certain extent, so it stayed. Of course, I couldn't feel the cold anyway after a bottle of wine and that same daily activity was taking its toll again. I was drowsy as I lay there, in my usual, abnormal position. Half on the sofa, half not, as if I'd been shot just above it and crumbled lifelessly down. A copy of Sixtynine (it wasn't a porn mag) was clutched in my hands, a magazine I was confident was from the midlands but had somehow made its way to the seat of the train next to me earlier in the day. I didn't consider it in too much depth though, much the same as how I scanned through the pages. *Shit, shit, shit.* Endless pages of self-indulged celebrities and abnormally unattractive models. *How do they always seem to pick the ugly people* I thought? *Maybe I should go in there.* I continued to flick through towards the end, the TV still blaring as I made my way towards the end. I noticed the article of the month: Travelling around the world. I sat up slightly, suddenly becoming uncharacteristically interested as if part of my childhood had been reinvigorated. I pushed aside the drowsiness in order to read a little of what it said. The article was gorgeous, the author immaculately recreating the beauty of travelling, the highs and lows and the undisputed, undefinable aura that comes with it. For the first time in ages it provided me with warmth, I have no idea why, but it felt as if a fire had begun to burn inside me once more. By the time I had travelled through Tibet and Venice I began my adventure into the Brazilian culture in São Paulo, totally engrossed. The article flew by and suddenly I was at the end, article finished, fire put out. I looked up, slung the magazine away slightly agitated by the rushed ending and thought little else of it. The TV news reel continued to scroll, the new topic subject read: *Mental health, the UKs biggest killer*. The newsreaders face was serious, and he spoke, in a threating tone as if I was being told off, about finding a way of counteracting the negativity - a passion. I thought about what I had just read and heard. Could travelling be the light at the end of the tunnel? I considered all the travelling I had done with Jasper, around the UK and even into Europe. They were the greatest years of my life, flashing down winding roads in our Polo, scaling mountains, and venturing through forests. It was as if a get out of jail ticket had been forced into my hand unexplained and unexpectedly, a lifeline to redemption and peace. Then, before taking it any further, I remembered the newsreader was a cunt and turned the TV off, eradicating my consideration with it as the screen went black.

You know when they just read obnoxiously, looking down their nose like it's the barrel of an RPG. *Please, blow me up, save me from having to watch you.*

Chapter 6

The fucked-up colour wheel

I dreamt for the first time in a while that night, about the colours of the article I had read, a colour wheel of the world. I was living in a subdued state above the wheel, watching it spin slowly. Life sprouting from each slice of colour. The amber and red tones lined up with my vision, hosting fire, and passion, festivals, and spices. It was a Brazilian samba parade, people dancing and laughing, floats hovering slowly down the road in tandem with people decorated in magnificent displays of fancy dress, recreating animals, nature, and leaders. It was immersive and the feeling was electric. The incredible South American music blaring in time with the samba dancers that lead the way. I became mesmerised by the lively and rhythmical dancing, feeling an urge to jump down and join the culture and the party. I remained subdued in the air, paralysed. I struggled but couldn't move, my life was no longer in my hands. I became panicked, screaming for help as I tried to wriggle free from an invisible hand clasping me in place, nothing. The salsa band continued to play below me, wheeling along the largest drum I had ever seen, one hit causing the wheel that I was looking down upon to continue spinning, slightly faster this time.

I was no longer in Brazil, shades of green erupted in front as the wheel begun creating a vibrant jungle all around. I could hear the exotic birds surrounding me but saw nothing, all hidden above the tree foliage. Monkeys swinging from vines hanging metres away in front. I began to sweat from the humidity, delicate particles dropping from my brow. I couldn't wipe them away, my hands still paralysed. Birds and butterflies continued to hover above, observing me, before a Blue Morpho Butterfly came to rest on my nose. Its beauty unimaginable, fluttering as if to show off its iridescent wings, almost arrogantly. I was consumed by the wave of blue, a deep-sea blue and before I knew it, I was transported once more.

Hanging above the ocean, I found myself watching dolphin shimmer across the surface of the water, barely breaking the tranquillity of the world they lived in. They were soaring great distances alongside whales, both equally beautiful. The whales breaching, the movement of leaping almost entirely out of the water, their unimaginable length only then proving a challenge for my mind to accept. I felt a sudden desire to see such beasts up close, one of nature's true gifts. I was so immersed I didn't see one coming up to the surface and producing an explosion of water through its blowhole, soaking me through. I closed my eyes to prevent it going into my eyes and reopened them to darkness. Gone were the bright colours and magnificent beasts. Poof.

Images slowly began to return after a while, like an old TV static finding its picture. It tuned and I was met by a greyscale picture, nothing like what I had just witnessed. I tried to move closer to get a better view, nothing. Though it was dark, I started to recognise the room, the lamp by the sofa flickering on and off, the disgusting mosaic rug on the floor. It was my living room. I looked forcingly to the left, a figure in the shadows. As I acclimatised to the darkness, I saw myself prominently, as if I was looking in a mirror. Accept was it me? My eyes were dark, as if I had been punched. My hair wet with sweat, the source of the salty river that continued down my face, tributaries from either armpit and various glands accumulating even more sweat, eventually meeting the mouth further down my t-shirt. The great river suffocating the t-shirt and draining its non-existent shade. My wrists displayed the only colour in this new vision, the same amber colours I had witnessed moments earlier in Brazil, but they were a lot less appealing in this context. My wrists were slit, the left hand retaining its grasp on the offender, nothing special, a Russell Hobbs kitchen knife. Blood trickled down to my fingertips and stood there grasping onto my nails, droplets falling slowly. The floor I lay on was something of a Tarantino film, the mess merging with the rug in the middle of the room. The picture, frightening. The reality of my nature juxtaposed the world I had previously seen, beyond the four walls that I lay in, slumped against the far wall. Dead. I felt my body become free as the hand finally released me from its satanic grip, I turned partly to refrain from seeing the image in front and partly to see the perpetrator of this horror. As I turned, still floating in mid-air, I turned from one nightmare to the next. Jasper.

Chapter 7

Thanks Tony

I began my journey to work the next day trying to disregard the horrors of the night, to little success. My drained face imprinted in my mind, the colourless expression, and suicidal temptations all too real to collate. And Jaspers face, controlling the episode like the prince of darkness, leaving me feeling betrayed and neglected. I stopped at the pub along the way, as it opened for breakfast. *Get me a drink* I muttered to myself as I entered.

The Royal Oak was one of those awfully furnished pubs with out-dated carpet to go with the out-dated beers on the taps. I would usually grab the red wine special, four pound for a glass, but I remained dazed from the night and instead opted for something that might pick me up a bit. I was greeted by the toothless smile of Tony behind the bar, a middle-aged fella, balding on his head and a typical boozer, big belly, and chubby hands.

“Ahhh!! What can I getchya, the usual?”

I found it surprisingly difficult to talk for some reason, leaving me with no option but to shake my head viciously, anymore and it might have fallen off. *Nicer way to go than the kitchen knife* I thought. In my furious shaking I forgot to answer him.

“Then what?” He said abruptly to break the strange silence my actions had summoned. He tapped his fat fingers across the bar as a gesture that he was waiting.

“Vodka on the rocks,” I blurted quickly.

"Eh, rough day already is it?" He said making a quick dart with his eyes toward the clock.

"Something like that."

"I'll give ya a double on the 'ouse," he said with his trademark toothless smile, littered with more holes than a golf course.

"Thanks Tony." I took the glass and spun to find a seat, my hand shaking viciously as I did so.

*

I sat at the edge of the pub for close to forty-five minutes, in a booth semi-protected from the other pathetic people at a pub before ten. On the wall by the booth was an old painting of a devil and I did my best to look the other way, convincing myself it was just a coincidence, I remained unconvinced. I tried to face the situation by thinking about the night before. The news, the article, the dream. It all seemed too conveniently close together in time to just be disregarded. The dream highlighted how beautiful the world was but travelling still wasn't a massive appeal to me. I did my best to remind myself it was just a child's dream, what I had once said to Jasper, as I finally rose from the seat and walked out of the booth. Though I'd regained my composure, with gratitude to the silky Russian concoction Tony had given me, I felt the same fire inside me from the article I read the night before. It wasn't quite put out; a gentle fan and it might just be re-stoked to some great magnitude. *What was this feeling though? A fire for what? Perhaps I was being stupid. Perhaps it was just the Vodka. Yeah, blame it on the vodka.*

*

I continued the journey to work a little past ten, taking the journey length to a running total of two and a half hours. I finally arrived and managed another one of my unconvincing smiles to Claire as I strolled past, she was on the phone and looked agitated, so I decided not to pursue a conversation or response, continuing towards the stairs. Excited by the prospect of another day of shit.

Chapter 8

22 + 20

Jasper continued to circle my head for the weeks to follow. Nightmares continued to raid my dreams leaving me propped up on my palms in the middle of the night, distressed and sweat dripping from every corner of my head. My hypothalamus letting me down on more occasions than not and a dream anxiety disorder and sleep paralysis often getting the better of me. I began to fear sleep, urging myself to stay awake as long as I could. More often than not I'd get as little as three hours sleep, while a couple of times I refrained from sleeping at all. It was these few weeks that were the worst for me, paranoia spinning me into hallucinations and a comatose state and my mind beginning to blur the boundaries between sleep and reality. The fire I felt in the Oak had been similarly comatose and put to the back of my mind. I waited for it to re-emerge with patience. Subconsciously, I waited with anticipation and hope.

*

I caught a glance at myself in the mirror one morning, taping it up with duct tape to make sure I wouldn't again. That resembled the biggest change I could conjure in my life, knowing I would need something much bigger to tackle me to safety now. My face seemed to have aged somewhat twenty years, making me forty-two and I'd somehow lost the colour in my eyes. Usually an emerald green they appeared dark and disserted as if the soul inside had given in. Shut up shop for the day or closed for the year. *Maybe forever?* My hair remained the mousey brown it had always been, showing no signs of grey. *For now.* But it too managed to make me look older, its wiry appearance portraying a delicacy and fragility. I began to form lines across my face, laugh lines I think they're called? That made me feel cheated. I had barely laughed, and it had still given me them. *Fucking cunt.* Yeah, I was in a bad way.

My drinking problem had continued perhaps even been ramped up, and I dreamt I lived in the Royal Oak. I probably would have thought it true if Tony hadn't been dressed in a housemaid uniform, massive tits and wearing a blond curly head of hair. He was still fat, so the massive tits looked at home, but the hair made it some augmented reality. He wore a thick pair of square black glasses, the type Austin Powers would wear and a juicy red lipstick that made his lips slightly attractive if nothing else. His staggered walk in the big black heels resembled how I felt in reality, only difference being I was there to catch him as he fell.

Chapter 9

The Prophecy

Another day came around, beginning like any other, fucked off with the world and an abnormal quantity of suicidal temptations, the lift, walk, Tesco meal deal, the Royal Oak, Tony, Big Issue guy and the Mayfair Journalisms revolving door. I was literally going round in circles. I hadn't seen Sandy since my remark about her hair, or lack of. I guess that was the only positive from the morning. As I began up the Mayfair Journalist stairs, I noticed a coin on one of the steps so instinctively took it given it's lucky to do so. Hell, I could do with a lot of that. I glanced briefly and saw the two-pound coin, disregarding it into my pocket with little interest, and continuing up the remaining steps.

I fumbled the coin in my pocket throughout the day, spinning it round self-consciously like I was preparing a magic trick, though it was intended more as a procrastination technique than anything magical. I continued to do so in intervals, before properly taking notice of it at around three, when the thought of leaving work early began creeping into my head. I spun it slower in my fingers, brushing my thumb across the face of the coin, it didn't feel like the Queen. Not one bit. I couldn't quite work out the pattern, but it was certainly thinner than a two pound and a hell of a lot lighter. How had I just noticed? I pulled the coin out my pocket, adamant I was mental. I was not. Written on the face, Nepal. What I presumed was one rupee, worth about fuck of a pound. Not quite the luck I was hoping for but another sign to add more stress onto my fucked-up mind. I studied the coin hard, wondering how it could ever have got to the stairs of Mayfair Journalism. The coin was a copper colour, slightly dirty preventing it from having a nice shine, instead giving off more of a matte colouring. I brought it closer to me to inspect the drawings on the face. On the side with Nepal written was Nepali writing, I had no idea what it said but presumed it to also say Nepal. Underneath the scribbles of the middle eastern writing (which is so much more beautiful than English) was a picture of a farmer following his cow, a sacred animal in their culture and probably why I was looking at it on a coin as opposed to a great emperor or influential person. I flipped the coin over, mountains covering the entire side, one huge peak rolling into the next. It paid respect to the great mountains of Nepal, the Himalayas. Mountains that covered most, if not all of the Nepalese land from border to border. I couldn't quite tell but presumed this coin displayed the mountain of Everest on the China-Nepal border. At twenty-nine thousand feet, Everest was a world-wide attraction, climbing it would fulfil a beacon of individual supremacy, supposedly. The coin instinctively reminded me of Jasper and his desired adventure through Nepal. He was never interested in Everest; I recalled the conversation we had about it.

"It's not something humans are built to achieve," he said.

"But wouldn't you love to see the view from the summit."

"Well sure if you can promise me my safety up and down, but unfortunately no one can. It's the Earths sacred spot I suppose, somewhere nature doesn't want us to go." He was right, as always. Parts of the Everest expedition are so gruelling people die climbing up there. Not that that scared me, dying didn't really faze me, more the light at the end of the long dark tunnel of life. Still I didn't want to climb it, even I wasn't particularly thrilled about the prospect of freezing to death. Instead of Everest, Jasper was in search of charming hill villages and golden temples. Somewhere the tourists or lonely planet hadn't discovered, where peace and prosperity ran its course. A viably simple way of existence where life was as beautiful as anywhere on the planet. I pictured tiny cobbled streets arching up the mountainside, an epicentre of colours, bright yellow and blue rural housing stuffed into either side of the paths with a plethora of flags introducing even more colour across streets that measured no more than two metres wide. A picturesque Balamory carved into the jungle on the edge of a mountain. Even the thought of a Nepalese Balamory made me smile, I couldn't remember the last time I had done so, Nepal really did appeal to me. The thought lingered futilely; *I wonder if Tony accepts Nepalese rupee at the Oak.*

Chapter 10

Up in the clouds

Over the next week I thought of Nepal an ungodly amount, I don't know why. I guess it was its appeal that linked me to Jasper. I didn't like thinking about Jasper but sometimes I couldn't help it, his face flashing in and out of my mind like a yo-yo. I dreamt of a day I could smile at the thought of him but figured I'd never actually see the day. *Shame.*

One day the following week, Wednesday or Thursday, I can't quite remember, I decided to pass the Royal Oak in the morning and head into the coffee shop further down the street instead. The coffee shop served a delicious breakfast explaining the chaos inside, till queues reaching the doorway and only a handful of free seats available across the shop floor. I stood in the queue, watching the world go by. A couple holding hands across the table, staring into each other's eyes, an infant throwing a tantrum in a pram, and an elderly couple sitting mute looking out the window and into the distance away from me. I couldn't see the elderly faces but could tell they were peaceful, content with their love for one another and in no necessity to speak, happy in one another's company. I scoffed, maybe a little too loudly, making the people queueing in front turn around and look at me but I didn't give too much of a fuck. Instead staring back at them like Medusa threatening to turn them into stone, my hair transforming into serpent heads. They turned away pretty quickly. "Pussies," I muttered towards the two mothers and their young children.

It was pretty childish from me I have to say.

*

I finally made it to the counter, I had scanned the blackboard behind the deflated barista for some time unable to decide what to have. In typical fashion my mind decided to wander towards the alcoholic beverage list. Rather counter-productive, I could have just gone to the Oak. I pressed on regardless, ordering a pint of Budweiser and making my way to one of the few empty seats in the shop. By the window. *Perfect.*

As I drank my ice cold sud, I remained pretty oblivious to the world. I enjoyed getting away from it as you can probably tell, there wasn't much excitement in my boring, shit, waste-of-space life. Instead I stared at the floor whilst hundreds of people entered and left the shop. That was probably a slight exaggeration, but I wouldn't know as I wasn't paying attention.

There was a mother and son sat at the table behind me, also by the window, who I'd only noticed when the mother began to weep slowly and quietly so no one would hear. I did, deciding to ignore it, instead rolling my eyes as if it affected me massively. It did not. "Don't cry Mum," the boy whispered gently, soothingly.

The Mum continued to do so, trying to hold it in, causing her breathing to become distorted and sound almost painful. It pissed me off. *Shut up dear.*

"It's only for a while, six months at most."

She continued to weep. Head in hands on the table. *Shut the fuck up you cow.*

"I've always wanted to travel Mum, you gotta let me go n' do this. I'll be fine."

I understood now, the baby leaving the nest for the first-time motherhood trait. *How ridiculous.* The boy rattled off where he wanted to go and whilst the mother sounded apprehensive about it, I couldn't help but feel a sense of jealousy. It shocked me. Over the past week my brain had rekindled a pathway for me, a pathway I considered I was too old for. It was a child's dream but a dream nevertheless and perhaps one I wanted to have? One I needed to have. For the first time I sat there seriously deliberating it, should I, shouldn't I? I considered what Jasper would say. I told you so, probably. For the next ten minutes the angel and devil fought each other for different decisions in my head, although I had no idea who was fighting for what. I continued to sit there letting the argument unravel. As it became fiercer and more consuming, I felt a tap on my knee. A child peering over the table at my face, I remained silent unsure how to address the little prick. He'd just interrupted the most exciting deliberation I'd had for a long while, I didn't care how young he was, he was a prick. He stood there still eating his cheese sandwich, chewing the bite in his mouth almost too much and leaving it gaping open. I saw it all. I looked around for a parent, nothing. "Are you lost kiddo?" I drew another one of my pretentious smiles that I seemed to perform too often, he saw right through it.

"What wrong with you?" He was only young, maybe four, his teeth still growing, one of those late bloomers. He hadn't quite mastered the old English language either and occasionally missed a word or letter as I embarked on one of the most influential conversations I'd ever had.

"Nothing lil one, why do you say that?"

He nodded towards the Budweiser. "Mumma says too early for tha' to ma Daddy," then preceding to waggle his index finger as a sort of tut-tut.

Whilst he'd just released an incredibly condescending gesture, I couldn't help but be amused and became guilty for considering him a prick initially. I mean he was, but I liked him. "Well your Daddy is a good boy then."

He nodded.

"What have you got there?" I said motioning toward the sandwich in his hand. I'm not sure why I continued the conversation on, could have just left it there, be done with the kid. I got the sense of comfort, having someone else to talk too and felt he had something to teach me. A proper odd feeling that let me tell you, a fucking four year old. I guess in his naivety he hadn't gathered the judgemental concepts that came with adulthood, whilst most people would avoid a rough looking man drinking a beer in the morning, he did not.

He tilted his head, continuing to gaze up at me as if he was seeing through me, I felt slightly uneasy, like you do when you're with those psychics in the local fun fair. All of it's a load of bollocks though.

"You no answer me," he said. "What wrong with you?"

I sighed. "Adult problems I'm afraid, I'm a bit sad." I displayed an exaggerated sad face showing my bottom lip.

"Why, you need joke?"

I chuckled. "Go on buddy."

"Wha' happen to the people who jump out plane at really high place without parachute?"

Fucker, he was psychic. I flashed my memory to Jasper in a similar situation and I felt myself become sick. "They'll fall and be gone forever unfortunately," I said partly to him and partly to myself.

"Uh-huh an' no. They fall an' die," he said as if I hadn't quite understood. "Bu' they don't fall or die either, stay up in the cloud with all our friends and ma' nana and look after us!" He spoke excitedly and I didn't want to let him down by telling him that maybe that wasn't the case, so I didn't. It wasn't really a joke either, but thought I'd keep that to myself too. As I smiled and said thank you the mother came rushing up out of nowhere. Maybe ten years older than myself, but better dressed and beautiful. I smiled pleasantly but was greeted by a cold, hostile look. Yep I knew it, bitch. She scanned my appearance with a new frightened look and apologised quickly before grabbing the toddler's hand and rushing away, the toddler still facing me and scrunching his hand as a good-bye. I stuck my tongue out in recognition and he smiled. Then he was gone.

*

I couldn't get the frightened look of the Mum out of my head as she scanned my appearance, I remembered what I had looked like before I taped the mirror in my bathroom but couldn't accept I still looked that bad. I sighed. *Maybe worse*. Either way I moaned and tutted for the rest of the day considering how shallow a person could be to build an assumption off of an appearance. *Maybe it was the day-time alcohol?* Then I considered the kid, and suddenly I couldn't get it out of my head. Not in a perverted sadistic way, I was suicidal but never that, it was the way he looked at me, genuine and friendly, as if he'd known me all my life. I began to resent his Mum, the embodiment of the western world, her judgmental nature – one of the components Jasper insisted the western world had. Jasper. The kid had also made me think profusely about him, the words *look after us* echoing in my head. Was he right? Everything that had happened in the past week, the article, the news, the dream, the coin, the coffee shop today, was that Jasper, protecting me from what he was afraid I'd do? Did he want me to travel the world? The kid nodding towards the alcohol was the nail in the coffin, another sign to change. That coffee shop left me with more questions than I wanted, in doing so only answering one. *Is it fate for me to travel the world?*

Chapter 11

Aquila

The wind whistled past my ears and the bitterness of the breeze left my face numb and red. I looked up; the stars shone brightly. Since a young age I was fascinated by star constellations, the augmentation of stars in a way that embodied a mythical character or shape. I studied the sky for a while, not daring to blink, whilst the picture grew bolder and more defined. Orion and Aquila's star constellations both became visible, glistening with pride. I smiled, it brought me satisfaction and warmth. For one moment I considered those stars were burning just for me, gifting me a moment of joy in an otherwise miserable world.

I noticed the wings of Aquila begin to flap, stars moving millions of miles in order to do so and suddenly I was moving. Sweeping through the canyon, the breeze suddenly feeling irrelevant and unnoticeable. The jaded rock edges became dark and difficult to see, but I felt a security in knowing where I was going, I could close my eyes and I'd be fine. I kept them open, scared to miss some of the natural beauty flowing below. A river lay amidst the canyon walls, glistening and providing the only light other than the stars above my head. I was sandwiched in between, like two torch lights illuminating me as If I were performing on a stage, the centre of attention. Though it wasn't raining, thick thunderbolts began to pierce the canyon on either side of me. it was beautiful, and I continued to stare, gliding between the strikes. The sky continued to produce more thick torches of light, the thunderbolts illuminating an invisible runway through the canyon. I continued along it, flying. I was Aquila, the Eagle that carried the thunderbolts of Zeus in Greek mythology and I felt invincible. My wings spanned across the canyon either side of me, stretching two metres each way, thick with feathers. Each feather was perfectly placed and coloured a tree-trunk brown with spirals of white intertwined to create aborigine patterns. The wind swept over my wings causing a ripple effect, all moving in unison like a choreographed dance. All the while, thunderbolts continued to rain down around me. Sometimes I absorbed the light, stoking a fire inside me, the world getting brighter as it did so and other times, I left it to sink into the futile earth below, ripping through it like paper. I watched the earth crumble for a couple more minutes, watching the destruction below helplessly. Trees smashed to insignificance, animals fleeing from the inevitable, vast plains of nothing being demolished right down to the soul of the world. Except, was it helplessly? I wondered, and then realised.

Only I was able to save my life that existed below. It occurred to me only then, did I want to?

Chapter 12

Alexander SuperTramp

Before I knew it I had done the unexpected, cast the life I had made off into the abyss, in the hope I'd shine brighter elsewhere. I figured even a mere glimmer would be more successful than the journalist life I so admirably led. I took great joy in dismissing the mandatory leave notice that the bastard boss set and I also took great pride in revolving those fucking doors one last time. In my head it had become a vivid ultimatum, get busy living, or die trying.

I booked flights on the way to the airport with nothing but my mind and the bag on my back. Perhaps the latter was the more reasonable voice to listen to. What the fuck, I had no idea what I was doing.

*

I had pictured Jasper faced with the decision of what to have from the buffet displayed across the hall of the Virgin Atlantic premium lounge when we'd left him at Heathrow a few years ago now. He'd somehow expertly conjured a way past the front-desk attendants without having to pay a penny, leaving him faced with the choice of pain au chocolat, a full-English or a granola bowl. In reality, it seemed a little more difficult. Four attendants, a great glass door to push through, and a blue backpack to give me away. My plan was at a fork head, *do I make an anonymous run for it, skipping the queue and heading straight for the door or do I blag my way with the attendant?* Both had their benefits, the first idea bringing an aura of confidence and understanding, the second a respect for the attendant whilst emanating the belief I am allowed to be here. I opted for the second under the grounds I couldn't show confidence if I wasn't particularly feeling it.

My eyes that prowled the floor would have given my guilt away immediately anyway.

I queued for what must have been fifteen minutes, giving me time to reflect on the past four weeks. I had gone from near suicide to standing in Terminal five of Heathrow. It wasn't quite the picturesque reincarnation of life yet, I still had tendencies to kill myself and would no doubt be wishing the plane windows were large enough to squeeze through and fall or even better, get churned up by the engines and displayed across the plane windows for everyone else to see, a mixture of blood and annihilated organs. I also wasn't too sure why I was on my way to travel the world; I didn't have a huge desire to and dreaded it more than anything. The prospect of talking to a load of self-invested arseholes on a little island in Asia that you can't get off of didn't particularly fill me with joy, not like it did once upon a time – with Jasper to lead me. It would have been easier to not set forth travelling, remembering how Christopher McCandleless ended up at the end of Into The Wild. *Silly fucker*. I would have turned back then and there, heading for my apartment and back to the despair of journalism, both sounding not so bad in that instance. *Was I heading way out of my depth?* But then I remembered the signs I had encountered, that had enlightened me. The advert, the article, the countless nightmares, the coin, the kid, Aquila. Jasper. The real reason I was doing it, not for myself but for Jasper. Sure, I could go home and kill myself, it probably wouldn't bother me, but I'd have let my friend down, something too difficult to do. Something I wouldn't do.

Why? I guess I could consider that one on the flight.

*

I'd reached the front of the queue relatively quickly in the end and was beckoned to the front by Emilia, youngish lady, brown hair, and dressed like an air hostess. That slightly confused me, they weren't air hostesses. They didn't even leave the country.

"Welcome to the Virgin Atlantic Premium Lounge, how may I help," she said in a soothing Irish voice.

I'd had time to consider what to say amidst my thoughts of Christopher McCandleless and didn't appear to hesitate or stutter, that aura of confidence that I thought impossible to conjure. "Hiya, yes I'm looking to head into the lounge before my flight."

She began clicking away on her computer, almost as a baseline to the drumbeat her gum chewing was concocting, it only needed a melody, I guess that was the voice. Although it wasn't all that melodic, the soothing voice had soon turned boring.

"Have you pre-signed in?" Her chewing becoming slightly jarring. She continued to avoid eye-contact with me.

"No but I was told it was included in my ticket price when I booked the flight through your website." Lie.

She chewed.

"Can I see your boarding pass please."

I obliged.

"I'm afraid the lounge is only included in the tickets for business class and higher, you can purchase a lounge pass at twenty-nine ninety-nine with your ticket."

Fuck that I thought, I continued my attempts though. "Oh, that's funny. I rang your helpline up to make sure I was allowed and they said yes of course," I pulled a surprised face to go along with my fake anecdote.

She considered this.

"I spoke to Simon I think." Simon was just to make the story more convincing, and even I stood there for a moment wondering who Simon was. That meant Emilia would definitely be lost in my make-believe Virgin Atlantic help centre. If she was, she didn't show it, disregarding poor Simon almost immediately.

"Did you use a voucher when booking your flight?" Her chewing was becoming really irritating.

"I did but unfortunately I don't have the voucher anymore."

"What was the voucher?"

I stuttered and it would be reasonable to believe that it was at this point that I lost the prospects of the lounge food. "Errr," I considered. "Just tryna' remember, sorry."

She looked up at me for the first time.

"Free lounge experience when you purchase any Virgin Atlantic flight," I said slowly as if I was making it up as I spoke. I was.

It must have been laughable and I'm sure I saw Emilia flash a cheeky grin whilst looking back down at her keys as if to cover her face momentarily. She regained her composure sublimely quickly and I was almost impressed when she resurfaced moments later and apologised that there were no present or expired vouchers that were similar. *How the fuck did Jasper do it*. I became frustrated, feeling my sadistic ways breaking through my skin like Venom did when he surfaced from inside Eddie Brock. Of course, Emilia did not see anything similar with the exception of a screwed-up face maybe.

I played my trump card.

"Oh that's so odd, I'm sure it was similar. Is there not anyway you can let me in please, I'm on my way to see my Mother in San Francisco, she has terminal cancer and I'm worried sick, I feel really awful," I clasped my hands in a begging motion.

Yeah, I'm a prick, my mother wasn't in San Fran and she definitely didn't have terminal cancer. Emilia's cheeky grin had vanished replaced with a stone white face, an expression that told me I had reached into her problematic past as opposed to mine. I thought she was going to start crying and I couldn't be bothered for that, so I grabbed my boarding past from the desk, and quickly began the tantrum of an unhappy customer storming off.

"How immoral of you, that makes me sick!" I yelled as I turned and made for the exit of the reception area, wagging my finger in the air as I did so.

I think I heard poor Emilia begin to sob as I made it to the terminal corridor, but I couldn't be sure. I made a left and headed to the rest of the economy travellers at JD Wetherspoons, wondering how Jasper had managed to get into the lounge for free without upsetting anyone. A direct contrary to my experience and clear evidence I had so much to learn. Of course, I never really knew if Jasper had made it in or even tried, that was just my imagination.

Chapter 13

Typical fashion

I scouted the terminals impressive array of shops for an indulging hour and a half. I'd stopped at Mr. Wetherspoons' fine establishment for a well-earned pint following the run in from the lounge receptionist Emilia, before scouting the latest magazines in WHSmith and purchasing a bottle of tequila at Duty Free. I didn't get a bottle of water, only had enough money for the essentials. Before going to the gate, I needed to head to the foreign exchange, so I did. I got a relevant amount of US Dollars and Mexican Peso's, the two countries I was to travel first, and decided I'd get the other necessary currencies at a later date. By that point I sensed it was time to travel to the gate, I looked up at the monitor, in awe of some of the places on the list whilst searching for my own. Tel Aviv, Cairo, Toronto, Rio De Janeiro, Sucre, Christchurch, the list went on for three pages, I won't bore you with all of them. San Francisco, VS twelve-ninety-eight, my flight, was on page one and was apparently boarding at gate nine. The boarding now sign was flashing, which didn't bode well so I tightened my backpack chords to stop it jumping around too much and began to run towards the gate in typical fashion.

I couldn't help but consider that in that exact moment I had perfectly summed up the rushed nature of the western societies. I couldn't wait to rid myself of it. If I could.

Chapter 14

Eleven hours and five minutes

I must have been one of the last to board the flight, there was no one queuing when I got there, sweaty and out of breath. The air hostess laughed at me as I came rushing up to her and told me to calm down, it would not leave without me. She seemed a lot nicer than her Virgin Atlantic colleague Emilia and I wished I could have spoken to her about a free lounge experience instead. As I made my way across the bridge, the air hostess waiting behind to welcome the final few stragglers, I composed myself, the magnitude of the trip starting to settle into my head and making me nervous and a little terrified. I wondered if the sweat was from all the running as I had first presumed. I was welcomed on the plane by a cluster of flight attendants, their robotic smiles and greetings scratching at my eyes and ears. *Urgh,* how tedious.

As I made my way through business class and then the waves of seats in economy, I tried to identify what plane this was in an attempt to rid myself of the nerves that had settled. It could have been a Boeing seven-eight-seven but was probably the classic seven-seven-seven, a plane that loved transatlantic American flights. I was never much of a nerd in terms of planes, but I vividly remember speaking to a classmate about it in year eight, he knew almost everything about them from back to front and I was mightily impressed. It was one of those strange conversations that occur with random people and just never seem to leave your memory.

Most people were already sitting and clearly agitated by my late arrival as I began to swan down the aisle. I gave them one of my pretentious smiles and continued as slow as I could. For the first twenty rows I would stop here and there looking for my seat, although in actual fact it was a lot further down, I just enjoyed annoying people. I eventually got to seat twenty-nine A, meaning I was by the window, the only positive to a dire situation. On the aisle seat was a Dad and to his left the kid, no more than eight. My seat meant the lil one was my neighbour and I could tell just by looking at him he wouldn't stop yapping the entire flight. *Fuck.* I was soon relieved to find that my prejudicial feelings weren't as impressive or true as I anticipated.

*

Planes are a funny experience, hundreds of people soaring through the air at high speeds, most of them taking it for granted. A few people here and there would look longingly out of the windows, gawping at the views of the world we live on, and a few people would be white ill with a sick-bag crammed between their hands. Most people though would shut their windows and take the time to sleep or become absorbed in something they could do on the ground like a book or music. I didn't mind it at all, as long as they didn't snore or sing, but thought it surreal that many people didn't even appreciate we were flying around thirty-five thousand feet in the air, I've always considered it mightily impressive. But perhaps that's just me.

This particular flight was incredibly uncomfortable for a number of reasons. I'd been on many flights before, but this probably conceded to being the longest, which meant I couldn't gaze out the window the entire time and had to find other ways of occupying myself. I also couldn't get Jasper out of my head. He had been following the exact route as this and therefore at some point I might be travelling over his wreck. That made me feel cold and a little ill. I wasn't scared about the possibility of death but the thought of finding out what happened to Jasper terrified me. As if I was holding on to hope that just maybe he was still alive. It was probably stupid.

Another reason I found it uncomfortable was I had one of those plane cunts in front of me. The ones who stare at the seatbelt signs after take-off, ready to rip the buckle apart and sling their seats as far back as the hinges let them once the sign vanishes. *Arseholes*. I respected the discretion other people used, taking the seat back an inch or so every half an hour, in this instance it gave the person behind time to acclimatise to the shrinking leg room and still left the culprit with over half the journey with the seat at the full one-twenty ish degrees as oppose to the common ninety. I was one of these. I would have made a scene at the ignorance in front of me but for some reason I felt obliged to carry some manners since I had a kid next to me. I guess it was some sort of newly found respect I had for them after the coffee shop incident, but I couldn't quite put a finger on it.

*

I sat for the first three hours staring out the window. Virgin Atlantic offer free beverages so I had two gin and tonics in that time, but it turns out those little sample bottles didn't satisfy my alcohol lust, if anything intensifying my addiction. I contemplated many things as my mind wandered out of the clear window, onto the plane's wing and jumped off soaring through the sky once more like I had when I dreamt I was Aquila.

I thought of my family initially. I didn't much like thinking about them, as I considered it the start of my spiral to shit end. Growing up I had gathered a plethora of happy memories with my family, we often went on holidays or day trips down the coast or to a funfair. I remember my passion to find the best ice cream in England, me and Dad had created a chart where we would rank every ice cream we had out of ten. We once travelled three hours for one ice cream, to a town called Studland, between Poole and Weymouth, just so it could go onto our chart. I remember both of us jumping out of the car with excitement, like two kids instead of just one. It was a windy spring day, with shades of summer making ice-cream tasting a necessity. The sun trying to force itself through the blanket of cloud as we ran up the road towards the ice-cream shop, hand in hand. Dad had said it was a world-famous store, which surprised me considering the half-broken shutters and peeling paint on the cabin. But I didn't suspect he was lying, after all it was forbidden in our house. I remember being so excited that I couldn't make up my mind and ended up going for a Mint Choc Vanilla.

The ice cream lady laughed. "We don't have that one yet I'm afraid sweetie. We do have Mint Choc Chip and Vanilla though, would you like a bit of both?"

I put my hands over my face in excitement and nodded frantically, looking at my Dad for approval. He laughed and rustled my hair as I looked back to the lady and took my gigantic ice cream with both hands. It was too big for me and the weight made the cone topple over and the ice cream to fall onto the floor at my feet. I cried for what felt like hours but realistically was only a minute or so before the lady kindly replaced the ice cream.

"It's got special ice cream glue on it now, so it shouldn't fall off. You can't have it until you've stopped crying though."

I coughed and spluttered, wiping my eyes and nose with the sleeve of my coat, leaving a trail of snot behind. I reached out and retook the ice cream, my smile returning to its former glory.

"Fank you," I said as I struggled once more with the weight of it. My Dad took his and we both set off for the beach, heads submerged in two mountains of ice-cream.

However, soon my parents were working day and night to make all the money they could, it turns out we had enough to live well but they continued to work hard in order to buy the best things and live a life of wealth. Life has taught me money doesn't always equal happiness and this proved true as my parents started arguing at one another and paid little attention to me, at a time when I particularly needed them most. It was following the news of Jasper's crash, when they truly let me down, a shrug of the shoulders from my mother and a heartless pat on the back from my father deemed enough to help me with the hardest years of my life. It took me to the stage of suicide, in need of the love we had once shared but it felt lost and I rented my flat to get away, leaving my family, memories, and ice-cream chart behind. I haven't spoken to them since, neither do I intend to. I'll just have to make it on my own. The chart remained pinned above the desk in my room like an important entity for years, so everyone would see it as they came in. It was my pride and joy, signifying the happiness of family and I'm sure it still exists somewhere. Maybe one day I'll find it again, the chart, and the happiness.

*

The plane hosted a universe of inflight entertainment; music, TV shows, films and books on the screen coming out of the seat in front. I flicked through the selection of books, prodding my fingers excessively hard on the screen to give the seat in front a few sudden and out of time judders, I thought that would annoy the cunt, maybe even wake him up. It was pretty childish to be fair but fuck it. With my prodding I clicked on dark humour books. My cup of tea I guessed. I flicked through the highly recommended and clicked on the first one despite not having heard of the author. The blurb sounded appealing enough as did the five golden stars that glistened above the review section, so I opened the first page and began to read chapter one. Wise Words From Will.

*

I was pretty engrossed from the first page and was nearing the end of the ninth chapter when the hostesses began to wander up and down the aisles distressingly. Like me, half the plane seemed to follow them, eyes adjusting to the dim lighting throughout the cabin. It was almost midnight, so most people had just woken up, their hoods up and dazed eyes scanning to find a sign that something was wrong. Muttering began throughout the plane, but I couldn't quite tune in to the conversations to understand what was up. The buckle light above came on, I obliged and clicked my belt into place in unison with the rest of the plane. We sat like school kids, waiting to be told what was happening and if we were in trouble. Perhaps I was heading for the same end as Jasper?

The captain began to speak. "This is your captain speaking, please don't be alarmed," he said trying to convince himself as much as us passengers. "I request you put your seatbelts on and shut your blinds immediately."

This was met by a moment of commotion, why would we need to shut our windows if we were crashing? I obliged again, as a good school child should, reaching for my blind. It was dark so I thumbled around for a moment trying to find the handle, in doing so I felt my hand shaking, the brink of death clearly getting the better of me. That surprised me. Then I noticed something else, out on the wing of the plane. It was dark and at first I thought it was a shadow of the engine underneath, then I considered a bird, both were wrong. I looked closer. My face now squished against the window. It reminded me of a child in a playground, sitting on the swing, waiting to be pushed. His legs were swinging in turn, his head bobbing from side to side as he sat there singing a song, relaxed. I screamed and he looked at me, it was the kid who had been sitting next to me, now sat on the wing of the plane. He must have heard my scream as he stopped singing and looked over, directly at my window and waved. His face trying to smile but being stopped by the pounding wind, his curly blond hair being pulled back and looking slightly darker from the water vapour outside. I began smashing the plastic window franticly, a way of being able to get to him. The air hostesses grabbed me by the arms and pulled me away from the window like a child having a tantrum screaming and shouting.

"No," I yelled. "Help him you fuckers, help him!"

"There is nothing we can do, please calm down."

"Help him, help him!"

My voice became croaky from the screaming, my eyes had started to water as I continued to focus on the child's eyes staring back. "There must be something!"

As I said that I thought I saw him tumble over in a backwards roll, the wind becoming too much for him. He fell into the engine and blood splattered the windows like I had considered myself doing in the queue for the lounge back at the airport. For some reason I thought I'd seen that, and I wept like a baby, the first time in ages. That didn't happen, my mind playing tricks on me even in the most horrific moments. He continued to sit there for a few minutes longer, swinging his legs joyfully before getting bored and beginning to stand up. I'd just about composed myself from the vision of blood and churned guts that I had nothing left to do apart from watch, still being held by the hostesses who were equally speechless and also watching in shock. As the kid began to push himself up off the side of the wing and onto his feet, I thought about the joke I was told in the coffee shop back in London, hoping that he might stay up in the clouds like the other kid had suggested. I closed my eyes, refusing to look anymore. I was furious with the hostesses for not helping and I was even more annoyed at myself, wasn't there anything I could do? I squeezed my eyes shut hoping to find it was just a dream and trying to force myself to wake up. The hostesses let go off me and I opened my eyes, scampering for my seat to look out the window. I felt dead inside as I looked out, watching the child somersault helplessly to the ground.

*

I must have passed out from the shock, horror, and pain as I woke up back in my seat, twenty-nine A. My hands shaking and my head sweating. I looked out to the wing, nothing. Then I looked around, at the two empty seats next to me, unsure of where the Dad had gone. Then around to the rest of the cabin, the tranquillity shocking and disturbing. I began to cry quietly so no one would look at me. And used my hood to cover part of my face as I leant against the window.

I got a tap on my shoulder after a short while. "You okay?"

It was a kid's voice and I looked up. His face and curly blond hair so distinct. This time it wasn't wet. I continued to cry softly and hugged the little man spontaneously. His Dad could see my distress and, like the kid, thought nothing wrong with the hug.

"It'll be okay," he said slightly shocked as he patted me slowly on the back in reassurance. "I was scared when I first went on a plane too."

I chuckled slightly, still holding the kid. "It's very high."

"Sure is, very beautiful though, like a birdy."

I let go and looked at him. "I'd love to be a bird."

"Me too," he said. "Big colourful one."

His Dad chuckled in the distance. "You've got a parrot at home haven't you Louis?"

I didn't hear Louis respond, instead I was focused on his Dad, wishing I could tell him how proud he should be of his son. I didn't get the chance then, nor did I for the rest of the trip. But as I looked at him, I knew he was, and I just hoped his pride lasted longer than my father's.

*

I'm not too sure where the rest of the plane journey went, I must have dozed back off again, this time evading the nightmares. The rest of the journey I worried about having them, they were becoming frequent and even more realistic after each time, like hallucinations when I was asleep. I particularly worried about this one, not being able to wake up when I tried was a scary thing, powerless in my own head. I guess that was one of the things I wanted to change with this travelling, become powerful in my head, rid myself of the negativity and find something to smile about. It seemed like a child's fantasy, a child's dream, but we'll see.

I'd never really spoken about it either, but I guess sitting on this aeroplane, nearing my destination, it dawned on me. The nerves and anxiety I had felt earlier were returning and I considered maybe it wasn't a fear of stepping into the unknown but a fear of grief. Since Jasper had died, I never grieved my loss, my family forming a hard shell and my compliance to do the same meant I only ever cried on a few occasions, never pushing myself out of its perils. The suicide, negativity, and alcoholism all by products. Sometimes I lusted for the life I had before, but I couldn't bring about the change necessary to make it happen, comatosed in grief. It was only now I considered I was finally trying to tackle it. As the seat belt signs dinged on and the cunt reverted his seat to ninety degrees, the plane began to descend, closing in on my new beginning. I fastened my seat belt, as if ready for the fight to begin. And then I waited.

Chapter 15

Auto Club Speedway

Luggage collection felt like the craziest Nascar race ever, I seemed to stand there for hours watching Dale Earnhardt chase Jeff Gordon with some of the most absurd tailgating I'd ever seen. Of course, this was far from reality, they didn't even race in the same era. Instead I was stood there watching luggage go around in fucking circles, waiting for my token car to finally get out of the pitstop. When he did finally show up, he wasn't very impressive, an old, battered Lowe Alpine walking rucksack found on eBay. He was bright blue, but his age showed giving off more of a faded and dirty tone. I didn't mind it. It's like a pair of shoes really, they always look better once they're used. I grabbed him with one hand and slung him up and over my shoulder as he came past me, his contents rattling and falling as I did so. There was plenty of room in there as I hadn't packed a lot. Only the essentials, toiletries, spare clothes, Jasper's map, and a few other survival accessories, as I never really knew where I would end up. I then began heading towards the lights of San Francisco and the heat, buzz, and exploration that came with it, hoping this adventure would be worthwhile.

Chapter 16

Rules on the Walls

I decided to head to a hostel in San Fran, down at Fisherman's Wharf. I liked the idea of being by the wharf and always opted for the sea over the city. It turned out the wharf was right near the Golden Gate bridge and I felt myself drooling over it as I walked up to the hostel. Its sheer yet minimalistic structure illuminating the backdrop of the entrance.

I stepped inside and was immediately taken back. As hostels go this was extremely luxurious and for a moment I figured I'd walked into the wrong hotel. Of course, this was my first ever experience in a hostel and I was taken back upon realising that hostels weren't all just dingy scout huts for travellers of any age. I had pictured a cramped reception area and a dilapidated lift in the corner, ready to whisk me into the unknown. Therefore, I was pleasantly surprised. The reception was brightly lit holding a sort of modern, vintage look with quirky chandeliers emitting yellow and white lights adjacently across the room. Neon signs consumed most of the walls with corny and supposedly inspirational traveller quotes whilst the rest of the walls had wacky aboriginal patterns splashed as a background to the neon signs, much like the patterns on Aquila's wings that I had seen in one of my dreams. There was a low murmur of music being played, a slow sort of lullaby in the background, I think I heard What's Up? By Four Non-Blondes being played, you know the - hey yeah yeah yeah, hey yeah yeah yeah, what's going on? one. I couldn't hear it too well though, the buzz of travellers over the top making it a hub of peace signs, long beaded necklaces, and braids. I grimaced in the pain of it, it was tragic. Within all of it though, I did get a sense of empathy, jealous of their happiness and how beaming it was. I guess I could say I wanted that, maybe even needed it.

I walked up to the front desk with what must have been a face soiled with my problems as the receptionist looked up and gasped. *Fucking charming.* He soon recovered, sensing I was in the right place for change and welcomed me with open arms and a huge smile. He genuinely looked delighted to see me, as if he knew I had come to face my problems and tackle grief.

"Welcome to Fisherman's Wharf, my name is Matthia. You look ready to discover memories of a lifetime am I right?"

"Uhh. Ermm, I guess so. I was more ready for a quick doze to be honest." The jetlag had begun.

Matthia laughed at me. "A doze I can give you my friend. You need a bed for tonight?"

"I sure do."

Matthia looked down to check the availability, giving me time to study him closer. I was expecting an American to welcome me to America so was pretty shocked to find an overly enthusiastic Italian. He seemed nice enough though, I got the sense that his enthusiasm came from his own experiences of travelling and how beneficial a welcoming face can be to morale and perspective. I liked that. He wore his long brown hair tied in a bun at the back of his head, a pencil behind his ear that had a few piercings in, I noticed the piercings did not stretch to both ears though. *Oh, that would be far too much.* He must have been at least forty, which made me presume he owned the place and wore those John Lennon-esque glasses. He was a cunt. *No. Be more positive*, I said to myself. He was pretty fucking cool, eventually priming my face with the smile he so clearly wanted to see as I chuckled at the demons fighting one another in my head. *Cunt. Cool. Cunt. Fucking cool.* I guess he didn't mean to put a smile on my face in that way, but it was a smile nevertheless.

He looked up to catch it. "What a beautiful smile you have, you must show it more!" His Italian voice sounding almost sexy and making me blush. I figured he was bent. "I'll give you a bed in our mixed dormitory, the best place to meet people. There's a European group in there that'll love to meet you. You shall go in and introduce yourself immediately, payment can wait!"

He rushed energetically around the front desk and grabbed me by the hand. *Definitely bent*. He whisked me up the stairs in the corner of the room that I hadn't initially seen, hidden by a beautiful green plant. I wondered where he was taking me, his hand so lightly holding mine I wondered if I was taking myself there. *Suicidal and gay, fucking brilliant.*

In actual fact, Matthias wasn't fucked in the head like I was, he was an amazing man and looking back on it I respect him very much, grateful for his presence and hospitality. I wish to note that my homophobia is unacceptable, and I am ashamed of what I used to be, but I was what I was.

He rushed me to dorm four, once we'd got the landing, and knocked a special password onto the door, a tune too fast to be able to follow. It was like some secret ritual, like when Harry Potter knocked on those bricks when he first found Diagon alley with Hagrid. It wasn't met by anyone opening the door instead more of a get ready I'm coming in knock, I presumed, given Matthia's few seconds delay in opening the door. As he did, we were met with an eruption of noise, screams, cheers, and excitement. I was taken back and didn't initially follow Matthia into the room until his hand dragged me in. It turns out the eruption was for me, and that was enough to once more plaster a smile onto my face. *Twice in the last ten minutes, shit I must have been drugged on the plane or something*. I stood there in shock as eleven faces came up to greet me; a Portuguese, two Canadians, three Germans, an Italian, and three Swiss, I couldn't quite tell where the last one was from. A south east European country, maybe Serbia?

It turns out dorm four is a special dorm and has its rules plastered on the walls. Rules on the walls. Whoever the twelve individuals in the dormitory were had to travel around San Francisco together for however long they were there, it wasn't up for discussion. Apparently. The great eruption was recognition of the completion of the group and their final member, me. After all their greetings they beckoned a speech. I flushed red, embarrassed.

“Hi guys, thanks for the welcome, I’m-”

A call rallied from the group of new faces. “Our friend is English!”

There was a cheer, as if an English person fitted the mysterious puzzle that came with the rules of the room. I never presumed the Europeans considered us English too highly, but I guess that was just a presumption.

As I stood there laughing with my newly found friends, I never considered the prospect of suicide, for the first time in years. It soon came back of course, would take a lot more than that but I wondered; perhaps the journey Jasper would lead me on would resurrect my soul and peace. Protect me from the nightmares I lived in? Recover some happiness, that beautiful smile? Only time would tell.

Chapter 17

Cream tea

The entirety of dorm four made their way down to the beach that evening but to my disappointment Matthia had to stay and work at the hostel. I had grown quite fond of him in the little time I knew him, which surprised me considering his sexuality. Not that that should have made a difference, but it did. The beach was beautiful, long white plains and a deep green and blue sea bobbing up and down. We stayed till it was dark listening to music and dancing, a celebration of meeting each other that night. The atmosphere was electric which I put down to their energetic and bubbly characters, the alcohol probably had a hand in that too. I felt calmed by their spirits, much like I did when I spent similar moments with Jasper, the company I felt I was missing, longing for my best friend as I sat their sipping a tropical lager from California, Tidal Wave. As much as I thought about Jasper at the start of the evening, I tried to keep it hidden, small-talking and wandering between different little huddles of the group. They weren't so much cliques as of yet, it was more people just getting to know each other. This wasn't me though, I was rubbish at talking to people, no confidence and nothing interesting to say. Just boring. I was sat on a small mound of sand, with the comfort of alcohol in my grasp, looking out to sea. I drank and I drank. The unsuccessful remedy I had turned to for help in the past few years, again working its magic. The golden gate bridge dominated my periphery vision on the left as it absorbed the final shards of light that the day had to offer. I took a deep breath, calming myself as I felt my head clouding under the alcoholic strain, the golden gate bridge beginning to move in time with the waves that bobbed underneath. I don't know why; I didn't feel stressed as such but the wafts of beer and my alcoholic ambiguity a deep reminder being here with these people didn't mean my problems were solved. The battle had hardly begun. One of the Canadians must've sensed my anxiety and sat down beside me slowly, as if I was going to refuse his company. I wanted to but managed to stop myself.

"Hey dude, must have been quite a shock for you back there in the room eh?"

I nodded. "Caught me off guard." I wanted to say something else but chose not to.

He pointed out to his Canadian buddy, who was currently drinking a beer upside down with the help of the Germans. "Me and Felix were five and six to arrive and we got quite a shock, so I can't imagine being in your boots. Hey, you don't mind though do you? Tagging along in the group n'all. We asked everyone else but got a hell of a bit excited seeing the last person, you." He pushed my shoulder, knocking my balance slightly which I managed to gather without looking too pathetic.

I smiled. "It's nice to feel wanted," looking at him for the first time. "Thank you."

He chuckled, got up and began mocking my English accent. "Oh, do you hear that fellas, the Queen and her little dog want some cream tea."

I don't know where he got cream tea from, nor why poor Elizabeth was brought into it. It was absurdly quite funny. I didn't show it though, instead rolling my eyes as the group began to laugh, a couple of them also trying the imitation but to lesser success.

He looked back down at me and winked. "Name's Stu."

I took his hand, and he pulled me up onto my feet as I replied. "Noah."

*

The evening raced by, and soon it was midnight. Everyone was still up on their feet, dancing round in a circle, thirteen shadows but only twelve strangers. The music continued to blare, and laughter continued to echo through the night sky. The thirteenth shadow belonged to someone who wasn't a stranger, their long hair tied into a bun, a bit of a giveaway, even in the darkness. Jasper. He stood there dancing with us for hours, as real as Stu and Felix either side of him. I was shocked by his presence, wondering how and when he had got there, my mouth open, speechless. I wanted to run up and give him a hug but thought it would ruin the atmosphere between our new friends, so I didn't. I smiled at him and he smiled back, I guess that was enough. After a while, I noticed Jasper looking at the figure of the young Serbian, or so I guessed, in the sand a few metres away from the rabble of young dancers. So, I gestured that he go speak to her, he did. I watched as he walked over, curious if the girl would be able to see him or if he was just a hallucination.

"Do you mind?" He motioned to the space next to her.

She looked up and met the question with a shake of the head, not too strong but enough to push her hair across her face. It struck me how she had never met this man but let him sit with her, a bravo to Jasper. He was always good at talking to strangers, doing the same here again now. She was a pretty girl called Mikky, hair in a blonde wavy bob down to her shoulders. I didn't fancy her, but she was pretty, nevertheless. She was scanning the sky, as if she was hoping to see something.

"What you looking for?"

She remained silent for a moment and I wondered if I and Jasper had both wrongly presumed she spoke English. The egotism of the English. *For fuck sake.* I was going to ask again for him, maybe a bit slower, but then she spoke. "Friends, family, those I lost." She smiled and pointed up to the brightest stars. "There, there, there, there. All looking on me."

He nodded agreeing and I felt myself nodding slowly and hesitantly in the background as I continued to eavesdrop their conversation.

She must have noticed as she asked. “What about you Noah? Have you lost anyone?”

I was confused how she knew my name, word gets around fast apparently and then I considered why she had asked me if she was speaking to Jasper.

I saw Jasper thinking about the question and nodding, about to talk. “No,” I blurted quite suddenly.

Mikky didn’t seem deterred by it though. “You’re lucky you know, a horrible feeling and a pain that doesn’t go away lightly. Still makes you the best person you can be, grateful that your life is still yours.” She turned to me as she said it. “Never forget that Noah, whenever anything awful happens just think of me. I’ll help guide you.”

I’d never understood how wonderful Mikky was to provide comfort and safety like that, I wish I had thanked her mercifully but in that moment Jaspers face lay imprinted in my mind and I thought of little else. He looked rejected when I had blurted out the lie, as if he had failed. His eyes looking toward the ground he was sat on as if he was afraid of me, as if what he’d heard was a nightmare. I noticed he looked up to meet my gaze briefly and then shook his head in the same disappointment he had shown before. It made me feel sick. And then poof, he was gone. Mikky seemingly oblivious to the disappearance next to her. My mouth gaping and my mind lost. I was insane.

*

I don’t quite know why I didn’t tell Mikky about Jasper, it seemed so true and perfect to mention in that moment, a bond that we share but she will never know about. I would have loved to have told her, but it didn’t feel right. I couldn’t bring it up without the emotion that came with it, and I wasn’t ready for that, so it stayed deep inside me, lingering. Never gone, atleast not yet. Jasper had some work to do.

Chapter 18

I am a river

I woke up the next morning with little recollection of the night before. After Jasper and Mikky spoke, my mind went all fuzzy and I couldn't remember how I got home. I didn't have to wait long to find out. Stu and Felix bombarded my fragile head with laughter and stories of our adventures the night before as soon as my eyes opened. It turns out I hadn't gone home, instead heading into San Francisco to check out the nightlife with the two of them. I felt a sort of guiltiness as Stu and Felix looked down on me.

"Gheeez buddy you sure know how to drink."

"Yeerr man, you've got a problem or something."

They both released a torrent of laughter as they reminisced. A few of the others were sat up in their bunks listening to the comedy duo, and chuckling away in unison, others remained asleep.

"Fuck, was it that bad?" I muttered after a few of their stories.

"We had to carry you home, never seen anyone drink as much as that. Ever."

They must have noticed I wasn't finding the recollection as hilarious as they were.

"Frigging fun night though ey Noah, did you enjoy it?" A smug grin forming over Felix's face, as if he knew that I hadn't a clue what had happened.

I was still in bed at that point but remember it being no more than five seconds between my feet touching the polished wood floor and my head being over the toilet bowl, leaving the laughter in room four as I staggered along the corridor and across to the toilets. Beads of sweat formed across my brow as I lent beside it, spit dribbling across my bottom lip and cascading down my chin. I felt like a river was about to be released, rising from inside me like it was magnetised by my tonsils. It rose slowly and that made me gag a couple of times. My whole body heaving under the pressure like one of those wave machines you get in swimming pools. I looked into the bowl of clear water I was about to vandalise. *Fuck, sorry Jasper.* I chundered three or four times. The acid rising and filling my mouth, bastard of a taste. It was pretty liquidy, evidence of the sheer volume of alcohol I had drunk the night before. *Fucking state. Fucking Cunt. Fuck.*

*

I sat there for a fair while longer, partly because I couldn't be arsed to move and partly because I didn't want to go and face the smug Canadians. I hadn't spoken much to Felix last night, at least during the parts I could remember so my first memory of him was that smug face as he stood there looking down into my bunk. It wasn't painting a flattering impression of him in my head. *He's a twat.* I continued to consider the previous night, trying to piece together small parts of my memory. To be honest, I think I was just making things up.

*

I sat there even longer. Thoughts filling the room. I was a mess, I was worthless, an idiot, uninspired and encumbered. *Fucking irrelevant.* I considered who would miss me as I did so many times back in the hole of London. I knew no one in San Francisco so the list didn't reach beyond my already dead best friend. *One. He's fucking dead Noah. None.* I felt my head twist, no one needed me, I was merely one of the empty souls that filled the world. I wasn't the first suicidal twat and I wouldn't be the last, but I couldn't bare it anymore. Let the darkness take me, the darkness is turning lighter. I wanted it. Nothing could change the way I was, this was me. *Suicidal Noah. Dead fucking Noah. I'm going to kill myself* I thought. *End the suffering, end the pain.*

I was now looking at myself in the rectangle mirror above the sink. The pain and emptiness both staring back at me. I smashed my head against the mirror causing it to fragment. My head stung. I did it again, this time harder. The sound of glass smashing rang in my ears. I did it again. The first sign of blood on the mirror. Again. My head began to throb, liquid rivers began forming from the top of my head, running down my forehead. Again. And again. I looked at the mirror, it was in disarray painted a dark red and mosaiced into tiny parts. Again. I looked beyond it and saw myself, the top of my head seeping with blood, running down my face either side. That didn't bother me. Again. I began feeling dizzy, the room was spinning. My face changed, becoming grey and lifeless. I blinked and my face was gone. Replaced by that of my best friend. I managed a slight smile, let this be the last image that I see before I go I begged. I continued to spin as the face was replaced once more. Still Jaspers only grey, lifeless like mine had been. One stark difference though, he was now dead. I collapsed unconscious. Unconscious, but not dead.

*

There was a knock at the door, quietly so I presumed it wasn't the Canadians coming to take a look at the idiot Englishman.

"I'll be a minute," I manged to croak.

The door opened anyway but I didn't look back, don't think I could have managed it. Still, I thought it was a bit fucking rude opening the lavatory on someone.

"What the fuck do you not get from I'll be a minute." This time the croak had a bit of anger in it, a flash of what I was like in my English Mayfair Journalist life. I hid my face, the fuss that would come with the blood would fuck me off.

I struggled to see clearly, the blood impairing my vision, the person came round to face me and begun wiping it out of my eyes delicately using toilet roll.

"Take it easy man."

It made me feel even worse than I already did, my shoulders had dropped at the voice. Not what the voice said, I didn't give a fuck. It was who said it that got me, my shoulders continued to sink, lower than the floor I was laid out on.

"Get out of my head."

"Take it easy."

I was confused. *What the fuck does he mean by that?* "Take it easy? You're not even fucking real, leave me alone."

He wiped my forehead clean, leaving a vague hint of blood.

He slapped me across the back and somehow that made me chunder again.

"Fuck off Jasper." My head throbbing.

"You need me. Don't make me be your mum Noah."

"I don't want you here, I'm going fucking mental. Leave me alone. I don't want to be here."

"What I'd do to be here now-"

"Just fuck off."

"It won't end like this, we'll get you better. You didn't come all this way for-"

"You'll be doing fucking nothing. Get lost."

He didn't reply. That made me feel slightly guilty for drinking and trying to kill myself, as I felt when Stu and Felix had told me I had a problem, what now felt like hours ago. I hadn't come halfway around the world for this, collapsed in a hostel toilet with blood all over the place and a weak attempt at suicide. Jasper had taken the moral fucking high ground on me, like Obi-Wan had against Anakin in Revenge of the Sith. I probably looked as bad as Anakin aswell. *Oh god I better not turn into Vader,* I guess that's what Jasper meant when he said I needed him. That I did. I had failed again and when you fail at something over and over, it starts to mean something. Right? Perhaps it's not meant to be? I highly doubted that and was confident that I would no doubt try again but for now Jasper had won. I hoped he wouldn't give up on me, I told myself I would apologise next time I see him.

If he ever returned.

Chapter 19

Reality Check

It wasn't the start I wanted to travelling. I was keen to get away from my problems and negative nature and find peace once more. I wanted to want to be alive, a strange desire, one that most people don't understand. I'd been living in a rut of grief and despair for years and wanted to rid myself of it before I rid the world of myself. It was one or another. Like a tug of war between life and death. In those years between Jaspers death and my decision to travel I looked on like a spectator, unsure of which side would win. My arms were the rope, my body being dragged this way and that. Just never the way I wanted to go. Then again, it would have helped knowing which way I wanted to go. So, as I sat there on the floor of the hostel toilet, I figured I had to expel my possessed thoughts, alcoholism, suicide, negativity, and grief. I concluded Jasper was here for them, I'd continue to see him until they were gone and then I'd feel better. We'd feel better. A load of bollocks? Maybe. Did you have a better idea? Thought not. I had to try. Not for myself, as I've said so many times, I didn't give a fuck. But I had to try. For him.

*

I stormed out of that toilet like a man on a mission, I'd chucked out the last alcohol I'd have in at least a year and I was ready to cast the spell of life on myself. Live and prosper. Stu and Felix saw me coming and laughed once more, only to stop quite suddenly when they saw my face. I didn't realise it at the time, but I was biting my lips, my eyes pierced with fire. And it wasn't till even later when I noticed my lips were bleeding that I'd understood the shock on their faces. I grabbed my bag without saying a word and made for the door.

Eleven faces staring. Come to think about it, maybe it was the swelling and remnants of blood that startled them.

“We’re heading to the Marin headlands today on the other side of the Golden Gate, do you fancy it Noah?”

I stopped as I reached the doorway. My hands clasping both sides of the door like a slalom skier ready to begin his descent. Only I was beginning a long gruelling ascent instead. I turned to face my new friends, eleven faces continuing to stare at me, some standing, some sitting and some still half-asleep. I felt one of the cuts begin to drip blood down my face.

“I’ve got something I need to do.”

I turned and never looked back, the same approach I used in the months to follow.

Bear creek gifted me my first look at the giant Redwood trees I'd been so desperate to see. I didn't have time to get a tape measure out, neither did I even have one, but I remember the awe I was in. We were in.

"Pretty fucking beautiful eh." Jasper stood there underneath the branches of the Redwood I was ogling up in the sky, his back resting on the base of the tree and his hands on the back of his head like he was sunbathing whilst sitting up. He looked tranquil, composed, beautiful, and I found myself jealous at the serenity of my best friend. Of course, this was after his appearance had given me one hell of a fright.

"Fucking hell Jasper, you scared me shitless."

He laughed. "Why? I've been with you the whole time."

I had come to the realisation that he'd keep popping up in my head back in Francisco, but I wasn't quite ready to tell him that or accept that he was doing what I was doing. "Spare me the bullshit Jasp."

"You didn't think those cars had cat called you did you Noah?" He laughed.

I scoffed. "Who else is there for them to cat call?"

"I'm here too," he said as he punched my arm in a friendly gesture.

I ignored it. "You're dead Jasper."

He smirked. "How can I be dead if you can see me?"

I sighed. Here I was talking to my dead best friend. "Fuck knows Jasp, I'm a fucking loony, I'm mental."

"You know the truth Noah, I'm here by your side till we're ready," he shrugged and looked at the pines on the ground, fiddling them with his feet.

"Ready for what," I said as I glanced back up to the high branches, the sun now glistening through the small holes in the foliage. I became mesmerised as I waited for the answer and slurred "ready for what," a second time, but still no answer. Poof, he was gone. I guess that meant he didn't fancy the hike to Lomond. *Meet me there then you lazy bastard.*

Chapter 23

Machines

I arrived at Lomond just after eight, making very good time during the day and meaning I saw the last of the sunset as it disappeared underneath the tree line, the light fading with it. From what I saw the lake was beautifully tranquil and untouched, the last shards of golden sun ricocheting off the almost perfectly flat surface and a few schools of fish the only disturbances underneath it. I admired its naturality and begged the rest of California would amount to this level of beauty. Lomond almost deserved a sandy beach or cove to finish its perfection, but I have to admit the lonely rocks jarring out far into the lake and the great redwoods and pines growing right on the shores gave it a unique, picturesque setting and I wouldn't have changed a thing about it.

Once my admiration for nature's beauty had peaked I decide to begin finding an area to camp, I presumed a lake like this would have rangers so decided to head into the closed section, telling myself it wasn't closed for any particular reason. I figured the rangers wouldn't look in these areas, leaving me safe to camp without a permit of whatever bullshit document you would otherwise need. I wanted an area close to the waters edge and not much past eight thirty I found it, a wide area that was open apart from the tree canopies above, which formed an intertwined ceiling over the space. I spotted a few holes in the canopy as I gazed up and I looked forward to its dappled sunlight raining down on my camp in the morning, nature's alarm. I began on the tent, something I hadn't done since me and Jasper voyaged into the wilderness. Now he'd left me to do it myself. Luckily even in the fading light it wasn't the most challenging build, the two poles under a metre long at either end kept up by bright yellow guide ropes, the extent of difficulty I encountered. I remember thinking the end product looked much like a triangular cave, but normal people would refer to it as a triangular prism, I guess both create a decent enough picture. The end by the door had a separate compartment to the main area, a vestibule, where you just dump all your shit basically. I finished stamping the pegs into the ground, which proved more difficult than I envisaged, the ground foundations rockier than visibly suggested. Also, the successful input of camping pegs relies on a strong mallet or hammer to direct the force in a straight motion to prevent any unexpected curvature of the pegs, my abnormal technique of stamping was none of the above. So, the five minutes it took to conduct a less than satisfactory job had unfortunately brought my anger out, cussing at anything and everything. I think I remember swearing at the flies that flew overhead, watching the pegs bend underneath my foot and getting pretty annoyed with life, for that moment forgetting I was in the haven of California and pulling my past back into view. I took a seat on the ground by the lake and tried my best to focus on nothing and everything. My breathing, the trees, the birds, the silence. I had to regain myself, or I may as well have gone home. In the end I decided it wasn't quite windy enough to be blown away and accepted defeat in true David and Goliath fashion, besides I hadn't eaten since snacking on a few trail nuts as I made my way out of Walmart, towards the Los Gatos Creek trailhead. *Fucking camping.*

*

I ate tuna and rice that night, and whilst it wasn't quite a pièce de résistance, it certainly filled me up, a good source of protein, vitamin and carbohydrate. I ate it so quickly I began to feel cramp in my stomach and leant forward clutching it and wincing.

Jasper laughed, deciding to appear next to me, sat on his walking backpack like I was.

"Nice of you to join," I said through the pain.

"Wouldn't miss your cooking for the world, never were much good were you."

"Fuck you."

He chuckled a bit more then fell silent. I looked up, worried he had left me again, but he hadn't, and I felt a huge wave of relief, something mesmerising about watching him rock back and forth on his pack whilst looking up at the sky. Something mesmerising about his company. That was the something I guess I missed, the light that had gone out in my life.

"Why do you miss me when I'm always here with you."

I hadn't been looking at him in that moment so didn't quite understand what he meant. "But you're not here Jasp, I wish you were but you got taken away from me and now I've forgotten how good it could be to feel alive."

"Not here here, but here."

I looked back to him this time, the plethora of 'here' becoming some sort of puzzle for me to decipher. I was no Turing but turns out it wasn't all that difficult in the end, he was pointing to his heart and then in turn pointed to mine, reaching out and tapping my chest. I felt his finger digging into my tshirt and pressing against my ribs, the bodyguard of the heart. I felt a fire and for some reason I suddenly feared I was having a heart attack, *stupid bastard*, I'd forgotten what emotions truly felt like. I sank back into my pack after shooting upright in fear, my force almost pushing me up onto my feet.

"Don't neglect it Noah, you don't grow immune from emotion, it's something beautifully unique about humans. Don't let anything or anyone take that away from you, happiness stems from not giving up." It lingered in the air for no more than a split second. "I can't wait for your emotions to explode when you see the Californian birds."

The final sentence stopped the seriousness of his mood from filling the air around us, something he knew I wouldn't appreciate. For a moment though, I didn't lust the Californian girls, the impact of his words drilling into me just like it did back at the house in Edinburgh with that family all those years ago. His power and positivity resonating into me like some mystical force. Then I sat back and began lusting the Californian girls, hot blondes, confident brunettes. I was midway through wonderland when Jasper held out a hipflask, I took it, not considering it odd that he owned one, he was never one for excessive drinking and this was the tool of exactly that, an excessive drinker. I had a swig without thinking about what I was doing. The liquid hit my lips, its heat warming my mouth and down my neck. And poof. He was gone, the hipflask of rum still glued in my hand. I sunk deeper into my backpack, so low that I wondered if I was even still sitting on it. I'd failed him. *Fucking hell.*

At that moment, the lakes tranquillity was broken for the first time since I'd arrived, ripples running away from the area I last saw the sinking hipflask.

"Fuuuck!"

I screamed some more and then some more, my clenched fists stopping the blood circulation in my hands and my head battered with guilt, my pettiness and reflection whether there is much point in this at all. I remember considering the possibility of walking into the lake with Mr Lowe Alpine to drag me under as I began clearing the stove before jumping through the vestibule at around ten according to my watch. I was knackered from the hike and also wanted to get away from how shit I felt from that drop of alcohol. Despite my outbreak and dark imagination, the feeling of regret did emit some light. *Maybe I was getting better?* It simultaneously started raining, vanquishing any revival of hope and the perfect atonement for my sins. *Fucking camping. What an idiot.*

Chapter 24

Poor Mr Lowe Alpine

Despite the strange animal howls and screeches I slept relatively well that night. It was only once my bladder hurt that I began to toss and turn. I have never much liked getting out of bed once I'm in it and would often refuse to go to the toilet until I felt a dagger forced through the pelvic area. The first calls of exotic Californian birds marked that it was around five in the morning when I buckled under the pressure and went in search of the zip of the tent. Nature's birds that is, unfortunately, not the ones I had dreamt about throughout the night. Boy how I wouldn't mind waking up to them calling out. As I fumbled with the zip I thought of Jasper again, after the Cali girls of course, how I'd let him down once more and how I couldn't wait for him to appear once more to apologise. I was surprised he hadn't pulled me into another nightmare he'd concocted, *an undeserved night of respite* I thought. I managed to bundle my way out of the fucking tent after breaking the zip. Cheap shite. Strangely, I somehow found myself lying facing the canopy above, which was slowly becoming more active with bird movement. I exhaled and inhaled slowly, trying to find the peace I was after. In out, in out, in. The blade sunk deeper into my bladder marking the end of the melodic breathing. I jogged over to the lake trying to find a nice balance between a run and a walk that didn't make my bladder feel it would explode. I must have looked like some kind of drunk, but there wasn't anyone to care. I ripped down my pants and begun slashing all over the plants just prior to the lakes edge, closing my eyes and using natures noise to carry me through the thirty seconds of relief. I slowly pulled them up, now more cautious of breaking natures peaceful tones, As I began to spin on my feet ready for another hour or two of sleep, I heard a crack of twigs on the forest floor. Too loud to be the wind. They say you often piss before shitting and that was sort of the case for me, the scare almost forcing my bowels to move in a way only recognisable by a toilet. My body probably would have committed to the indecent act if not scared for the noise it would make, so luckily for me it did not. Twigs cracked again. I scanned the area for the sign of movement, an early walker maybe? It was still fairly dark so I couldn't tell, my face scrunched up as I squinted into the forest, no signs. More twigs. I began to take a step back.

"Don't fucking move Noah."

I retraced my foot back to the ground it was originally laid. Too my left, Jasper. He looked even more terrified than I imagined I looked, as if he knew what the noise was. I began to whisper back but Jasper cut me off.

"Sh."

I took his cue and then shrugged as if asking what it was and he mimed one word without breaking his gaze with the darkness, bear.

I didn't realise it possible, but the thought of a bear made me feel even worse than I did before, now I knew what I was looking for, I saw it a whole lot clearer. The bear was around six foot long, the size of a small car and probably weighed near six hundred pounds, at least that was my random heat-of-the-moment guess. He wore a huge black coat and used his huge talons to prod at my beloved vestibule. He looked in my direction as if asking for my permission, the cold whites of his eyes becoming visible, the fist-sized snout quivering as if smelling me from twenty feet away. He definitely didn't need it. He grunted as he stood up on his back legs before crashing back down with his paws crushing the ground, I had been lying on not five minutes earlier. The thought of being underneath made me want to turn and run as fast as I could but I found myself rooted to the floor, the only movement I could muster coming from my reverberating arms and legs. Jasper continued to stare, petrified and I felt my breathing become disjointed and found myself focusing on not spluttering. In out, in out. I felt my forehead begin to sweat but I didn't have the courage to move and brush it off. It ran down my face.

I stood rooted. The bear continued to stare at me, breathing in and out really fast to let out a sort of woofing noise, a technique they used to show power, it worked, I was powerless.

"What are we going to do?" I spluttered to Jasper, not sure if I even made a noise.

"Stay exactly where you fucking are."

I was content with the answer and my eyes turned back to the bear, my head slowly turning with the same caution. I didn't dare blink, aware of how fast the predator could be. It was like a western, waiting for the first move. After what felt like hours the bear began prodding my bag once more, exhilarating more force with each prod before it turned into huge swings at poor Lowe Alpine. It must have survived three of four huge blows and I wondered how many I could have survived, maybe one. Probably none. The contents flew out, trail nuts airborne in the morning breeze before resting across the forests surface. The bear had now lost interest in me and I felt myself stop shaking, though still unable to move. For the first time mine and Jasper's alarmed looks met each other, no actual words said. I knew if we weren't silent there would be a few 'fucks' and a few 'shits' echoing through the trees.

"Black bear."

This made me feel a lot safer. I knew from school they weren't as aggressive as Grizzly bears and tended to stick to nuts, berries, and insects. Very rarely did they ever attack humans and only when provoked. I continued to stare at it though, my eyes beginning to suffer as a result of the lack of blinking and I felt myself forced into a momentary image of nothing. Then back open. In a way it fascinated me and I almost grew to enjoy the harrowing, life-threatening experience, something I'll never forget. The animals force and magnitude something not often seen on land in this world. I felt privileged in a way and like to believe I almost swanned over and paid my respects to the animal. In actual fact I was still slightly terrified. Slightly another word for extremely in that context. I did continue to be mesmerised by its beauty though, its nose scouring the floor for the scattered trail nuts, twitching uncontrollably. Its huge paws grafting away at the ground pushing the nuts into accessible places to be able to eat them from, all the while occasionally looking up at me.

I don't remember exactly how long I was there, stuck like stone, but my body ached from being cramped in the same position when Jasper finally allowed us to move, after I'd watched the stocky back of a bear plod away, satisfied with my kilo of trail nuts. I was also aware that it was light when we did finally move, the birds were chirping and the dappled sunlight that the foliage had promised me the night before was living up to its expectations.

"I… I don't know what to say," I said to Jasper. But he'd gone, poof. Like some guardian angel. My apology would have to wait once more.

Chapter 24

The Good, The Bad and The Ugly

It was a mere four hour walk to Santa Cruz, equating to twelve and a half miles, and my early start meant I arrived at the West coast around noon. The walk had given me time to encapsulate my meeting with the bear and I pondered why It hadn't ripped my head off. A few weeks ago I would have wished it had, but now I felt a strange desire to find an alternative way out of the gloom and nightmare I had been living in for the past years. Perhaps it was fate? Perhaps it was the American heat?

I hadn't quite planned what to do when I got to Santa Cruz and after polishing off a classic American sub, thick with meat and sauces I wasn't familiar with, I found myself down at the boardwalk wondering what the hell to do next. I figured I'd done enough walking for the last two days so wouldn't begin the trek down the West coast just yet. That meant I was resigned to another night at a hostel, take two. I headed to an internet café to look up what Santa Cruz offered me in terms of a decent sleep.

As it turned out, the city of Santa Cruz, or town or whatever, isn't as enthusiastic about hostels as its bigger brother, Francisco. That meant stumping up a little more cash to get a room in a local inn. I found Howard Johnson by Wyndham not far from the coast and at a bargain price so went to check it out.

*

Poor Howard was an ugly fucker, a sort of sandy, beige brown colour coated the walls of the inn and vividly reminded me of the Chicken Korma I'd often have at the local Dynasty curry house, Raj and his buddies now a thousand miles away. Of course, like any decent person I'd moved on from the Korma to the Masala and then further into Indian cuisine around the age of fourteen or so, just so there are no prejudicial valuations of my taste.

As I walked in I could only presume Howard had burnt his budget on the location and had little to spend on furnishing, the spectacular view of the Cruz boardwalk and beautiful Californian waves through the reception window being tainted by a tacky sofa, broken front door and an ugly middle-aged receptionist. I remember wondering whether this was all that California had to offer and whether the girls I'd dreamt about so many times were nothing more than pigments of my imagination. I wondered then whether those uplifting and positive thoughts I'd encountered, away from the gloom I'd suffered for a number of years were nothing more than minute flashes. Of course, the introduction of Scar the next day would completely contradict that fear.

The receptionist immediately reminded me of a less enthusiastic Claire and for a moment I thought I'd stepped back into the Mayfair Journalist. To be fair to Claire, she always tried to be happy, this woman was content with a face like a slapped arse. I looked down at her obligatory name badge: *Say hello! I'm Sharon.*

"Hello Sharon!" I said maybe too enthusiastically, which can't have been considered anything less than mocking her. In reality I was just trying to keep away any disappearance back into the shell I'd been so comfortable in over the years since Jasper's death.

She was staring at her computer but her eyes moved up to meet me. "What d'ya want?" She said in her thick West accent.

Fucking rude cow I thought, she was pissing me off already. How far I could last before my old self collapsed in on her? "There's a lot of things I want in life dear Sharon, meeting you was one. How are you today?"

She clearly wasn't the most flirtatious type.

"Better before you walked in."

Don't crack Noah, don't crack. "Awww Shaz don't be like that. The sun is shining, the sea is beautiful, and we have had the fortune of meeting one another."

She grunted. "You English are so pathetic."

Now I'd often insult the English stereotype, a lot of us are pathetic granted, but to hear Sharon's fat arse say it made me angry, and I collapsed inward. My new embodiment unable to resist the possessed soul that scratched at the surface anymore. My skin split and the demon broke out, something out of Hawkins, Stranger Things. Jasper wouldn't be happy and to be honest, it wasn't a very impressive attempt at resisting my obligatory evil.

"Oh fuck off you fat bitch, give me a room as far away from this reception as possible, I couldn't bear to have to sleep anywhere near your lardy arse."

She looked up, her facing hardly reacting at all. She clearly wasn't shocked. "There it is."

"Go and jump off the end of the boardwalk you boring slapped up cunt, doubt you can swim but do us all a favour and put some rocks in your pockets anyway." In hindsight I'd probably taken it too far, but I couldn't be bothered to feel ashamed. "Now book me a room and hurry up," I paused and sunk low. My body shrunk before the reception desk till I could no longer see over the top. My hands grappled the edge as I stood on tiptoes, like a kid peering over. "Add a tip for yourself, calling you a cunt was a bit far."

She stared at me and leant back in her chair. "This is going to be the most expensive single room of your life."

I sighed, my outbreak getting the better of me. Lesson learnt, so me and my wallet hoped.

Sharon had taken redemption of justice into her own hands as she said she would and generously gifted herself a two-hundred and fifty dollar tip, a bit extreme even for the word cunt eh? I was in no position to argue though, the shame I'd tried to cover earlier getting the better of me as I passed over three-hundred dollars. "You have a lovely day Sharon." It sounded condescending again despite no intention of doing so this time and I wondered if I would ever be able to change, I was a puppet on some ropes and had no control of myself. I wish Jasper had control of the ropes, not fucking Satin.

*

I chucked the key in the door and walked in, it wasn't quite awful, but it wasn't anywhere near nice. The duvet cover standing out as one of the ugliest décor choices I'd been alive to witness, it was one of those old, multi-coloured quilt covers and worked in tandem with the yellow walls to make the room look like something out of nineteen-eighty. The rooms redemption feature was the huge windows on the far side, looking out to that beautiful view I noticed in Sharon's lair, not ten minutes earlier. I had time to focus on it a bit better now, and pondered over to it, opening the window as wide as it could go and sticking my head out. A subtle breeze hit me and wooshed my hair over my face as I breathed in the sea air. The palm trees stood tall, I hadn't noticed them before, but they now took residence along either side of the beach boulevard, which welcomed crowds of people – tourists, skaters, lovers, surfers, runners. It was like a scene from GTA V, except I wasn't there running up to people and knocking them out like I did so many times on the game so in that sense it was so much more beautiful. Time flew as I stared longingly out of the window, watching the sun fall below the horizon, the shades of amber and red striking the middle of the sea and bursting out into every degree of the one-hundred and eighty that the sea occupied. I continued to admire the scenery until it grew dark and the sun was lost, then I went and got some Californian grub.

Chapter 25

Peace, Pancakes and love

The evening had flown by and before I knew it my alarm was ringing at seven-thirty, breakfast closed at nine, so I had to get up and ready before then. I'd spent the evening strolling through Santa Cruz downtown and along the boardwalk before sitting on the beach for half an hour or so in an attempt to cleanse my soul following my run in with Sharon, fuck knows if it worked. I was also contemplating my next move; Jaspers plan was to scale down the west coast and that was also my ambition but the trek down to LA could take ages by foot. I considered train and bus but both had the likely prospect of missing some beautiful coastline and views. I then pondered hitchhiking but didn't consider myself outgoing enough for that. *You fucking pussy Noah*. In the end I gave up debating it and walked back to Howard, ready for an early-ish night, I'd worry about it when the time came.

Well at seven-thirty I guess the time had come and I deliberated my possibilities whilst sitting up in bed, I didn't conjure much partly because I was hungry and partly because of the distracting view out the window, the boardwalk already buzzing with early risers. I figured I'd think better with a full stomach, so I got up, showered and chucked on some clothes, white t-shirt and my usual cargo trousers. I also grabbed some sunglasses in the hope that if Sharon was down at breakfast, she wouldn't notice me. It was a bit of a futile attempt really, my long wavy hair a bit of a give-away. I guess tying it in a bun would have been a more reasonable attempt at anonymity, but I couldn't bring myself to finalise the cunt look, not just yet. I probably hadn't even earnt it. I left poor Mr Lowe Alpine in the room, even more faded than at the airport and with a few holes in the roof and side of the bag from the bear, I'd come and get him after breakfast.

*

To be fair to Howard a decent portion of the budget must have gone into the breakfast, the selection was vast and I found myself stood there considering what my appetite desired, the availability giving me a conundrum I enjoyed. I discarded cereal and fresh fruit without a second thought and yogurt soon joined them. Pancake or pastries? I looked back and forth at them, like a tennis game. It must have been match point as it seemed to go on forever and I decided to grab a coffee while my decision continued to be contemplated in my head, at least they didn't have a glass of red wine for four pound like the Oak. In the end the pancake won the point with no explanation other than I really fancied giving that huge pancake machine a go, my eyes googling it like it was Christmas Day. The machines are relatively simple, and I soon got the jist of what was going on, batter in, lid down, red light, green light, lid up, pancake done. I dowsed it in maple syrup, or golden syrup, fuck knows the difference, and then surprisingly went back to the fruit which I had so quickly disregarded and chucked some of that on top, made me feel a bit healthier, I guess. It looked beautiful and reminded me of the classic white girl instagram story, only missing the caption, *With my besties xoxox* or *Breakfast with my girlies x.* It reminded me of how much I did not miss all the egotism and attempts at fame and it made me chuckle that some people could get so engrossed in the way they look on social media. Sado's. I didn't take a picture for the gram, instead tucking in and beginning my struggle to an empty plate.

*

It was probably around fifteen minutes later that Scar, Ralph and Alec came into the food hall, making a bit of a racket and causing a few heads to turn, including my own. The two boys were laughing out front as they walked in clearly amused at something. Scar was just behind them, smiling but more composed, as always. I loved her smile, little did I know at the time. She never showed an overload of emotions, just a subtle show of satisfaction. Her blonde hair tied in a ponytail made her face look beautiful, her tank top accenting her perfect tits, whilst showing off the small shell necklace she wore round her neck. It was the typical surfer, traveller look that I usually snorted at but here I admired it and thought it nothing less than perfection. Her tank top was tied up around her belly showing off a small slither of tanned skin before a small denim skirt that further showed off her tan with her long legs. I can't remember what Ralph and Alec were wearing that day so it's safe to say I fancied the holy shit out of her immediately. Of course, I had no idea of their names at this point.

Fate had it (if you believe in that shit) that they came and sat on the table of four next to my table of two, still talking abnormally loudly in comparison to everyone else in the room and unintentionally I found myself listening to their conversation, the thick Norwegian accents making it hard but not impossible to understand. To this day I still wonder why they weren't just speaking in Norwegian, as I did when I began listening. Jasper insisted it was fate.

"No, I found this guy down the boardwalk yesterday."

"Who is he?"

"How the fuck should I know Alec you idiot, I've never been here before."

"Is he legit?"

Ralph, who's name I didn't know yet scoffed. "I don't know you fucking idiot, I've never been here before. He said he'd show me what he had later today though, he gave me his number."

"Have you messaged him?"

Ralph pondered it before replying slowly. "Not yet."

The boys fell silent, Scar remained silent.

"Meh forget it, we don't need that shit we've got enough weed to last us till next year."

Scar spoke for the first time, her accent just as beautiful as her appearance. It wasn't as thick as the boys' and I figured she was only half-Norwegian and maybe half-American. It turns out it didn't take long to find out her name, hence why I knew it. "What time are we leaving for Big Sur?"

Ralph shrugged. "Sooner the better I reckon. Unless you gotta see the lover first Scarlett?"

She rolled her eyes as my heart sank. "He was about fifty, and I'm pretty sure he was hitting it on with Alec anyway."

Thank god, my heart was revived as Alec's face turned red.

"Male or Female, no one can resist these looks." He pointed to his face and muscular frame as he said it rather unconvincingly and Ralph gave him a nudge.

"You self-absorbed prick."

As they began tucking into their plates for the first time since sitting down Jasper began speaking, he had appeared in the seat opposite me.

"Excuse me lads. And girl, I beg your pardon." He gestured to Scarlett and followed up with a smile toward her. That made me jealous. "I couldn't help overhear you talking about the Big Sur. I'm heading along the coast myself, all the way down into Baja California over the Mexican border, how are you guys making your way down the coast? Is there a local bus route or something?"

They sat there for a moment, speechless, as strangers do when you interact with them for the first time. I also sat there, slightly embarrassed particularly when he spoke to Scarlett. Then there faces turned to smiles and they all looked at each other for a few seconds, I'm sure I noticed them nodding at each other as if agreeing telepathically.

Ralph spoke up. "Well hell man, you're in fucking luck!"

Jasper disappeared when Ralph spoke and left me to perform some unconfident introductions to these three new strangers, I introduced myself and they did also. Turns out they owned a campervan and had been touring all-round the North West before heading into California. They were also heading down across the US-Mexican border and it made me wonder whether Jaspers introduction was because he knew this already. Ralphs friendly persuasion to 'tag along' made me forget about the *don't get into a car with a stranger* slogan and join in their adventure. The boys were overly enthusiastic about more company, rambling on about surfing, weed and where they had been previously as if they were on drugs. I remember it somewhat resembling twenty-one questions, and I felt flustered trying to keep up with the conversation. Scarlett on the other hand remained silent, not quite formulising the same kind of energy as the other two. She was more peaceful, controlled and that's what made her stand out. That, and the fact that she was fucking mega hot.

Be cool Noah, be cool.

Chapter 26

The RV

We met in the car park, an hour after we'd left breakfast, the boys had told me that their RV was the best thing since sliced bread but I didn't take that as a necessarily positive comparison, I also noticed Scarlett rolling her eyes behind them as they ranted how incredible it was and made me wonder if it was all that. As it turned out, it was not. They presented their banged-up VW Campervan with a drumroll and a roar once they'd climaxed the drumroll, I couldn't help but laugh and noticed Scarlett smirking in the background too. Alec ran around the van like paparazzi pretending to take pictures of it whilst Ralph climbed on the roof and started jumping on top. These guys were fucking nutters. I turned to Scarlett and took a split second to stare at her beautiful features, her hair not in a ponytail anymore but curling down instead, her bright blue eyes filling my world. I could have stayed their staring forever and I did find myself accidentally staring for a second too long as she turned and noticed me. I was worried my mouth had been open and I'd been drooling but I assured myself I was not.

"Are they always like this?"

She chuckled quietly. "Sure they are, like two little kids, I hope I don't have to look after three now." And finished it off with a slow, delicate wink. Safe to say that finished me off and I just stood there smiling for a while, unable to formulate proper words. In my mind it marked the first time in ages, that I considered the prospect of ending my life as impossible, and the meeting with this energetic bunch my lifeline to survival. I am forever in their debt. Funny what a pretty girl can do to you.

*

The van itself was a Volkswagen seventy-two bay window camper. It was clearly on its last legs and the bright, vivid paintings on it didn't reflect its condition. The bodywork was interesting, hand done, most likely by Ralph, Alec and Scarlett. It was actually surprisingly good, and it reminded me of a psychedelic Picasso, they'd each scribbled a little message and their names somewhere on the van and I was standing next to Alec's so noticed that first: *Find your vibe and never let anyone change it, Alec.* It surprised me. I hadn't seen the serious side of Alec yet but looked forward to it very much. *Maybe I'd learn something off him?* I tried to find the other two but figured they must have been on the other side as the rest of Alec's side was just swirls, flowers, strange symbols which I later figured to be the Buddhist chakras, and a big yellow sun with a face. It was a typical surfer van and I fucking digged it. They introduced their boards with names, Birdy, Chakrain and Julia, before tying them to the roof to allow room in the back of the van for us to sit. Each board had a different meaning behind their name, but they told me they'd explain that later.

Back in the breakfast room we had agreed on one term of residence within the van, I had to get a board, seemed like an offer I couldn't refuse so willingly obliged. We jumped into the van around ten thirty, aiming to get to Pfeiffer Big Sur State Park by lunchtime.

The van was fairly plush inside, symbolic throws hung over the ceiling and across the windows as curtains. The seats were comfy and doubled up as the bed when pushed back, I hadn't quite figured out the sleeping arrangement but wished the only space was next to Scar. That was a bloody bold wish, one that unfortunately didn't come true. I didn't have to much time to observe the rest of the surroundings as I was hurried in like cattle entering a field. I reached for the buckle on the far seat, sitting behind Alec in the driver's seat, it didn't move.

"That one doesn't work."

I moved to the middle seat, next to Ralph, Scar was in the front.

"Neither does that one."

We laughed, and I returned to the window seat and looked out as we began hurtling towards my Surfing 'quick fix', as Ralph put it, at legendary Uncle Tom's Surf Shack. So legendary I'd never heard of him.

"Somethin's make goo'd secrets n' sometimes y'want t'keep things for y'self, I wanna choose who rides my boards n' then I wanna that person t'choose my board back, like a two-step authentication, y'know what I mean?"

We didn't really nod as we didn't quite understand.

"Why did you choose Noah?" Alec asked curiously, I was considering the same thing.

"Why did you invite him into your van?"

We gasped as if Tom was psychic although in reality the three Norwegian accents and a London accent probably gave it away. That and the little TV showing a live feed of the car park in the corner of the room.

"One lucky fucker." Alec replied almost dejected that it wasn't him, but Tom soon shook his head.

"This guy isn't lucky." He said, driving a comb slowly through his messy, silver hair. "This is his revolution, his redemption." A rather awkward silence grew until Tom turned and began wrapping up the board for me to take home, aware of the silence he had created.

The guy was like a prophet.

Tom had insisted I look after his board and gave me a board bag for free with the words, always wrap it up. Hmm. We all took our time to thank him and then left slowly, as you do when you really don't want to leave somewhere. Tom followed us to the door before waving us over the bridge and returning to his rocking chair, a zoot back in hand, ready to immerse the next lucky surfers. I felt an enormous jealousy as we walked past people in the alley of vines, the dappled sunlight seemingly illuminating the board bag under my arm drawing their attention and elated looks. They had the shack and Tom to look forward to.

Chapter 28

One last gesture from Tom

We had jumped back into the van, my board strapped tightly to the top like the others and then we checked the straps and checked again to be sure before setting off for the Big Sur. There was no clock on the van dashboard, but my digital analogue watch read twelve forty-three, meaning we'd probably been in Uncle Tom's surf shack for near an hour and a half. It felt like ten minutes. The entire way to the Big Sur we reminisced our adventure, how insane the shack was, perched in the middle of the lake like some sort of temple and how awesome Tom was, an aura of confidence yet tranquillity, his consumption of cannabis probably playing a part. Then we discussed my board which I greeted with the biggest of grins, to a point that I felt my cheeks would explode, a supernova. Maybe I'd had some of Toms weed too? I thought about how he offers his boards to very few people and how he knew about my path to redemption, as he put it. I thought I'd feel threatened that someone would be aware of my past, but it felt comforting for Tom to mention it, in a bizarre way. He was right, this was my revolution. I needed change and I'd make that change happen. I already felt the suicidal thoughts going, leaving a trail of bad blood behind me. Hopefully soon the blood would run out and I would no longer leave a trail, nothing to be worried of. That's what I hoped, that's what Jasper hoped too. I wondered whether Jasper had told Tom about me but I disregarded it sure Tom would have worked that out for himself.

In all my excitement I'd barely thought about how much I paid for Toms board, offering over my card and letting him process the payment behind his makeshift till of a stack of boards, as I clung to my new purchase to be. I dug out the receipt from my pocket, the one I had scrunched in earlier without looking at it. It was an almost blank piece of receipt paper but for the uncle Toms surf shack logo at the top of it, a simple circular picture of the shack on the lake with Toms Shack written over it and the price printed on at the bottom, in typewriter font. Zero, zilch, nothing. I gasped quietly, the paper was thin and I noticed writing on the other side so I turned it over. It read: *My friend, my gift to you. Go and find what you are looking for. This world is too great to give up on. Carpe Diem.* My throat stopped, a lump catching in it making me splutter, I'd hardly realised that I hadn't paid a penny, more focused on the words and meaning. Sacred words addressed to only me. I tried to cover my face and looked out the window not ready to show the others. My sight grew bleary as my eyes welled and I continued to watch the world go by outside, the note now folded in the palm of my hand, hidden but safe. I let loose silent tears, rivers of water slowly inching down my cheeks, no sound to accompany them other than the distant conversation going on in the van. Then I thought of the words Carpe Diem, something I hadn't said since my departure with Jasper and his departure from the world. It was our phrase, every trip we travelled on, every memory we made, carpe diem to accompany it. I didn't know whether to mourn or smile, so I did nothing, continuing to stare out the van window as the tears rained down my face. I thought again, it was as if Tom had known, it was as if Jasper had told him.

*

Tom was one of the many people who restoked my spirit over my travelling adventure, people before that moment and after, but he was one of the most special. I believe that day marked the turning point for me, and I am forever grateful for those four, special people. I can never repay them for what they did for me, as good as saving my life.

Chapter 29

The Big Sur and My Big Sir

Pfeiffer Big Sur state park is located on the western slopes of the Santa Lucia mountain range and its peaks tower above the Big Sur gorge down below. It's a vast paradise of rocky edges, rolling hills and nature, residence for the Californian famous redwoods as well as maple trees, sycamores, conifers, oaks and willows. There's a rare peacefulness in the Big Sur, away from busy California. The commercialisation of LA and Francisco lost at the park entrances, like huge security barriers protecting it from the way of life so many people are used to nowadays. It's the haven me and Jasper dreamt about, you could stand still and hear nothing but the trees speaking and birds squawking for miles, a place I considered a sacred spot in a violent world. We'd spent the past few days there, driving our campervan to campsites in the woodlands, spending the days hiking through the woods and rendezvousing with other campers at camp in the evening, sharing tales of the day and the tastes of a barbeque. We'd then light the sky with bonfires, singing and dancing, the ferocity of the fire equivalent to our enthusiasm. Those evening were some of the best, I felt light, dancing around the fire, a smile etched onto my face like the Joker and his scars, not a worry in the world. I don't know what came over me, my worries torn away by nature. Maybe after all this time I just needed some company?

We'd made the small journey to the coast one morning, leaving some beautiful people behind on our trip of tranquillity, joy and embrace. We found a campsite on the beach, away from the tourist hotspots. It was called Saddle Rock Campground, visible if you zoomed in close enough on Google maps but deserted from the rest of the internet, not even coming up if you search it by name. Perfect. It was just south of McWay Falls, one of many beautiful coves along the west coast.

McWay had a waterfall draining into the sea, coming from the heart of a group of redwoods on the cliff above the beach that made it particularly special. The cliff itself appeared to have been broken after years of waves smashing against its face, leaving huge rocks the size of small islands creeping into the sea, as well as deep caves and tremendous underpasses. Tourists could only see the falls from a distance, the beach impenetrable. Saddle Rock itself resembled the tranquillity of the woodland campsites, only the bird and tree songs replaced by the crashing of waves at the bottom of the winding path down to the sea. For all its beauty however, there was one particular thing about heading to the beach that got me unimaginably excited, Scarlett. I knew she'd be hiding a perfect figure, my incognito staring for the past days building a faultless perfection in my mind. I was adamant I would fancy her even more than I did already if I saw her in a bikini, something I wasn't too convinced was possible when I first met her. I'd been with the gang for a few days now and still hadn't the courage to have a proper conversation with her, only managing small remarks and the odd smile at her. *Fucking pussy Noah.* We parked up at the campsite and jumped straight for the boards, getting changed once they were all off the roof. Us boys got changed quickly and stood outside the van shouting Scar to hurry up. Of course, I wanted her to take her time, make it as perfect as possible. As we waited, I noticed how starkly opposite Alec and Ralph looked, Alec was huge, bulky and a typical Californian surfer, long blond hair (sort of similar to mine), tanned and a pretty good jaw to top it all off. I figured he would have girls flocking after him and that made me sort of jealous. Ralph on the other hand was dweeby, about the same height as Alex but not a bit of muscle on him. Pale white skin and long skinny legs, the only defined thing about him were the bones that stuck out highlighting his ribs, knees, ankles and back. He didn't look like the typical surfer at all but from what was said on the van down to the big sur, Ralph was the best. I found it hard to believe. I myself was the middle ground between the two, albeit an inch or so shorter than their six foot two figures. The years of calamitous decay and drinking had left me with a greater belly than the other two, not huge but noticeable. Yet, apart from the mid-life drinker look around and above my waist, I wasn't in awful shape and for a prick that had given up for a few years, I was fairly ripped. My shoulders and arms were reasonably bulky and my face seemed content to remain fairly slim throughout all life had thrown at me, or I'd thrown at myself. I respected that. Still, I chose to stand next to Ralph as oppose to Alec, not fancying my body against his.

I'd almost forgotten what I'd been standing waiting for until Scar opened the campervan door releasing waves of subtle fragrance from the back cabin, it was her perfume, elegant and sweet, setting the scene perfectly. She then stepped slowly out. I'm not sure if she actually was walking slowly or I just imagined it, slow-mo like in those really crude films. It was probably my imagination as at the speed she was going I'd have expected her to lose balance. I certainly would have and almost did as I caught my first glimpse, my legs nearly buckling from underneath me and sending me plummeting to the sand, that wouldn't have been too impressive. To be fair to me I stood firm, rigid, paralysed, but upright. Rigid. I was mesmerised and was adamant I'd be unable to wipe the drool from my face had I opened my mouth. Scar continued to step out, her long-tanned leg almost creeping round the door into view, like a striptease. I felt suffocated. Her other leg came and then so did I. No, not quite yet. I glazed from the bottom of her leg up as she continued down the single campervan step, her body coming into view. A beautiful white one-piece swimsuit, it was plain but for a singular hole on the side of the suit and a solo shoulder strap on the same side that the hole appeared from. The hole itself was carved to show her belly button and went from her hip up to the bottom of her tits and across about three-quarters of her body, in an almost D shaped cut-out. Very erotic. She stepped onto the sand for the first time, her body becoming enraged by the sunlight which turned her a glowing brown as opposed to the delicate brown she had worn a second earlier. I noticed how tight the suit was on her, pushing her tits up to create the perfect outward V shape underneath the jutting collar bone. Her neck was in beautiful proportion to her face just above the collar bone, one side which lay underneath the single strap that ran from her chest over her left shoulder and rejoined at the back. She spoke but I had no idea what

Chapter 31

Sunset

The boys headed back out for another quick surf at around seven that first night down at Saddle Rock, I was too tired to be able to follow them and Scarlett didn't fancy it either. So, it was just us two, sat down in our camper chairs watching the sun descend behind the mass of ocean. It was like some cute outdoor cinema date, watching the boys miraculously weave in and out of these huge waves that stood over them like the redwoods had done back in the Big Sur forest. Scar had changed out of her incredibly appealing swimsuit, now wearing a cute floral dress and flip flops. Her blonde hair was now wavy from the sea salt and she hid her eyes behind a pair of quirky round sunglasses, with golden arms and lenses that matched the bright blue of her eyes behind them. She still looked stunning which had prompted me to put on a white, cotton shirt, buttoned halfway up in the hope she might look at me even half the way I did to her. I also wore my black shorts and chucked my now incredibly faded red Forty Niners cap on, my hair curling out the sides and back of the cap.

It was silent for a while, both keen to breathe the fresh air and listen to the low rumble of life all around us, the waves, the wind, the trees, the birds, all creating a layered scope of the beauties that life can offer.

"This is beautiful eh Noah." Her body in the upright position that it had been for the past few minutes, leg over the other and head back toward the sky.

"It sure is." I replied, and she chuckled. It wasn't funny to be honest and instead I began kicking myself to allow the conversation to dwindle that easily. *Fucking hell Noah, lay it on.* Jasper took over and that sparked an anger once again inside me.

"It's like a perfect painting, isn't it?" He said as he stared out to sea. I glared at him as Scar chuckled once more.

"Am I in your painting Noah?"

That confused me, why would she ask me? It wasn't a fucking painting it was a view of the sea, it was just Jasper saying stupid things. I kept my cool, somehow pushing the anger down and following Jasper's dire cue.

I blushed slightly as I turned my attention back to the conversation, but I didn't think she was looking, "Ermmm no, well yes but. Do you want to be?"

She then turned to me and moved her chair closer, brushing my arm with her hands. "Oh of course, may I! As long as I don't ruin it?"

"You'd never ruin it, you're beautiful." I thought out-loud. I was taken back by my forwardness and sudden confidence which was met by a short silence and I started getting angry at myself. *What a stupid cunt.* "Ermm I didn't-" Lost for words. "Shit sorry."

Scar grinned and then leant over and kissed my cheek, I'd noticed her coming out of my peripheral vision but didn't have the guts to turn my face to meet her, I wasn't sure if she wanted that either and I couldn't decipher whether it was a friendly kiss or something more. It was beautiful though, soft and crisp, life returning to slow motion once more. I felt myself go to mush, sliding down into my seat. Then she pulled away and leant her head against my shoulder, her hair brushing my face and almost going in my mouth. I didn't mind at all though and wished the moment would never end.

"I'm so happy you have come with us Noah, I would be so bored with those two kids."

"I'm not a kid?" I asked, in a bid to move on from my spontaneous compliment.

She chuckled, a contagious light chuckle, not one of those that got annoying after a while, one that you could hear and love again and again. Forever. "No Noah, you are not as stupid as those two. That's why I'm so happy you are here. I think you have saved me." It was met by more silence for I didn't know quite know how to reply. It was only brief though. "Hey, may I ask you something?"

"Sure," I replied coolly.

"At Uncle Tom's surf shack, he said that this was your redemption."

I nodded slowly, not quite understanding the question, she continued. "Well I wondered why he had said that, what does he mean? Are you running from something?"

I didn't want to lie to Scarlett, her head coming off my shoulder to look at me. Our eyes connecting, as if a vow of secrecy. But even then, I found it impossible to tell her, unable to draw the nightmares and problems out of me, happy for them to lay dormant at the bottom. I began searching for a suitable response that wouldn't stray far from the truth but wouldn't give away my secrets, that way I wouldn't feel as guilty for lying to the girl I loved. And then Jasper spoke up for me, bringing my truths with him like some sort of dictatorship.

"You could say that it's a sort of redemption."

I didn't say anything, instead sat there staring at him angrily. He sat between me and Scarlett, ruining my biggest moment with her and releasing my biggest secret at the same time, one I had begun to fear. How dare he. I was so shocked at his appearance and betrayal that I didn't cut him off nor speak over him, instead sat there letting him flood my problems onto this beautiful girl. *Fuck sake Jasp*. I felt myself losing my temper again as I listened to him.

"There have been some struggles in the past," he said looking down sadly. Scarlett beckoned him to continue, so he did. "I lost my best friend a few years ago, a plane crash."

She gasped. "I'm so sorry."

He ignored her. “It drove me into a dark tunnel, a labyrinth with no map of how to get out. My family neglected me, as my friends and colleagues did. I was all alone, the darkness consuming me. I’d have spells of pain and anger that I tried to hide, but it only meant they’d grow bigger and more ferocious.”

I felt myself becoming even more angry at his impersonation of me because it was so perfect, as if I was looking in the mirror.

“Still no one offered me support, so I guessed it meant I had to get over it.” He gave a light chuckle and stared into the sunset once more. “It’s not that easy. I began to turn to drinking to numb the pain, it growing more and more excruciating which only made me rely on it more and more. I’d drink each morning, lunch time and evening, the sobriety bringing the pain and anger back in a flash. I became sleep deprived, starving myself as protection from the nightmares, where my suicidal thoughts would feast and grow. They eventually occurred beyond sleep, my life becoming unimportant and unnecessary. I grew to hate myself as the people around me did, this dark shadow burdening the room they were in.” He shrugged.

I listened to him jabber on with an air of jealousy. I wished I could speak as openly as he could, seek the help and tackle my problems straight on. But I couldn’t find it in me. My best friend had died, but that airplane had killed two people I knew that day. I was now as good as dead. I cursed Jasper for bringing the topic up, I had almost felt alive since meeting my new friends and all this had brought me back down to reality. Hell.

Jasper continued. “I felt maybe it was easier if I wasn’t here, the beauty of life vanished, replaced by the boring spherical nature of the monochromatic, western world. No excitement, no joy, no happiness. Just black and white.”

Both me and Jasper looked at Scar, tears running down her face the only evidence that she had been listening. I imagined myself beginning to take over from Jasp, a sense of relief beginning to brandish as I clawed with the darkness, dragging it out of me and into the light where it vaporised into nothing. We both continued to talk but he became quieter as I began to notice my own voice over his, like a dj blending a song from one to the next. I imagined that, but I just couldn't do it. *What a failure.*

"I found myself trying to kill myself, but I couldn't. Something wouldn't let me, someone?"

Now it was just me speaking. "I continued with life, little things pointing towards the road of redemption, to find what I had lost all those years ago. So eventually I decided to take the plunge and booked to come travelling, doing what my lost friend was coming to do. If things were different, he'd be sat here looking out at the sunset." I raised my hands in a V shape, tears also slowly falling down my face. "To re-evaluate the worth of life. To find my peace with my friend and to tackle life in a new state of mind, a new beginning. That's what I seek." I sighed. "So yeah I guess it's a revolution, Tom was right."

I looked over at Scar, her head down covered by her hair. I could hear her sobbing and I touched her arm delicately with my palm, somewhat a gesture of reassurance. She looked up, her eyes red and soaked, tears lined down her face and I wondered if I'd gone too far with the emotional truth.

"Have you ever told anyone that?"

Both me and Jasper shook our heads and she flung herself on me, pulling me in to her circle of sweet perfume, arms tight around my chest and her head plunged into me, as if listening to my heart. I'm sure it was fast, but I couldn't decide whether that was from the anxiety I had listening to my story or because of her. Probably a bit of both. I put my arms around her too, not missing the chance as I had done with the kiss. I buried my face in the nest of salty hair and began to sob loudly, almost like an acceptance of what I had been through the past year. At first, I figured I was being weak, but it's ok to cry. Everyone cries, a show that actually there is some emotion in me. She began squeezing me tighter and more passionately as Jasper took his leave.

“I’m so sorry Noah.” She whispered as she cried, the dying sun illuminating us both one last time before it hid underneath the sea, the road to redemption contrasting the evaporating light of the sunset.

Chapter 32

Darkness

Ralph and Alec came wandering up the path laughing soon after me and Scar had swapped our tears for a bit of laughter and a smile. She'd returned her head to my shoulder and the boys were none the wiser about my past, perfect. After releasing it and feeling so enlightened, I was confident I would be able to tell them soon, by myself. No Jasper. I figured Scar knowing was enough for one night though.

The boys reached our camp.

"The waves looked feisty," I said, keen to stop them thinking anything was wrong.

"You missed something down there Noah let me tell you," replied Ralph. "She was killing it."

"She?"

"Julia."

I became confused and looked around for support from the others who paid no attention to the spontaneous appearance of a girl, I looked behind the lads expecting to see Julia appear. I figured she would be another Californian stunner, not Scar but a stunner nevertheless. It reminded me of an old friend at home (wherever that is) who would brag about the name, Julia, being saved for only a few girls that were really hot, as if they had to earn their name. There was no one behind and I sat delirious for a moment, then Ralph said her name again looking at his board and holding it as if it were a girl, arm around its waist.

"She's a beauty."

I forgot their boards had names.

I'd read somewhere a long time ago that surfers gave names to their board but figured it a load of bollocks, so as you can imagine I found it quite amusing to discover each had given their boards a name. As mentioned, Ralph had gone for the name Julia, a memorial to his childhood crush back in Tromsø. He referred to her as the dream girl and remained definitively set on returning and marrying her. He tried his best to describe her and his taste in women surprised me; shy, brunette and petite. I figured a tall, energetic, loud-mouth like him needed someone equally mental, but I guess opposites attract. Or so he hoped. He had it all plotted out to be fair to him, an average job that paid enough for him to get by. His joy would be at home, a big house by the coast, three kids and his beautiful wife. I admired his optimism despite the other two laughing at him, and I wondered if I was perhaps slightly envious, I'd never thought of my future, I guess for the most part I never considered I had one, the road of depression taking its toll.

Scarlett had called her board Birdy, formulated from her spirit animal, a bird. Rather vague if you ask me, but who was I to tell that to the beautiful girl with her head on my shoulder. She also drew a comparison to the way she flew through the water, and I had to agree with the comparison, her technique effortless like a bird when it flies. Both not leaving a trace of their presence when they'd been and gone. She also told us about the peace and tranquillity birds found, how she admired them for staying away from the carnage that descended below, we all nodded agreeing with her choice of words. The brutal but true insight into modern civilisation, so similar to the rants Jasper use to conjure.

And then there was Alec's board, which he called Chacrane. He told me how it was a conjunction of two words, Chakra and Crane, seemingly pretty proud of the adaptation of the two words. I guess it worked. He referred to it firstly as a respect to his Buddhist beliefs in the seven chakras, which pull mental and physical challenges onto the

Chapter 33

The Album of Life [Remastered]

As expected, the newly wedded name was met with a scene of confusion, and to be fair to them, it wasn't easily dissected. What the fuck is Cee-Dee? What about Jasper? Or Aquila? Mayfair or even Mikky? So many things that have influenced my life and left their mark. No, too easy. So, I'll describe my thought process to help you understand why Tom's board became Cee-Dee, as I did for them that night on the coast of the Big Sur.

As I sat there thinking, it was like an extravaganza of emotions, a flashback of all twenty-three years I'd spent in the world; happiness, sadness, reflection, compassion, remorse, anger, and too many more. Like an excessively large rainbow lighting up my head. For some reason in the middle of the muddle of words, emotions, and experiences, I considered the spherical nature of the world, as I had done strolling towards Mayfair Journalism a few months earlier. How life can become so predictable and continuous. As a ball does, life keeps rolling on, rarely providing anything too dramatic nor spontaneous, as if someone has pushed it down the smallest hill that goes on for years, the ball neither picks up pace nor does it slow down, continuing on the same path it was once pushed down all those years ago, perhaps against its will? One day it might hit an early roadblock and stop before it's reached the end of the hill or it'll ricochet off a pothole and continue down the hill as it had before. I guess that's where I got the circular idea from, the hill of life and the ball of a person. The journey was mine to make.

Then I considered a CD, though it's not a sphere it is still rounded to reflect a continuous cycle, the album getting to the end and then going back to the start, a process of repetition and similarity.

However, each CD is unique, externally, and internally. Externally, most have art on the front, what I considered an expressive decoration of life, your life, my life, whoever's CD it is. There is something beautiful about their art, like a book cover or painting, it belongs to the artist and no one else. I liked the idea of having my own art, decorated with whatever the fuck I want. No one to tell me I can't have it.

Then I thought about a CD internally, the album representing a story, an electronic life, cut into chapters. The individuality of the chapters decided by the artist, me. Only that person can choose what each song contains, will it be a continuation of the preceding song or will it be different, greater perhaps? The greatest gift an artist has is their ability to choose how long each chapter lasts, what happens in the chapter and if the next chapter will be better or worse? I reflected on my life, a dark hiatus around song four, with song five beginning here in America. It filled me with comfort, the change in mood from four to five, the bold introduction of a new chapter of life and a new continuous climb to greatness. There were many songs left on the album, I knew we'd hardly started. It would continue whirling around in the player until the day I die, a story of triumph, peace, and reflection. I hoped.

A final thought popped into my mind as I became more set on the name Cee-Dee, the initials, CD - Carpe Diem. Seize the day. The greatest motto of my life, and a tribute to Jasper.

Jasper ignored that as if he hadn't heard it. "But I'll still be with you, you know that."

I nodded and we fell silent for a while, letting the conversation disappear into the night.

"It's a beautiful night."

"Sure is."

"Come to the falls with me," He said as he sat up on his board, his guitar now nowhere to be seen.

I looked over to the cliff which McWay Falls was hiding behind, shaking my head. "It's too far and the currents are so strong round the cliff, Alec said it's near impossible to get round there."

"Near impossible, not impossible," Jasper said as he winked at me and made for the cliff, beckoning me to follow. It didn't take long for me to follow, and it gave me a warmth to know I was following my best friend again after all these years. *So what if it's impossible, I'll die trying.*

*

Alec was right, the journey round was pretty treacherous, and I was in two minds whether to turn back or die trying. That was under the assumption my imaginary friend wouldn't save me. In the end I didn't need to pick either, as we made it to the small cove of McWay Falls in one piece, albeit tired from fighting against the current. The cove itself was untouched, not a single print of life over the sandy floor. It was illuminated by the moon above, and the glistening of the sea bouncing off the beach. The cliffs rose high and seemed slightly menacing in the night, a huge dark wall of jagged faces and broken land. The falls itself was the near side we paddled round to get to the shore, its water crashing down eighty feet onto the beach and forming a pretty impressive river along the sand towards the ocean. It was something of a rare artefact and turns out you can't get to the beach unless you do as I had, via the water. It was beautiful to know it wouldn't be ruined by fucking pathetic, picture seeking tourists. I stood in awe whilst Jasper headed straight toward the falls, getting underneath it and letting the great plumes of whatever crash down on him. He looked so peaceful, his head leant back facing the top of the cliff, his arms stretched out almost reaching either side of the waterfall, but not quite. He looked so real, so perfect, and for a moment I wondered whether he was here, living the dream together, our dream. Sadly not, and for the second time that night I found myself in tears at the thought of my bereaved friend. Picking up speed on the road. I walked over to him and stood in the same spot as him, walking through his body and causing him to disappear. Except he hadn't because I heard him say. "Noah, isn't this the life?"

"Fuck yeah Jasp, this is it."

Chapter 35

Surrounded by the night, and you don't give in

We sat there for a few hours, chatting through the early hours of the morning as we had done many years ago. Nothing was different, I felt myself pulling off this décor I'd plastered myself with, making my positivity visible once more. It was illuminating, and I felt as bright as the stars above. I hadn't felt like this in years, hardly able to even imagine it. In those moments with Jasper I had no worries, I was free, almost recovered if you will. Jasper was sat next to me, cross legged on the sandy floor, breathing deeply, a sign of relaxation and meditation. I sat and listened to him, as if he was real. It was only when he got up and vanished into the darkness that I began replenishing the décor I'd felt myself pulling off earlier, all the problems of my past coming back. I was suddenly lonely again, no Jasper to comfort me and I began to cry. I missed him, his laughter, voice, aura, even just sitting under the stars again. Everything. I'd never really cried over Jasper's non-existence, until I was sat on that beach under the stars and waterfall, and then I did. I cried for ages, silently, loudly, in as many different ways as you can cry. My heart hurt, my head was heavy and my eyes bulging with pain. It hadn't struck me properly until now, the suicidal thoughts and alcohol almost blinding me from it. I should have felt awful as I sat there, breaking down into more pieces than I could ever have imagined I had, I did but I also didn't. Confusing right? It was like a weight being lifted off my shoulders, pushing back against the toughest obstacle life can throw. For so many years I'd sat underneath this great weight but now I was rising from the ground pushing it above my head and casting it away into the darkness, hurling it miles from me as Thor would to his axe. Except his always came back, I would make sure mine did not. It would break and fall onto me, hurting me as it did but I didn't give in, kept pushing back adamant the pain would only get weaker, whilst I would only get stronger.

*

I sat there on my own till my watch read five-fifty. I listened to the waves crashing onto the beach, washing up to my feet and covering them in that white sea foam shit that always leads the wave onto the shore. The early risers had started up in the trees, squawking away simultaneously, like the worst choir I'd ever heard. Probably the first aswell. The sun began to appear from behind me, the furthest part of the ocean I could see beginning to glisten like a diamond in a shop window. The light at the end of the long dark tunnel of grief maybe?

I lifted myself off the ground, one arm on the knee like an old man and hauled Cee-Dee under my arm and then into the water. The water woke me up nicely and that tiredness vanished, replaced by a face full of water and goosebumps all over my arms and legs. The water was calmer than it had been the night before, so the treacherous route wasn't all that and I managed to paddle round relatively danger free, the only obstacle a bloom of jellyfish. Nothing to panic about, just a small diversion.

I got back to the campervan around six o'clock, all three still asleep. I tucked myself back into bed and closed my eyes, out like a light this time, now composed and relaxed, with my companions none the wiser. My red eyes were the only minute giveaway I'd been anywhere else other than a dream, but itself near impossible to notice.

Chapter 36

And a giant leap for love

We stayed at Saddle Rock for a few nights more, a smile etched on my face throughout those days. My meeting with Jasper and the few hours to myself down at the falls did me a world of good. Of course, I had felt myself only just beginning to mourn Jasper's death and I found myself sitting alone, crying, pleading and praying a number of times. I wasn't even fucking religious. I guess I just hoped. Not sure what for, just hoped. But importantly, I had begun to grasp how fortunate I was to be alive, to be where I was and to be with the people that surrounded me. It was special, they were special, and I was beginning to realise, I was too. Never forget that. Everyone is special, never let anyone make you think any differently. Okay? Good.

On the Thursday of that week, we decided we had outstayed Saddle Rock and all huddled round Ralph's map, stabbing at different parts of the west coast as if it were alive and attacking us back, where would we stay next? It was another beautiful night on the west coast, the sky was once again an amber orange, the sun retreating behind the miles of water that I was so grateful for. The separation between my past and present. It was this point, after large consideration, that we decided Los Angeles wasn't for us, I was compliant with the decision that LA was for paparazzi and shit celebrities, nothing too special, and agreed that it could be missed. I remember wondering what Jasper would have done. Morro Bay and Avila Beach on the other hand both enticed us to stay on the coast as we'd expected, and Santa Maria just south of both seemed like a fitting stomping ground for a night or two. The lack of campgrounds sent Ralph into a rage, as he moaned about the inadequacy of hotels, which only resulted in the rest of us laughing at him, getting him even more wound up at the prospect of a hostel or hotel. It was settled, early morning rise and a drive to Morro Bay for the day, crash in Santa Maria and back to Avila Beach the following day. It was also settled that the waters of Saddle Rock would experience one last surf from us that night before we crashed into bed for an early night.

*

The boys were running down to the water before I'd even got out of my chair and I noticed Scar was also itching to get down there, but something was holding her back, like a secret magnet forcing her to linger between the surfboards and me. I was the magnet.

I'd notice Scar had changed since I'd told her about my problems and I feared it had shot my chances with her, however slim they were already. She'd grown more quiet, happy to not talk for hours, as if she wasn't quite sure what to say to me. I noticed her looking at me now and again, as I had done to her so many times since meeting her in old Harold, Santa Cruz. I'd meet her eyes with an embarrassed smile, and she'd return it with an even more embarrassed smile or wildly moving eyes trying to cover her tracks. It was useless, I'd seen her everytime. It was either she was scared of me and my past or she felt something for me, I remained adamant it was the first. Well, that was the case until I noticed her lingering here, her eyes shifting like a naughty child, not sure where to look and not sure what to say. I walked up to her and grabbed her arm to knock her out of the weird trip she'd entered, as if she was on drugs. I'd grown used to being around her now and felt I could do something as small as touch her arm without spunking myself. *Small steps Noah.*

"Scar, are you ok?" I asked softly as I looked down into her eyes, which met me startlingly quickly. The sun illuminated her vibrant skin as she shrugged off my hand and caught it with her own softer version as it went swinging to the ground. I was surprised and almost pulled away, it clutching mine like a pillow wrapped around it, her fingers interlocking mine and squeezing tight as if she was expecting me to resist. I didn't, obviously, and I was sure I noticed her face and hand relax when she realised this, as if she was shocked that I wanted to hold hands with her. I felt myself go to jelly, raspberry jelly, bright red and unsure of what to say or do. A lump appeared in my throat and I swallowed it down with difficulty. Nothing else went down and I begged she didn't look that way. Instead she shuffled close to me, our bodies now inches from one another, her fragrance filling my nose and my entire world and the air suddenly getting stifled and dense, I struggled to breath. She looked up at me, her eyes prowling slowly from my eyes to my lips and back to my eyes as girls often do. She bit her lip for what I consider no other reason than to look sexy. As if she needed that, her blue swimsuit doing that sufficiently well, as the white one had also done to the same effect. She leant closer to me, a few millimetres maybe and then she became the magnet, and I was drawn in, a sudden confidence as I met her lips with mine. Slowly, beautifully. It was as if the rest of the world shutdown, which it may aswell have done, for everything else was so meaningless. Her lips were acute, not too small but neither overwhelming, subtle. Perfect. I felt her hand come up to the back of my head, grasping my hair slowly between her fingers and in her palm. She then guided it toward my face, stroking my cheek and following my jawline down in the most delicate way, to a point I was wondering whether I was imagining it. I didn't dare open my eyes, the threat of ruining the moment to severe. I was in only my swim shorts, so her hand continued to where the jaw met my chin and then it slid down my neck and onto my chest, the pressure on my skin still equivalent to nothing more than a spider or ant. Her caressing made my hairs stand up on my arms and the back of my neck, nervous of what might happen next. Turns out I had nothing to worry about, it wasn't to be that night. Her hands circled my chest a while and then she stopped kissing me, her lips moving away slowly mimicking the feeling that I'd been left stranded on a desert island. She gave a little chuckle and rested her head on my chest, where her hand had been moments earlier. I wondered what was funny but didn't want to break the moment, my arms coming up across her back and holding her in. I felt her lift her head slightly off my chest and kissed it with slightly more force than she'd shown me earlier but not enough to leave a trace.

"I'm sorry, I've wanted to do that for ages."

My heart sunk. *Fucking dammit Noah, should have moved sooner.*

*

I'm not sure how long we stood there watching the sunset, but it was sort of becoming our thing. As if we were growing closer without even having to speak, it's something I've only ever had with my best friend, that connection of peace, joy and self-effacement. It didn't quite compare to that obviously and I don't think anything ever will, but I guess there's something about a decreasing sun over the Pacific Ocean on the top of a cliff with a beautiful girl that puts me at ease. It didn't hide the feelings of mourning I'd felt at the waterfall and if anything amplified it, but I knew for sure Jasper would be stoked to see me sitting there with Scar. *Hell, he was probably watching me right now, a beer in his hand, and a smile on his face.*

"That's my fucking boy Noah, that's my fucking boy."

Chapter 37

I want a Camaro

We arrived at a Motel Six night in Santa Maria at around eight o'clock after having spent the entire day down at Morro Bay tearing up the waves and having a fucking blast. I had had a pretty positive day, staying up on the board and it not being awkward with Scar after our kiss sure helped. And my day would soon get even better.

We strolled into the motel lobby like four homeless, all windswept, slightly sunburnt, and knackered. If it wasn't for Scar's incredibly convincing demeanour and our four smiles still printed in bold graphic, then we'd probably have been turned away. Scar dealt with the booking and Ralph and Alec peered over her shoulder, not sure why. Intrigue maybe? I couldn't be arsed so left it to them and went and found a seat over by the vending machines. To my delight there were X rated magazines straddled all over the coffee table and I alarmingly looked around the lobby, anxious we might have set foot in some sort of sex dungeon. Nope, the magazines looked seriously out of place, the lobby holding a similar feel to old Howard back in Santa Cruz. Shit, but not a sex dungeon. I was shocked but that didn't stop me from taking a peek, my masculine and animalistic nature prodding through the pages at a rate only acceptable from someone who was worried they would be caught.

I found some interesting and fucked up pages on sex positions, and some even more interesting pictures of the female anatomy, modelled by some pretty fit models. I continued to sift through, eventually becoming indulged in a bunch of horny car washers soaping up a Chevrolet Camaro, aswell as their tits. Their white crop tops now transparent and raunchy. I began studying the minor details of the picture, desperate to take it all in, hence why I didn't notice my three companions standing over me for what they later described as ages. Scar was stood with her arms crossed and her face scrunched up, the first time I'd seen her annoyed. She still looked beautiful, strands of hair falling over her face, making her blue eyes shine over the lines her face had adopted from being so angry. Alec and Ralph stood either side, torn between laughing and joining me for a closer look. In the end they resisted both, their faces trembling under immense pressure to hold their bursts in. *Baited.*

There is good news to that story, whilst I had been goggling a solid thirty-four F pair of tits, Scar, Alec and Ralph had decided the two boys would stay in a double room and me and Scar would also. Yeah you read that right, and I didn't need to lift a fucking finger. I figured that sex position reading might actually come in use as I put the magazine back alongside its counterparts on the table. Ralph thought the same.

"Bring it with you," he chuckled. "Might come in handy."

"Not a fucking chance." Scarlett hissed as she pierced her eyes at me and swivelled in one motion, heading for the room. Girls will be girls.

Chapter 38

Woman

We got to the door of the room and said our good-byes to Ralph and Alec, who were a few doors further down. She barged through the door a little more forcefully than necessary, confirming my sense that she was still annoyed. We entered the room and I felt myself getting angry again, resurrection of my pity. *Fuck off.* My feelings, not the girl. They would not.

"How can you be annoyed at me?"

Silence as she walked away.

"And you're just not going to speak to me now? That's mature."

She turned in a huff. "I thought you were different Noah."

"Different? What the fuck do you mean, different?"

"Pathetic Noah, sitting there reading that shit, it's fucking garbage. I didn't think you were that childish. You're as bad as the other two."

My short fuse coming back to haunt me. I was on the verge of screaming. More at my life and everything that's happened to me than at Scarlett. I like to think she knew that.

"Fuck off, you don't know me. Maybe I am pathetic. Maybe I'm worse than the other two. I thought I'd begun to find a saviour, something I enjoy. Maybe I'm just even more fucking lost than I've ever been?"

She stood staring. Shocked.

"I fucking tried to kill myself less than a year ago, if you didn't know."

I hardly finished speaking and received a slap for my efforts. Scar was crying and the slap seemed almost justified. It stung my face and brought me back to reality, almost calming me down, like she had knocked my anger out of me. It shut us both up and we both stood there staring at each other for a moment, almost as if we were shocked at what we'd done. I began to move away, turning my back on her, disappointed in myself but she stopped me from doing so with her hands planted either side of me. To my surprise she then kissed me, a quick peck. There was no time for me to return the favour, but I felt myself go hazy again as I had yesterday, a feeling like I was a planet and she was my sun a million miles from earth but only a few from each other, alone forever.

"Didn't mean to tell you to fuck off you know."

She disregarded it like I hadn't even said it in the first place. A stern voice you usually heard from a teacher telling the naughty kid off in the back, her finger raised toward my face. "Whatever you fucking do. Never. Never talk about killing yourself to me Noah," she began to sob. "If you're going to talk about. That. I want you to leave now," she pushed me away from her gently, like she didn't really want to. "Because I will have failed, and I can't do that with you."

There was a shudder in her voice as if she was hiding something. I watched her as she sat on the side of the bed, resting her chin on her knees which were tucked up in front of her.

In that moment I learnt two things that I should have learnt sooner. One, the world doesn't just revolve around me. It isn't just shit for me. There are other things, other problems and other people that have to face them. I'd soon find out what was wrong with Scarlett, but for now I learnt about myself. Narrow-minded and self-indulged. Jasper smirked, I'd figured it out, and to make the smile even bigger, I wouldn't do it again.

She sighed, walking back into view, coming over to me and putting my hands in hers as she sat on the side of the bed. "You know Noah, bad things happen to anyone. And everyone." She put her head on my chest. "Suicide is awful. But you're not the only one to have tried to kill themselves. It's like when someone dies, except its way worse. You've watched them battle against some unnatural being, a fight against nothing. Yet a fight against everything. Do you know what I mean?"

I nodded and was surprised for her to acknowledge the gesture despite not looking at me.

"Meanwhile you've been there the whole way through oblivious. Unable to help. Like the worst friend in the world. Think of how you feel about Jasper. Mourning is awful eh? But imagine being able to prevent it and not doing so."

"You mean to say you've-"

"Can you imagine not even noticing anything wrong. Going about your life, inconsiderate of someone else's struggles. It's only when you look back that you see something was wrong, but you're already too late." She pulled her hands away from mine and lingered them mid-air before she clasped them together. "And. And then, poof. My best friend." Her hands fell apart, marking the end of a sacred life as she choked on her words.

"I-"

She cut me off again. "I've been there Noah. My sister. Only seventeen," she said trembling. "So, don't even fucking think about it anymore."

She turned to face me with a smile she'd struggled to impose onto her face and squished my cheeks together in a friendly sort of gesture. Probably to change the shocked, white face I was emitting. A single tear fell down her cheek as she continued to etch the smile through the pain on her face.

I was lost in thought, my head spinning like a yoyo getting longer, then crawling back up the string. I hadn't quite come to comprehend the significance of suicide on others, what I would leave people with. Scarlett had yet again opened my eyes to another dimension and if I'd paid more attention I'd have noticed Jasper sitting on the seat in the corner, his leg crossed over the other and his hands interlocked in mid-air, balanced by his elbows on the arm rests. He was leaning back, eyes shut and nodding his head slowly in agreement. Him and Scar both on the same page, like a reincarnation of my best friend. Boy how they'd have loved each other. Boy how they had taught me time and time again. I was slowly becoming grateful for these lessons. Jasper sensed this and smiled.

Chapter 40

Bienvenido a México

8 days later

I began my Mexican journey, around a week after my performance in Santa Maria. We stopped in the city of Tijuana for a day, keeping our precedence of beaches and surfing over tourism and business. I was unsurprised by the Americanisation of the streets, huge wide roads similar to its northern counterparts. The only noticeable difference being a distinct lack of funding in comparison, pavements littered with trash, and road signs bent and in need of refurbishment. It gave Tijuana a feeling of unsafety, living up to the high crime rate it has boasted for many years. The people nevertheless seemed relatively friendly to us tourists as we crossed the border into their culture and streets. I remember the pasajes being full of life, people strolling, people running, a whole spectrum of different paced life. We were among the strollers, taking everything in. The sounds – car horns in the distance, street-sellers shouting at passer-by's to try their local, fresh, best-of-the-best creations and the sound of hundreds of footsteps on brick paved flooring, like something from the streets of Rome as opposed to Central America. Then there were the smells - fresh citrusy notes reverberating along the pavement beckoning to be sold, surrounded by other local concoctions, great jugs with ladles serving margaritas and open ovens offering wide selections and adaptations of the classic Taco. Each giving off delicate but beautiful smells. The food was an obvious highlight that we had to test, and many family food street-sellers beckoned Tijuana the capital of Tacos. Who's to say they were telling the truth though? I still have no idea to this day, it sure tasted like they were the authentic original though. And finally, a plethora of people filling my gaze, different people - young, old, men, woman, beards, no beards, tall, short. How different each person was, each with their own story, background, and lives. How unique each person was, me and my three companions being four completely different protagonists to the rest of the street, the beauty of life. I guess it's safe to say, as I looked down that street I was certainly coming to terms with the importance of individual life, my life, all thanks to Jasper and his fucking map.

*

I vividly remember young Alejandro luring us into his stool, standing tall over the abundance of competition that lined the street through his confidence and warmth as opposed to his stature. Alejandro and his Father, who for the case of story will be known as Alejandro Senior, had been intrigued by three Norwegians and an English man travelling down the Baja California Peninsula and cursed staying anywhere but down around the La Paz area. They described it in immense detail, the rolling cliffs full of nature like something out of Jurassic Park, looming over the coves of transparent aqua blue water and pristine white sand. They sold it like they were selling the place, greedy businessmen of the Western world. Their English wasn't great, and only a few words per sentence were recognisable, yet these Mexicans were different. Their awe of the place was frightening even to a foreigner, like it was magical. They referred to it as paradise, one of the few English words they knew and that was what sold it to us. For absolutely nothing, clearly not the best businessmen. We were about to set off when the Father grabbed my hand in his. They were surprisingly thin and delicate and didn't match the age of his face, sign of the hard labour he'd been used to to his whole life.

"Friend Tito, Papa Tito, Don Tito. You find, please. My friend, old. And now yours."

I nodded, "You have a friend at La Paz?"

He didn't understand, repeating what he had said previously. "You find, please." He touched my forehead with the back of his hand and then pushed us away, shouting "Adiós mis amigos!"

I'm not sure why he touched my forehead, it was some sort of sentimental gesture of luck or good fortune. I would have asked him, but he was soon back to being his usual street seller-self, shouting at the passers-by and catching anyone he could, so I didn't quite get the chance, though I did eventually work it out at a later date, so perhaps you will too?

*

There was no doubt in my mind the beauty of Tijuana lay within those *pasajes*, the main streets were dirty and boring. Like a stripped-down American highway. We'd got lost in the *pasajes* for a large portion of the day, at first excited by the untravelled labyrinth but after many hours we became unappreciative and tentative in our directions. I was therefore happy to get back in the campervan and return to the coast once we had found a way out. There is something about relaxing on a beach with not care in a world that appealed to me. A new appeal I wasn't aware had dawned on me. Sure, I enjoyed travelling and visiting new places and cultures and hoped there would be a hell of a lot more of it during my travels, but at that moment, when the van trundled out of Tijuana, I felt an explosion in my head. A desire. Something that clicked, a part of Jasper maybe. I wanted to spend the rest of my life on a beach. Me, a boat, and hundreds of miles of water to discover and surf. Life on a beach. How about that?

We headed for the coast, travelling south down highway one to get away from the bustle of Tijuana and to find some peaceful waves to enjoy just the four of us, in this unknown, hyped-up paradise.

Chapter 41

Huevos Retcheros

The journey from Tijuana to La Paz was near enough twenty-one hours which meant it took the entirety of the night and morning of the following day to get there. The campervans utility meant the three of them could all take turns driving and sleeping and though I wasn't really legally allowed to, we figured we wouldn't be stopped on highway one in the middle of nowhere, so I also had a shift. Only stalled it a few times too, that's not bad going.

We managed a number of stops on the way, our first being the cute town of El Rosario, on the West coast, just south of San Quintín.

We then stopped again at Punta Chivato, a small town further south, at what must have been the early of hours in the morning. The sun had just about begun to rise, a cinematic to go with the orchestral crashing of waves across the beach floor and bubbly noise that followed as they neared their death. We had found a car park by the beach and jumped out to spend a minute sitting on Mexican soil as opposed to American that we'd been used to. It didn't feel all that different despite us now looking out into the Gulf of California instead of the Pacific. Of course, the waves weren't quite of the Californian magnitude we'd witnessed over the past weeks. One notable difference was the ruralistic nature of Mexico, sand dunes for (what seemed like) miles behind as opposed to the American forests and big concrete roads. That's not to say the Big Sur wasn't rural, just this part of Mexico was extreme, almost desolate. And beautiful.

Our final stop before Don Tito and La Paz was a little village called Villa Morelos to which we renamed, Villa More-A-Loss. It was seven streets deep and eleven streets wide, adopting the traditional

got up a few minutes later did I notice they were Manchester United ones.

I must have been so shocked that he felt it necessary to ask again. “Who’s Jasper?”

“I. Err he’s. Erm. No one.”

As it left my mouth, this young Mexican’s face began to change, malform into a new face, some sort of shapeshifter. Parts of his skin grew and bubbled, his skin tone changed ever so slightly, as did his hair. His brown eyes replaced by a beautiful blue, recreating something far more familiar, Jaspers face.

Failed, kaput, lesson learnt again. Must talk about my loss. Of course, I didn’t think about that right away, my first reaction was passing out from the horror of the changing face, falling back into the water, the waves cushioning my fall to the seabed. Out like a light, as immediate as a tv turning off. Darkness.

I was resurrected however long later by a slap across my face. My eyes opening both alarmingly and wearily to the young Mexican looking over me, his face no longer contorting into Jaspers. He was a good-looking chap, young but built strongly, much like Alec, only darker, that beautiful olive tan you can only get in Central America. He had one of those perfect jaw lines and whilst I grew immediately jealous, I liked him, the gratitude of him pulling me onto the beach probably at the heart of that. I could see him breathing heavily, his chest inverting in and out at a rate slightly quicker than to be expected, his forearms were full of veins, including one that raced up his bicep and into his shoulder somewhere. I guessed I was tougher to pull out of the water than he had anticipated. He rustled his hair then neatened it by adjusting a few strands either side of his head, it was mad. His hair. Curly, which in that moment I could only describe as like a large portion of curly fries. It was a dark brown, slightly darker than his skin and matching his eyes. His hair was somewhat wet, ever so slightly, meaning I couldn’t decide whether it was sweat or the spray of the water as he splashed about trying to pull my lardy arse out. He continued to stare at me as he began to control his heavy breathing, all in the time I painted this entire picture of him.

In the end I spoke first. “Thanks.”

“My pleasure Sir.” He stuck out his hand, which I met. “Seferino,” he said as he shook it enthusiastically, which in my groggy state seemed unnecessary. “But you may call me Seffe if you’da like?”

“Noah,” I replied.

“Say Noah, what were you doing out there?”

“Out there?”

“You were outa sea Noah, a twenty metres.” He pointed. “And calling, but why?” He frowned his face to suggest he couldn’t understand it.

“Fuck it if I’d know.”

He laughed. “Ha. Yes fuck it! This is what you say when you are annoyed?”

“I guess so.”

He laughed again and shouted this time. “Fuck it! This is better isn’t it Noah!”

I liked him and laughed along with him, his repetition of the word in those five minutes almost as frequent as me back in England. He eventually stopped laughing and began to panic, remembering I had fainted at the sight of him.

“Noah I am super sorry, I frightened you?” He put his arm on my shoulder, slightly condescending but I let it be, it wasn’t meant like that.

“No, it wasn’t you at all, I think it was sunstroke,” I lied. A white lie though, no telling off from Jasper for that. Seffe would have freaked out had I told him his face had transformed into a perfect replica of my late friend.

He wasn't quite sure what sunstroke was and pointed to the sun with a quizzed face.

I nodded.

"We must get you the shade, a drink. Please, with me. Can you walk?"

I pulled myself off the ground slowly and he greeted it with a huge smile.

"Good good Noah. It is not far."

He eagerly led me into the hills through a hole in the bushes, which I hadn't noticed until now. It was paved with small stone slats, and for some reason reminded me of the pathway to Uncle Tom's.

"It's not far." He insisted as he rushed ahead like the rabbit from Alice in Wonderland, desperate to be on time. On time for what?

Chapter 43

Those bastard bottles

Seffe sat me down in a café, restaurant, whatever it was and rushed off to fix me a drink, which made me presume he worked there, at the least. Only later on in the evening did I discover he owned it. Or his family did.

The freedom from Seffe gave me time to adapt to my surroundings, we were no longer on the beach, far from it. Yet a sort of beach vibe continued, palm trees and shade protecting us from the ball of fire above, the sandy floor playing the role of a plush beach café. In reality though it was a café tucked away from civilisation by a thick growth of trees and canopies. The entrance spread from one side to another of the vast café floor creating an open feel like you were eating or drinking in the trees. I could see a slither of glittering blue sea as I looked back toward the way we had come from. It had a beautifully naturalistic feel about it. I laughed, but for an illuminated path leading to the beach and the noise of the road the other way I'd have been convinced it was impossible to find let alone economically impossible to run. Then again, is it all about money? Ask yourself.

There was one other café guest, but I presumed him more of a family friend or something from his quick chatter with Seffe as we strolled in. Of course, I didn't understand a thing, it predominantly spoken in their native language but for the hello we both received as we walked in, which I presumed was for my benefit. He was propped up against the bar, one hand on his glass of spirit, a whisky or tequila, hard to tell, and his other hand on his knee propped up by the stool he sat on. He looked interesting and whilst Jasper would have gone and said hello, I did not, instead waiting for him to appear and make the move for me. A reliance that had spawned inside me. He didn't and the man eventually waddled off to the toilet. Chance wasted.

I continued to study the café which Seffe had brought me to. I was fascinated by the lights that dangled above. Almost a chandelier, but not. Tough to explain. Spooky but also warming. Maybe even mesmerising, something that pulled people into the café. That or the vast selection of alcohol propped up behind the bar. Even just the thought of alcohol made me feel like shit, reminding me of the shit I put myself through. The worst times of my life. It sent me on a train of remembrance, and hell, a resurrection of all those thoughts I felt and how low I was at the time. I felt my hands shaking quietly as they rested on my knees, but continued to stare at the bottles, as the train altered its speed accordingly, pulling into some sort of station. The motion blur of the train began fading as the train slowed, replaced with images of me in my room. Mid suicide. The bottles behind Seffe's bar grew blurred, until I wiped my eyes, streams of history flowing down my face. My history. The image outside the train was as gruesome as my dreams had once been, though this one was real. The prescribed tablets box I'd once tried to overdose on was sprawled across the floor, as well as a few escaped tablets on the other side of the room which had rolled away from me in their attempt to save me. Jasper's voice was acting as the train's conductor, coming out of the old speakers in the four corners of the carriage. Though I was in no headspace to listen to what he had to say. Not now, sorry Jasp, this is enough. I could see my discomfort as I rolled around on the floor in pain, sweat clearly under my arms and across my face, which worked with a drowsiness to scare me shitless. The harsh reality of a world I have lived in. I was distorted, twisted, my soul open for the world to see. I heard passengers laughing. Kids were pointing out the window, shouting to their mothers to come and look, their faces smooshed against the windows in awe. I wanted to shout at them, I was raging, I wanted to push them away from the windows. Cover their eyes. But I just sat there. It was a spectacle for them, and I grew grey in the face. I didn't want to look anymore. The face outside was dishevelled, uneven, and unrecognisable. Life wasn't in this picture nor would it ever be. I was lost. Lost to grief. Lost to everything. But most importantly, lost to myself. No one would bet there to be a way back from where this young man sat, in his room. Alone and all but dead.

The motion blur returned as I zoomed toward the next station, though in reality there was no blur only bottles of reflection facing me from behind the bar. They continued to grow distant as I was sucked away from my body into another world.

The next station was the aftermath of hearing the news about Jasper, footage of me in my room, behind the door barricade I'd erected. There was blood on the walls and a chunk of plaster falling loose in the middle of the bloody section. The structural consequences of repetitive punching of the wall. I was lying on my back on the middle of the bed, cradling my hand. It was completely fucked up, blood coated and malformed. Broken knuckles and a broken wrist, the physical effects of grief and mental health. Though for some reason that part of the picture wasn't the worst. My face was the most frightening, as if I, sitting on that bed then, knew what Jaspers death would do to me. My face was expressionless. A simple look of well fuck that's it for me radiating out of my white face and lost eyes. Again I found myself staring at the picture roll on as I continued to wriggle back and forth, cradling my hand. And again, I was lost. No way back. The children cheered, the parents raised a glass and everyone celebrated. The finale. I cried. Was it the finale? *Don't let this be the end Noah.*

My hands were shaking as they were back in Seffe's café and I couldn't tell whether they were for different reasons or the same. What do you think? I began to scream, in the café, in the train carriage and there in my old room, all three a scream of pain and horror. Back in Seffe's café it brought him rushing out from where he had disappeared moments earlier, an empty cocktail glass in his hand and a frightened look on his face. He was shouting but I neither turned to face him nor replied, continuing to stare at the bottles at the bar and screaming. I was in a sort of hallucination or parasomnia though I wasn't asleep, still very much awake. Seffe was now shaking me, his hands gripping me at each shoulder, his grasp getting tighter after every few shakes. His voice grew louder and more frightened and I wanted to stop my screams, but I couldn't. I was still on the train, Jasper's voice now booming through the carriage and the next platform coming into view.

This next one wasn't a memory, more a dream. I was on a plane heading for Francisco, Jasper to my left. The screen above told us we were around halfway through the journey from Heathrow and I watched the hostess' filling people's seat trays with food and replenishing old drinks. It all seemed so gentle. I knew what would happen next. I tried to scream but Jasper covered my mouth, and nothing came back. I looked at him and he responded with a smug look, as if he planned what was to come. A face of evil. I began trying to shake my head free of his grasp, though with minimal success. The lights then went out. The engines went off and chaos unravelled. Screams similar to those Seffe was burdened with in his café. Though I was a million miles away at that point. The nightmare began to flicker between two different visions, Jasper had replaced his evil-esk face with something like Seffe's petrified look, though he was incredibly calm considering the disaster unfolding. Then it would flicker to a new one, his panic visible and heart-breaking in this vision. He was looking around him, panicking and crying. Screaming, as watching it made me do. Even more than I had been already. Then it would return to the first vision, him remaining in his chair, peaceful and protected by composure. Like a bubble around him that no one else in the cabin could get near. The planes nose continued to dive as the visions flickered between them, both gathering speed toward the ground, both two logistical methods of dealing with a plane crash. The shouts of *Brace, Brace* erupting through the plane and getting quicker as the crash timer got closer to zero. My heart racing, tears flowing, screams echoing. I could have sworn in the final second Jasper looked over at me for the first time since the visionary dream had started and found a small smile which had no place in a plane-crash, but something as his friend I had seen all too often. It was a perfect replica of each and every smile he'd given to me over the years. I waited for impact.

I returned to Seffe's café just before the plane fell into water with a warm hand hovering over my forehead, something Alejandro Senior had also done. Though I had been slightly creeped out then, this produced a relaxing feeling and a sudden calmness that I needed to be able to control my breathing, support my overheating hypothalamus and focus my eyesight on the man who's palm was producing the magic ritual on me, after I'd rid myself of the tears. It wasn't actually a magic ritual, the man sat in a wheelchair in front of Seffe and I immediately presumed it a doctor. Wrong. He gave me a smile and pulled his hand away from my head, instead holding my hand in his, which also had similarities to Alejandro Senior, its delicacy and comfort almost identical.

Seffe began to speak behind the man, slowly and clearly, his Mexican accent so much more evident than it had been, fright still in his eyes. "Noah, this is my Grandfather, Papa Tito. He wants to know if you're alright."

"He is adamant that you get better here. He insists." Seffe gave me a look to suggest not many people refuse the hospitality of Tito and so I grinned unconvincingly and spoke to him myself, "Gracias. Erm. Tito."

Tito bowed his head in response and swivelled away in his chair, leaving me wondering who these people really were.

*

It had been agreed, though more decided by Tito, that Seffe would go and fetch the estranged Englishmen's Nordic friends, who I decided to mention based on the fact I'd left them on the beach a couple of hours ago with no communication or farewell. I wondered how on earth Seffe would possibly find them, as I didn't have the faintest idea, then I remembered how loud they had been when I had first met them and agreed to not accompany Seffe on his adventure. As Tito had insisted. This left me with the old man and began my insight into the complex understanding of Tito Garza.

Tito rolled back into the café just after Seffe had gone to find the others with only the fact that they were Nordic and loud as a description to find them. He rolled up to me and shook my hand again.

"Ahhh Noah Noah Noah."

"Erm, thanks for letting me stay Papa Tito."

He pulled a face, eyes wide and mouth all wobbly. "Dónde estamos?"

I somehow had the recollection to remember that meant *where are we*, probably from the hours Scar spent telling us the most used phrases in Spain and Mexico from her little pocket translator whilst we were on the road.

"Mexico Sir, just near La Paz," I figured he had a few screws loose, but I was quickly mistaken.

"Sí. Por qué hablas inglés?"

He'd reached my limit and I struggled to comprehend what he was getting at, my face going red with embarrassment as he waited. Eventually he sighed and spoke again.

"Why do you not speak Mexican if you are in Mexico? England is far away," he spoke fluently and in an almost perfect half Californian, half Mexican accent, or at least somewhere in the South West of America, Arizona or Nevada maybe. It took me off guard and I felt myself become even more embarrassed that I'd wrongly considered this man Mexican. He sensed my discomfort so continued. "Welcome to my café, are you ok?"

Fucking wake up Noah you twat. I pulled myself together. "I'm so sorry, I didn't think you spoke English."

"Why?"

"I thought you were Mexican."

"I am."

"I didn't realise you spoke American too."

"There are many things you don't know about me. You don't know me at all. So why would you presume based on first impression?"

First lesson.

"I. I'm. Shit sorry."

He laughed quietly, almost impossible to notice but for his slight movement in his body. "Dear boy Noah, all is forgiven," he said getting up from his wheelchair. "Walk with me," more of a command than a suggestion, I did so once I'd realised he was able to walk too, another assumption I'd got wrong.

Lesson revised. Lesson Learnt.

Chapter 45

Lessons with Tito

Tito Garza spent the afternoon understanding my problems. Jasper spoke to Tito whole-heartedly and I took a back seat, walking behind them, silently for quite a while. It was different to our talk with Scar, where I hadn't wanted him to get involved, or mention it at all. This time I did and felt weak that I couldn't speak about my problems myself, having to find support through a medium. Fucking hell Noah. I became agitated and frustrated at my exclusion. Neither looked round once, jabbering away like I wasn't there. I may aswell not have been. And they carried on talking about pure fiction.

After some time, I began trying to get a word in, but I didn't know how. How do I push myself to be confident like Jasper was? I had no idea, my thoughts muddled and confused. *What the fuck, this isn't even real. Jasper is dead. Wake up Noah.* I became annoyed. He was nothing but a pigment of my imagination, what I wanted to see but would never again. I was hallucinating. Surely. *Wake up. Wake up.* I became annoyed at the sight of him and pushed him in the back. *Get out of my head.* My hands grappled the air but nothing more, Jasper gone, replaced by nothing. I stood where he was, my hands outstretched in front as they had been when I pushed straight through him. My face drew shocked and Tito stopped walking to stand alongside me. He eyed my face, its hurt and suffering etched like fire in the night sky. Bold. Obvious. Painful. He smiled a soft smile.

"One foot in front of the other my friend. Slow and one at a time."

I continued where Jasper had left off, not hiding anything from him, beginning with my upbringing with Jasper. We strolled through the woods for hours speaking in Mexican where possible, as Tito insisted, though really there wasn't much to be impressed by. He listened for the majority, posing a few questions to me when I ran out of thought. It felt so easy to express my mind as I did and knew my dark secrets were safe with him. My soul felt open and vulnerable, but I kept pushing myself, I didn't want Jasper to come back and do it for me. I was a man. I had to grow up and take control.

"Where are you going Noah?"

I looked up sceptical of where the path was taking us.

He tutted. "No. No. Where do you want to go? What you want is far more important. So Noah, what is it?"

I looked up to the sky, the twinkle of stars beginning to dawn on us through the tree canopies above. Night-time had come. "To find peace, I guess. To want something, and to be happy. To get away from all the bullshit of the world and to feel like I'm not actually all that bad. To feel like I've learnt something," I scoffed, almost laughing at how ridiculous I sounded. "Pffff pretty long list. A load of garbage, right?"

"Never," He said quietly as if to mark the end of my laughter and to prove I was wrong. I didn't respond, marking the start of a moment of reflection. Perhaps he was right? Low and behold in that moment he let me reconsider what is right and wrong. Or more importantly the fact that whatever you want can never be wrong. Your dreams and hopes are only yours, only you can choose them because only you know what you want, and the special thing – everyone's are different. It was from that moment I began to consider what I wanted, why I wanted it and soon I would put it to good effect. The realisation of this idea almost as beautiful as the production of my ideas, my dreams.

Tito started up again after a few minutes of silence as we continued to walk through the trees, each foot becoming engrossed in the darkness of the forest floor. The sounds of the night around us were near silent, meaning the sounds of waves were just about audible, giving me a wonderful remembrance of where I was in the world.

"Do you find life difficult, young Noah?"

I did."

"And now?"

I sighed. "I haven't found life easy ever since I started tumbling. I figured going to the other side of the world would cure me instantly, but I was wrong. I still have moments of feeling unnecessary."

He looked up at me as we began to reach the entrance of the café. His face fragmented by the light but his bold eyes, glistening with life and warmth. I felt calm.

"Noah you must listen carefully. Whatever comes easy will never last long but life and happiness that last long will never come easy. Do you understand me?"

I nodded slowly.

"Never quit young man, for it will be your loss and mine also," he smiled a warming smile and sat back down in his wheelchair he'd got out of all those hours ago. "It looks like you have some visitors," he said as he pointed his delicate finger towards my three travel companions, who were sat round the same table I was at earlier.

Tito swivelled away into the darkness of the café off to my left, without welcoming Scar, Alec and Ralph as he had to me. He left me with many racing thoughts in my head and his words in my mind. I stood frozen for a moment, in reflection. My head wrapping itself as best it could around the inspiration he'd just invested into my soul as well as the confidence he so clearly had in me. In that moment he felt like the closest I'd ever come to a father figure, painting the most important things about life and the wonders of its individuality. *I just hope it's not too late for change. Fuck off, of course it fucking isn't.*

Chapter 46

Smiles all round

Scar was on me before I'd even made a step toward her and the boys, she had run up and hugged me so tight I thought I was going to faint again and to be honest I probably could have done at the sight of her, need I say anymore, beautiful as ever. To my surprise she had jumped on to me and wrapped her legs around my waist, the kind of intimacy she usually hid from the others, who were now looking on probably wondering how the fuck I managed to pull such a beauty. She then pulled away from the hug instead opting for a kiss and I could have sworn I heard Ralph cough and splutter admist a few little light-hearted digs to which I met with a beam probably too over the top. No one seemed to notice and I in turn hugged the boys as they strolled up and met me as Scar returned her feet to the ground.

"How you doing buddy?" Alec said calmly as if I was delicate and about to break apart in front of all of them. I didn't think I was that bad personally.

"Yeah shit man we heard what happened, Seffe told us the lot, you alright?"

I continued the emphatic smile I had done since Scar had openly kissed me. "All good here boys, just wanted to get away from you sorry fuckers."

There were a few half-hearted chuckles as Ralph lifted his fists. "Say that again, go on!"

I looked at Seffe. "So you found them alright?"

"You were right," he said as he pointed at Ralph. "Very loud."

Ralph shrugged innocently but clearly enjoying the moment of attention.

"Please come, I can give everyone a drink, please."

Seffe turned an ushered us all into the café where we sat chatting and laughing for the rest of the evening, my talk with Tito a refreshing reminder to enjoy life while you can. I like to think in that moment I did just that.

Chapter 47

Fear is no reason to run

Over the next few days, I became increasingly close to Seffe, when I wasn't with Scar. I spent the mornings helping him out with a vast list of different jobs. He insisted I didn't have to, but I felt I owed it to both him and Tito and also wanted to keep my mind occupied. In addition, as much as I enjoyed my connection with Scar, which had now become pretty obvious, I enjoyed the peace away from her and the other two. I guess more than anything being away from people makes you appreciate them that little more, and that ethos sure worked. I could feel myself falling in love with her someday, though I wasn't quite sure it was possible just yet while I was still learning so much about myself. I was however pretty convinced she had fallen for me, her constant hanging off my shoulder a pretty vivid indication as well as the words of Ralph and Alec, whom I both trusted.

The days I spent with Seffe highlighted his importance to Tito and I gathered so much respect for him in such a short space of time. The dedication to his grandfather was mesmerising and his gratitude to life was something I'd seen in few people, something that also resonated in Jasper. I guess that's why I got on with him so well. Seffe drove me into La Paz a few times for café supplies during the few days we were there, leaving the others to enjoy the Balandra stretch that carried on for miles past the café's unrecognisable path from the beach that he had dragged me down when I had first met him. It was at first glance a fucking disgusting place. Dirty and derelict, the sort of place you question your sanity after voluntarily visiting. Though Seffe to be fair to him did turn my head eventually, taking the time out of his busy day to show me around the Bahía de La Paz, it's beauty equal only to Playa Balandra. We strolled the seafront, passing palm trees higher than you can imagine and a plethora of tropical coloured cafes that looked like they'd been taken from the Caribbean. It was clearly the wealthier part of La Paz, with sailing boats and even the odd yacht cruising around the sun-soaked bay and in no rush to get anywhere or do anything. How life should be approached. Don't you think?

"This country is beautiful."

"The best in the world."

I smirked at his patriotism.

The sunset for some reason made me think of my parents, the times where we'd gotten on, how incredible the feeling of family was. One of those rare life drugs that keep you satisfied for hours, days, years. Though sadly not in my case. The scene of dropping my ice-cream down the beach at Studland with my father popped into my head as it had done on the plane to San Fran.

"Where are your parents?" I said to my surprise. I'd been thinking it but never intended to actually ask Seffe and immediately began cussing myself for my naivety. *You fucking prick Noah, what the fuck. Dickhead.*

Seffe was less bothered, in fact he wasn't bothered at all. "Not sure. Papa says they left before I was four, for various reasons that he's never told me," he shrugged.

"Does that bother you?"

He continued to shrug. "I'm happy. I'm relaxed. I have father in Tito. I need no one else."

I let it be a short conversation as I was left succumbed to consider the maturity of the guy. How I'd always considered myself unfortunate, which now left me feeling embarrassed with my own self-pity. I wished for resilience and determination like this younger, better person that was stood next to me. Something I can take from him, an experience, a learning curve and an improvement in myself. The journey of redemption in full flow as the heat of the mid-day sun beamed down on us both.

*

We'd returned from La Paz and I soon found myself stood in the shallow sea, a school of fish circling round my feet and a fishing rod in my hands. Seffe was five or so metres to my right, also fishing with considerably more luck. He'd decided we would spend the afternoon catching fish to put on the barbeque as a parting celebration for me and the others before we left for mainland Mexico tomorrow, though he hadn't mentioned how difficult it was to catch anything.

I stood there wondering where the days had gone, I had loved my time with Seffe and was gutted it had to end so soon. I guess we all had the itch to get back on the move and meet more wonderful people. Still I remember thinking Seffe and Tito are surely as wonderful as they come. There must be a limit. Right? I wasn't convinced I wanted to leave.

"This is fucking impossible!" I said as I looked glumly at my shitty bit of bait on the end of the rusty old rod.

"Nothing is impossible Noah, just to practice."

"Practice not catching anything? That'll work."

Seffe chuckled as he lifted up his next winner, like a kid in a funfair, a small Spanish Mackerel who'd made a decisive error in biting more than he could chew. Poor fella.

"Yes! Easy," he shouted as he flashed it in my direction.

I rolled my eyes. "Show off."

He laughed. "Perhaps Scar fancy me now instead eh?"

"You'd be fucking lucky."

The sunset took the conversation from us and we stood there in silence for a moment, I was in awe of the view but Seffe, who'd probably seen it all too frequently, paid more attention to catching his next victim as the warm glow illuminated us both.

“Hey Seffe.”

He looked up.

“Do you ever think of leaving here?”

“Not really, I think this is the most beautiful place in the world.”

I nodded. “You sure got lucky, beats my home.”

“Londres?”
I nodded again.

“Ahhhh Londres. It isn’t nice?”

“It’s a different world. Rushed, hostile, not the sort of place you can show weakness.”

He lifted his rod out the water for the first time and reeled it in before slinging it over his back as he thought. “The west is no place for me. I heard the stories, competitive and fierce. Where is living? It takes a seat for dominance, money.”

I looked over at him and spoke slowly, shocked and contemplating what he’d said. “That’s exactly it.”

“You don’t want to go back?”

I shook my head. “I’m scared of going back.”

“Ahhhh no? Fear is no reason to run, only hatred is a reason to run. I can tell you suffered there you know. It’s all over your face. But you are also strong Noah, don’t be frightened of a place because of the past, the future is always different - If you want it to be.”

Like grandfather and son. Guess the wise words run in the family.

“I don’t think there is anything there for me anyway.”

He shrugged. "So why be scared? Just don't go back, many other places to be and see."

"I think you're right," I contemplated.

"Perhaps one day you'll come back here and live, run the shop together." He chuckled. "I could do with a friend like you to help," he said in joking fashion, but I could tell he meant it.

"I'd like that," I said convincingly, though in my mind I was adamant Mexico, though its beauty was unbeatable in places, wasn't the home I was looking for. Still, I couldn't break Seffe's heart like that, his hopeful voice agonisingly radiating through my head as I finally caught one of the little fuckers swimming round my feet.

Chapter 48

A City of Reflection

We had a party that night, a magical moment in an unforgettable adventure. Stars flashed like headlights lighting up our faces, which shone just as brightly as the stars that lit them. We sat on the beach, embracing the moment. I like to think it was more from happiness and laughter than the light, but I guess not in reality. Seffe cooked the fish to what tasted like perfection and it resonated the only silence of an evening of songs and laughter, the barbeque-turned-campfire an illuminating and mesmerizing presence in our gang. Other than a rival gang of fucking midges fucking off, there wasn't much else that would have pleased me in that moment, the exhilaration immense. The power of friendship a bold illumination in my life, one that had been missing for far too long. It felt incredible and free.

I remember Seffe bringing Mexican margaritas down to the beach, splashed with more tequila than liqueur and juice. At least that was what Scar had told me, since I decided to stay away from them, instead having a fruit cocktail that Seffe had also brought down, seemingly aware I wasn't a drinker of alcohol (anymore) despite me never mentioning it to him. Strange huh? It much reminded me of the night in San Francisco, but for the stark differences of not drinking and no Jasper. Though I knew he was there in spirit. Or perhaps looking down on me, proud of how far I'd come. The sad truth, I didn't need him there, these were my friends and I guess he felt he didn't need to help me anymore, at least not in that moment. I was adamant he'd be back when something went tits up and I sure looked forward to that time, as I always would. But for now, no Jasper, the long-awaited feeling of accepting his death finally coming through.

I enjoyed watching the fire, always have done. I guess it was my newfound comfort of these friends and Scar leaning against my

shoulder that made me enjoy it all the more, a circus of heat and spontaneity. How the flames bend and twizzle in every direction they know, how the wood cracks leaving a few pops as the only evidence of its existence to a blind man. The sounds of fire almost as beautiful as the aesthetics. It's like it consumes your world, a sort of hypnotic sorcery, one that removes the world around you. Just you and the fire, an estranged date.
Scar continued to lean on my shoulder, her perfume slowly becoming lost by the presence of a new smoky odour, as I began to tune back into the life I was living, the sound of laughter becoming louder as I came closer to reality.
"Europeans are very odd you know," Seffe said in between his barrels of laughter which apparently hurt him a fair bit.
Ralph was up on his feet, dancing round the fire in his usual entertainer role. A fucking nutjob really. At least that's what I thought when I saw how he swanned around the fire, like a sloth with an unexplainably low centre of gravity. His long gangly arms swishing this way and that. The tequila had got to him.

*

It was as the energy around the fire and the fire itself began to expel that Alec got up and walked toward the crashing waves. He often took himself away and so it didn't cause much fuss as a result. In fact, it was as if no one had noticed him, and I looked around the fire half expecting him to still be there, a mere pigment of my imagination. No, he was definitely down by the water. I watched him swash his feet in the small waves, hands in his loose cotton joggers, deep in imagination. I decided I'd go and see him after a while, once he'd had considerable time to himself. After all, I guess that's why he took himself away in the first place.

*

"What you thinking?" I said coolly in a way that sounded like I wasn't really bothered by the response, as I strolled over to Alec. His head looked up and behind his shoulder in the same motion, his back-muscle bulging as he twisted his torso ever so slightly. He

looked away again when he'd greeted me with a welcoming smile.
"Just thinking I guess bud."
I nodded my response. "Would you prefer me to leave?"
"Not at all, you're all good."
We fell silent and I became the night dreamer that Alec had been for the last few minutes, looking up at the constellations in the sky. The fascination of how staring for longer would create a better picture. Like art really, how taking more time over a picture would give a better end product. I never thought like that and shocked myself by how deep in thought I was, but my shock was soon displaced by conversation.
"City of reflection."
I looked over at Alec. "Huh?"
He pointed to the stars, though a constellation I hadn't noticed. "Each star is a memory."
What the fuck was he going on about. I continued to follow his finger around the sky, like a dot to dot.
"The birth of my niece. My first lover. My first flight over to America." He then spun his finger round to the left and pointed to a small star, obviously further away than the last few but brighter and in some ways more attractive. "This one was meeting you."
My heart welled with warmth as I figured what he meant. He paints his best memories in the sky so they'll never be forgotten, explaining his frequent time alone and unmediated walks. A memoir of reflection, a city in the sky. The most Alec thing I've ever heard. He put his arm over my shoulder, as a best mate would do and we both admired the canvas he'd painted. A story of his life.
"You're doing good kiddo. Scar told me how difficult it's been for you, we had to dig it out of her when we were all panicking back at the beach when we'd thought we'd lost you. I hope you're not annoyed."
I wasn't. Not one bit. Been too annoyed the past few years for unnecessary shit, time to change.
"Not at all."
"Change is hard eh? I haven't been through half the shit you have, but I went travelling to change. I wasn't happy. Not unhappy, but not content. So, I know what you're sort of going through."

I nodded. "How did you find your peace? I want the same. You're always so. Happy."
"What I did and what you'll do will be completely different," he said, as he noticed my disappointment. "But you'll get there. Hell I've seen a difference already, you're double the man you were when I first met you."
I shrugged. "Sometimes I agree and other times I wonder."
"That's normal. I was the same, you'll be the last person to notice. Perhaps it will be something that makes you realise, a gift, an act. Perhaps it will be a moment, somewhere special where you're tranquil and undisturbed," he shrugged. "At first it's all I begged for but now I love the spontaneity of it. It's a beautiful thing. A jigsaw where you don't know what it looks like or what the final piece is. The hardest one in the world. But also the most fulfilling."
"Where was yours?"
He pointed to a star not so far from mine, the brightest one in the sky. "Strange you know. I had been travelling for two years; Thailand, Cambodia, the usual, even to Japan. But it was only when I got home and saw my Mum that it clicked. Like a home away from home is nice and all but. It's no home. I guess that's why I'll never leave Norway. I could be gone years, but I'll always go back. That's my peace," he brought his hand back down. "I called that star Eureka. What do you think?"
"Seems fitting," I muttered, deep in thought. Would mine also be my family? For some reason I wasn't convinced and the thought of that made me feel cold and shallow. I think Alec noticed soon enough, after all he had turned into a good friend.
"It'll all be alright you know. You'll find it if that's what you want. Just keep doing what you feel is right, even if other people don't agree. This is always right." He pointed to his heart and head simultaneously. People often say they are saying different things. That's a load of bollocks though, one entity means one honest opinion. One that out shadows any other minute opinions that you may conjure. I had to agree with him, I had to follow myself, do what I believe in. It's the only way. Besides, I had Jasper watching me. Perhaps I would have considered it even more if I realised, I'd have a dilemma along those lines the following day but I guess that's the

spontaneity Alec referred to, and the test that Jasper had been waiting patiently for.

*

We returned back to the fire soon after the conversation had ended. Scar gave me a look of curiosity but decided against asking any questions in front of everyone. We sat back down to the tranquillity of a roaring fire, I looked up to the sky, my mind absorbed by Alec's city of reflection and curious as to where and what mine may produce. Fucking scary but exciting as well. *Who knows what the future holds. Who knows where I'll be.*

Chapter 49

The Day of Reckoning

I woke up that morning five or so hours before we were supposed to get up to leave Seffe and Tito's, it must have been around two thirty. I woke up to a thud on the wall coming from the room next door, which even in my drowsy state I knew was the toilet. Scar also sat up next to me, alarmed.
"What the fuck was that?"
I didn't reply instead motioning her to stay where she was as I got out of bed and crept toward the doorway. According to Seffe, because of the heat in Mexico he decided to take all the doors off to create an airflow around the rooms, out the back of the cafe. I figured it was a good idea and seemed to work well enough for me and Scar and also meant I didn't have to struggle with the creaking door as I tiptoed closer to the sound, now regretting not picking up a weapon of some sort prior to beginning my heroic, albeit slow charge toward the unexpected, rather early alarm clock. I reached the corner of the doorway and peered my head round into the toilet. The room didn't have a window and was considerably darker than our bedroom meaning I had to take a moment to acclimatise my eyes, opting against using the light. I didn't bother for long as I heard the unmistakeable grunt of Seffe, on the ground some two metres away.
"Seffe? Seffe. Are you alright?" I whispered in a voice far too loud for a whisper but still spoken under my breath, as I raced forward with my hands in front of me like a blind man.
I found him slumped against the side of the wall, his head in a rolling motion, from the wall toward the ground then back up to repeat. I grabbed him by the shoulders and turned him round. Even in the dark I could see his face black and dishevelled. His eyes were bulging red and his mouth seemed to whimper, though no sound actually came

out. I called to him again, unsure whether he was conscious or not. "Seffe. Seffe." Nothing.

His heart was pumping really fast and it was only now that I realised he was really hot to the touch. I rushed oved to the tap and plucked a towel from the side, chucking it under the water before returning to rest it on his neck and back. The clattering brought Scar into the room.
"Shit Noah. Shit!"
Her disbelief annoyed me, the first time I'd ever been annoyed at her and the first time I'd been annoyed at anything for a while. I did my best to ignore her.
"He's really sick I think."
"No shit Noah. Look at his fucking face!" The terror of the situation seemed to have got to her more than it did to me, and she seemed to be taking it out on me. I remember her still looking incredible in that moment though and had Seffe not have been near convulsing on the ground I'd have trotted over and shagged her standing.
I ignored her terror, she didn't need the help. "Get me some water and something sugary," I beckoned to her, partly to get her to leave and partly because they might actually come in handy. Doctors might have laughed at the medicinal effect of sugar and water, but it always seemed to work for me. As she left the room, I immediately found myself able to think.

What to do. What to do.

In that moment, Seffe began convulsing rapidly, his body stiffening and violently shaking. A seizure maybe? I wasn't medically gifted enough to have a clue to be honest, all I knew was he looked in trouble. I did my best to comfort him, wiping the sweat off his forehead with the towel in my hand as his head lay on my legs. He fluttered in and out of panic and I wondered whether he'd have an attack so I held his hand and continued to tell him it would be alright. I don't think he paid too much attention to me, but it helped me calm myself down if nothing else as he drifted between consciousness.

He began to compose himself around the time Scar came back in. She was accompanied by the rest of the house; Tito, Alec and Ralph who all stood there in the doorway as Scar had done initially, albeit less annoying and panicked. Tito started praying quietly, there was no sound in the room other than Seffe's struggled breathing, so we all noticed immediately. Needless to say, we all would have done the same had we been religious. I looked down at his face, his head still propped up on my legs. He was still white and his face drained, though his eyes looked to be rousing some energy to open themselves past the minimal light they had previously been letting in. The hard floor begun turning my legs numb, that odd tingly feeling. I needed to get up and move around to shake it off but I considered that selfish so remained sitting and psychologically pushed the feeling into the abyss. A new selfless nature that had been born in me maybe? I didn't consider it in that moment, my focus solely on my friend. I found myself begging him to come back to us under my breath, as Tito had been doing and sure enough the plea soon worked.

"Where am I?" He croaked almost inaudibly.

We all jumped with excitement as he spoke, the Norwegians' youthfulness causing them to crowd around Seffe almost immediately, bombarding him with questions and showing their clear relief. Tito on the other hand was quite different. His composure struck me, and for a moment I found myself staring at him in the doorway. He was equally delighted at Seffe's resurgence, I knew that much, but his aura was almost conducive and expectant. He was like God. He drew a smile hardly visible, the side of his mouth twitching upwards minutely, so minutely I wondered whether it actually moved at all. He reached into his suit trousers and pressed his perfectly folded handkerchief lightly against his forehead, sapping the beads away from his head, the one sign of relief he showed. I never once considered why he was wearing suit trousers or his crisp cream shirt in the middle of the night, but that was Tito through and through, like a book that had got wet, the pages sticking together like glue. It was impossible to pull them apart and understand him more, turns out I was inclined to give it a good go anyway. Tito finally began to move toward the scene, though instead of going round to Seffe he came over to me, touched me on the forehead and leant slowly down to kiss the top of my head.

"Gracias."

I didn't have time to respond as Seffe spoke again. "What happened?"

They all looked at me.

"I think you fell unconscious and must have hit your head or something. I'm afraid I don't really know," I said, feeling almost embarrassed that I didn't have a better medical explanation. "How are you feeling?"

"Shit," Seffe muttered as he closed his still groggy eyes.

I nodded, agreeing with him unconsciously, he looked like shit.

Scar had come to terms with what had happened whilst the other two were still a little behind. Tito remained silent at the back, but I soon noticed him slide away out of the room, and I wondered why. No time to consider it though.

"Let's get him back into bed."

"Agreed," Scarlett replied. Gone was the terror and panic back to her usual confident voice that brought reason and calmness. She barged her two native companions back to reality and they both approved simultaneously.

*

Young Seffe was back in his bed soon after the decision to move him had been decided. In reality, Alec probably could have done it himself but the scene showed four friends all wanting to help, so we all took a limb, lifting him to his room with ease. Still groggy and not all with it, Seffe fell straight to sleep, leaving us four standing in his room watching him struggle with his breath and a thin layer of sweat dribbling down his face.

“I think it’s time to join him,” Ralph said in his usual volume, oblivious of the prospect of waking Seffe, as he made for his own bed. Classic Ralph.

Alec grunted and muttered the word Goodnight to me and Scar. He was always the one that was seemingly more respectful out of the two, this time toward our sleeping host.

I gave him a wave and he was off. Just me and Scar. She looked up to me and nodded toward our room. I put a gentle hand on her back as I spoke quietly in her ear.

“I’m gonna sit with him just for ten minutes, make sure he is ok.”

She looked quizzically back at me.

“He’d do the same for me.”

She didn’t bother arguing, just one of the reasons why she is better than the rest of the female population. Instead she shrugged and nodded in agreement as she squeezed my hand and walked away, leaving me standing there on my own without hesitation.

It was only now, being on my own, that I noticed my heart pounding and my own thin layer of sweat across my forehead. I walked over to the window to catch some fresh air through the insect repellent netting across the frame. I took a deep breath, calming myself down and trying to eliminate all the thoughts that raced through my mind. It was like a cluttered office, a messy bedroom. I had no idea where to begin, I thought of Seffe, Scar, leaving the following day, Jasper, Alec’s city. The one constant, I didn’t think about myself. Selfless and growing.

“You’re right.”

I looked out of the window, the source of the voice drawing nearer. I’d have taken a step back but there was no need.

“You’re right. I am proud.”

I managed a half smile as I continued to psychologically bulldoze the messy bedroom. "Nice of you to show up. I wouldn't have come this far south if I knew you weren't a fan of Mexico."

He laughed. That laugh. Opening his arms wide. "It's not my adventure Noah."

I corrected him immediately. "You're wrong. It's ours."

He smiled as he walked through the wall and into the room, arms outstretched ready to receive me like an old friend. "That it is."

*

Jasper sat with me that night as we looked over Seffe well past the ten minutes I'd told Scar. It was like an in-depth catch-up, we talked about everything that had happened since I'd last spoken to him on the Californian west coast. He was listening intensely as I talked him through the relationships I'd grown and the places I'd been. I talked about Scar. About that night, about how our relationship had evolved into almost a couple since then, and about how that feared me. I asked him if I was ready for that and he just shrugged, as if he knew the answer but wanted to remain tight-lipped and let me figure it out. I'd fluttered around with a few girls in my early teens but nothing major. Me and Jasper always saw it as a burden, a solitary handcuff around one wrist. You still have freedom, just not quite enough. I struggled to decipher whether this would be the case in a relationship with the free-spirited, light-hearted Scar. I wasn't sure, and I didn't know if I wanted to find out. I talked about the busy pasajes of Tijuana, about San Quintín, Punta Chivato and Villa Morelos, the little towns where we stopped enroute to La Paz, and about La Paz itself. I allowed myself the occasional laugh as I threw ridiculous anecdotes of my past weeks. The harbour, the beautiful clover-shaped bay with a mesmerising blend of aqua and clear water, the unmistakeably white sand and finally Seffe and Tito. How Seffe had dragged me from the water, and how Tito had immediately opened my eyes.

"You've had quite the adventure," he said after it all, as he stared out into space.

I wasn't sure what to make of that so remained silent.

"And how do you feel?"

I sighed. "You know after all I've done, the places I've been, the people I've met. I should feel on top of the world, there should be a crazy euphoria, an overwhelming gratitude and a massive smile on my face all the time. But there's not." I looked over at him and he beckoned me to continue. "I think I've changed, evolved beyond the darkness I was in back in London. But I still feel caged, penned in by my own frustrations. The worst part is, I don't know why."

"Two steps forward, one step back."

Thinking about my infuriation was making me frustrated now and I blurted rudely back at Jasper, in a volume Ralph would use. "What the hell does that mean?"

He remained unharmed, a tranquillity I lusted. "Don't run before you can walk. Don't jump before you can stand. It's not a race Noah, you'll keep changing till the day you die, and you'll be long content with yourself before then. Just relax, you'll find peace soon enough." He paused to consider. "Just keep doing what you feel is right, even if other people don't agree."

The exact words Alec had said to me just four hours ago.

Chapter 50

Even if people don't agree

Morning came around and I ended up spending the entire night in Seffe's company, asleep underneath the window that I'd noticed Jasper through. I was awoken by a nasty coughing fit coming from my young friend, his face still as plagued as I'd remembered it that night. His voice was hoarse and his eyes unnaturally weak for someone who had just arisen, which must have made my sleep-deprived face look considerably normal.

"Noah."

I jumped up, ready to look after him once more.

"Water," he gasped reaching out toward the half empty, half full glass on his bedside table, which was actually just a chair. I wondered why the fuck I hadn't slept on it instead of the hard floor but decided it was too late to consider it too much. I passed him the water, maintaining my grasp on the glass as he drunk, his hand clearly shaking and in no shape to bear the weight of the glass itself.

"How are you Seffe?"

It was met with another rupture of coughing and pain drawn over his face. This cough was like no other, it sent a pain through my body as I listened to the retching sound as he spluttered and splundered his way to the end, it coming out of him like something paranormal. He grunted as he shifted his body, as much as he could, to face me.

"What happened?"

"You don't remember last night?" I said calmly as if it was normal to lose your memory.

He shook his head and began to panic. I did my best to calm him, putting my hand on his shoulder and perching on the side of his bed. It did nothing. "Noah, Noah."

"Shh Seffe I'm here, don't panic."

He tried sitting up, which he did with incredible pain, I could see it spread like a disease across his face as it turned red then white. His heart was pounding, and his eyes were alarmed. "Noah. I. I. I can't move my legs."

I looked down at his legs equally alarmed. "Are you sure Seffe?"

*

What a fucking idiot. I've never understood that. When someone says something and you have to confirm it with them, why can't we as humans believe each other? It's my phone – are you sure? I have an appointment at two – are you sure? I am periodically paralysed in my legs – Oh Seffe, are you sure? What a fucking idiot.

*

The doctor came and tried to mediate an inference for Seffe's horrible turn that morning. Though I couldn't speak Spanish and therefore communicate with the doctor, it didn't take a genius to figure out he had as much clue as I did. By the time the doctor's naïve attempts to understand the problem had concluded, the sun had risen, and the Mexican heat was swarming the room. It was the day we were to be leaving, getting to Mexico City by tomorrow would already be a struggle as it is and so the crew packed up. But it didn't sit right. Not at all. In fact, their neglect of Seffe and Tito made me feel really uncomfortable. I sat down with Scar as she frantically packed her bag.

"Have you packed your bag Noah?" A stressed tone.

"Not yet."

"Fucking hurry up we're late as it is."

"But I don't-"

"Hurry," she interrupted as she made for the door.

"Scar."

She turned around and stopped, sensing the deflated tone in my voice. Her eyes pierced, almost expecting what I would say and the first step to her defence barrier mechanism.

"I can't leave with you."

"Yes. You have to." Her voice now suddenly trembling, making it difficult to decipher whether it was a command or a plea.

I walked up to her and held both her hands in mine, but she pulled them away instantly.

"You can't leave me." Her defence barrier became overwhelmed. Tears began surfacing and sliding down her face.

"I'm sorry-"

"Fuck you! You can't."

"I-"

"Fuck you. How could you?" She said sobbing as her clenched fists pushed me away by my chest. "You-"

My own barrier became overridden as I ignored the pushing away and pulled her in to me as she screamed and sobbed a few inaudible sentences.

"You don't want me! I knew it."

I sighed as I tried to compose myself, tears still following but my emotions holding off before the sobbing stage.

"Scar-"

"How could you?"

I closed my eyes and tucked my head into her shoulder, smelling her perfume one last time. My heart hurt, like it was being broken. I loved this girl, the time I had spent dreaming of her, being in her company. A natural spark that is so rare. But I had to do this, for me. For Seffe. For Tito. How would I ever forgive myself if I left these two people like this, two people who took me in when I needed them most?

Ralph and Alec came into the room and it prompted Scar to pull away once more, shielding her tears from the other to as she slinked out the room. I wanted a proper good-bye, not that, but maybe it was easier for both of us this way? They both pointed at her with their eyes.

"Everything alright brother?" Alec said calmly.

"I can't come with you guys today. I have to stay and look after Seffe."

Ralph looked shocked and disappointed. Alec nodded his head expectantly though remained equally as disappointed.

"Are you sure? Can we not get a doctor to look after him?"

I shook my head. "I asked the doctor when he left this morning. But no doctor will come all this way to look over him all day. I need to do this."

Ralph gave me a hug as he fought against the news and left as mute as Scar had, his emotions a pleasant surprise to me. Alec stood there in front of me for a moment, before breaking into a small smile. A mutual smile. He popped one hand onto my shoulder and squeezed it as our eyes both filled.

"Even if people don't agree?" He asked, his voice following the same trembling pattern that Scars had.

I nodded and he returned it content.

"Well. Good luck my friend."

"Thank you," I said as we hugged a farewell.

*

I watched the van leave, a van I'd loved in, laughed in, grown in. A van of memories and wonder. A treasure, one I'd never forget. I missed the three of them as soon as they left, tyre tracks and a single hoot of the horn the only evidence of our paths crossing. The colourful van faded into the distance, a single blob in the vast landscape. I realised only then that I never found what Scar or Ralph had written on the van and that thought alone filled me with sadness. But it wasn't really that which made me upset. It was the feeling of togetherness, solidarity and over everything, the feeling of being. I felt I could be myself, I felt I had a place, I felt loved. And I loved back. For the first time in years I had found it and for the most undecipherable reasons, I had let it slide through my hands. Like I had picked up a dream and watched it fall through my fingers as sand back onto the beach. What are the chances of picking up those same grains? It was all nothing but a distant memory.

Their emotional faces remained imprinted in my mind as I stood there, on the road for quite some time, fighting back tears in vain, a clear picture of the impact these strangers had on me. But that's not what they were, they were friends. Family.

I took a deep breath and closed my eyes, silent tears creeping down my face. "I have to do this," – even if people don't agree.

And then they were gone.

Chapter 51

Alone?

I lay to rest on my board that afternoon as the sun began to fade, floating quietly with just a few small schools of fish as company. The board made me think of my friends and I thought hard about the decision I had made. How would I know if it was the right one? Seffe was still seriously ill and struggled to understand that I had stayed to care for him, not much of the friend I had grown so close to was there to comfort me in my loneliness. I knew he'd have wanted me to go, see the rest of the world in my great adventure, but I also knew he'd be extremely grateful if I repaid his decision to pull me ashore by pulling him beyond the darks of illness. It wouldn't be fair to back down from a challenge like that, he needed me and perhaps I needed this?

*

I knew Seffe made dinner for Tito and himself every night, Tito was old and the agility required to rush around their small kitchen wasn't quite in his favour. Still, as I returned from the beach, I found him giving it a good go.

I walked up to him and smiled softly, taking the wooden spoon from his fragile grasp and insisting I would do the cooking. He began to fight back insisting he would be fine but I continued the soft smile which eventually made the old man back down. We engaged in chatter as he sat in his wheelchair sipping straight tequila. He was wearing a yellow long sleeve shirt, sleeves rolled up and a navy tie loosely around his neck, the top button undone. He looked like he'd just stepped off Wall Street into one of New York's finest underground jazz bars and was ready to settle there for the night, a routine he had performed every day for the last twenty years of his long, illustrious career. For a moment I forgot about my friends, Jasper, being in the middle of nowhere. It wouldn't be crazy to say I felt normal again but that suggests coming out here, meeting new people, smiling, and laughing isn't normal. So maybe its safer to say it just made me feel interesting, he made me feel interesting.

I hadn't seen Tito all day, he often disappeared in the early hours of the morning and today was no different. He knew little about Seffe's condition until he returned home, I talked him through it and asked permission to stay and help out with all Seffe's jobs. He smiled at me and spoke in Spanish before rising out of his chair and giving me a strong handshake, a sign of gratitude and respect, I guess it worked in similar ways to the kiss on the head that he so frequently gave. We continued to speak long into the meal, just the two of us sitting at the table. We got on well and the language barrier became weaker the more we subconsciously learnt about each other, pretty impressive skill of the human brain – wouldn't you say? I'd often check on Seffe during that time, no change. Asleep, drowsy, irresponsive. I'd then return to Tito with the update and he listened profusely but not entirely focused on me. Like something else was on his mind. I could see it ticking away, spinning, turning, deliberating constantly. A man with many thoughts and views, but a man who allowed very few to hear them. *What a strange man.* Perhaps he was strange yes, but exciting too. I decided that night that I liked Tito and would do everything to make sure I wouldn't let him down.

It was getting late.

"I will go to town tomorrow Tito, I know what supplies Seffe gets for the café, I will get them. Would you like anything?"

"I will leave a list," he said, pointing toward the kitchen. I understood. "Grazias, buenas noches." He rolled himself out of the room before I had the chance to reply, typically Mexican as I was beginning to understand. I followed him to Seffe's room where we took turns to say farewell for the day. I left Tito in the room with his grandson and stole a glance over my shoulder as I went through the doorway on my way out. A beautiful picture, a moment to cherish. It makes everything seem so futile when those closest to you aren't there. You find yourself lulling in memories and hope, it's like someone has taken a part of you. The full force of companionship. Many people insist they don't need people, some say they prefer to be alone. It's sad to think that they genuinely believe that. You always need people. They're the iron of the world, the heart of your soul, without that relationship, does happiness ever really exist? I went to sleep that night thinking about my own family and our memories. Life often passes you by without reflection, you often forget to think about the moments that have made you happy. But why? If you don't reflect on these specific moments, then what's the point in making yourself happy in the first place?

I made a promise to myself that night, a promise I intend to keep until my CD stops spinning.

Goodnight Jasper. Goodnight Scar. Goodnight Alec, Ralph, Seffe, Tito, Uncle Tom, Mikky, Claire, Tony. Goodnight Mum. Goodnight Dad.

Chapter 52

Challenges

I woke early that morning, too early really, so I passed the time by heading down for a walk along the beach. The wind had washed any signs of civilisation away and my prints soon became the first in the white sheet of sand. The wind was soft and the sun just a subtle glow, meaning I didn't have to squint. I liked that. I could see for miles. I strolled along for thirty minutes or so, mainly wondering how I was to get use to being on my own like this. I hoped Jasp would turn up, but he never did, and I was left let down. Too early for him maybe? I strolled back hoping Scar would be back at the café, ready to embrace me as she had done the day we had arrived. I was again left let down.

*

I must have been gone longer than I realised as by the time I walked back into the café and noticed Scar was not there, the sun was shining brightly and the warmth of the Mexican sun was now obvious. Tito was gone to wherever he goes, leaving the evidence in the form of a scribbly handwritten note and a bundle of Mexican Peso. A ten-thousand peso bundle equating to around three-hundred and sixty-ish pounds. From my experience with Seffe I knew the supply run cost no more than two-hundred leaving me with a plentiful supply. Why?

I got dressed, visited Seffe and made for Market Monday in La Paz, or Manic Monday as Seffe referred to it, a day he had warned me about a number of times.

I had accompanied Seffe the Thursday of the week before, but this was crazy busy in comparison. Sellers lined the streets with all sorts of shit that you'd struggle to find anywhere else. There were alleys and alleys of useless clobber, twelve to be exact and each felt like it went on for miles. I knew everything I needed was somewhere, but the arrangement of stools was a free-for-all so retracing my steps from last week would prove unsuccessful, so with this thinking I began down street one.

*

An Englishman wandering down the streets alone, imagine how that went? Sellers smelt the opportunity like lions to their prey. I stank of money, not to mention vulnerability and incompetence. I was immediately pounced upon, memorabilia and useless gadgets were shoved into my face, I was serenaded by weak English accents and greeted by various bits of clothing thrown onto me. I was flushed and grew nervous, the surrounding jabber of Mexican proving too much for my brain to translate. I was in the ocean and I couldn't swim, drowning. There was no escape around me. I stopped moving forward and closed my eyes for a brief second. A second long enough for my hands to be grabbed. I gasped in horror. Ready to fight. I looked to the culprit on my left, Jasper. I looked to the culprit on my right, Scar. I breathed a sigh of relief and looked onward, Seffe. A triangle of safety. It was then that I wondered if I'd ever be alone again, however alone I may feel. What a discovery. Remember that, you're never on your own. It was moments like that which pulled the end of the tunnel closer, small revelations that made life so much easier to live. Stand back and admire it sometimes, don't get caught in the rat race, just keep that head up, clear and above all, be happy. I wish I could say I remembered that same piece of advice in the months to follow.

*

I began moving forward, the armbands I had left on the beach now comfortably around my arms. I felt a resurgence of belief and propelled myself in search of the fresh fruit, cordials, juices, and alcohol that the café so desperately needed.

I quickly grew into the Mexican market extravaganza and soon found the alcohol. I exchanged currency for goods and even managed a crude attempt at a conversation in Mexican. The seller was poor in his English and even worse in my attempted Mexican dialect so called upon the help of his neighbouring touters, who got a real kick out of the lone Englishman, a sight evidently rare this far south.

I soon began to enjoy myself, taking in the various displays and hand-made luxuries as I ventured deeper into the chaos. I completely forgot about Scar, Seffe and Jasper who I'd left behind at the fresh fruit stool ten minutes before. I managed to find a few smaller alleys perpendicular to the main streets and these, unknown to me at the time, were typical of local cartels.

I soon found myself wading through a dingy street which saw candlelight and spooky lamps replace the beaming natural light I'd soaked myself in all morning. It suddenly felt like the middle of the night in a backstreet of London during the fifties, though the heat bore a stark exception, given the lack of space. Air vents jutted out of the walls of tiny bars on either side, pushing hot air and unnecessarily loud sounds out into the street. The bars revolved around a common theme of cannabis, sweat and tobacco, though there were other little similarities in truth. Some were littered with whores, leaving nothing to the imagination, whilst others looked like a home for brawls and bust-ups. I found myself metres from live sex shows and people being beaten up in street boxing matches. There were drugs flying around like planes coming out of Heathrow terminal five. Though the streaks of white were disappearing a lot quicker than the plane's vapour contrails. The more potent, chemically processed cocaine, crack, was also being smoked in huge quantities and I immediately understood how Cocaine is deemed Mexico's greatest addiction problem. My walking became a lot faster, though I didn't acknowledge my change in pace until I'd got well clear of the cartel country. There were more luxurious bars further into the darkness where people donned suits and these places went however close an underworld can go to being described as sophisticated. In reality these were probably the most dangerous places and that's why I did my best to stay in the light and keep the whores in my view. The drugs had been replaced by money, greed, and great cigars, which went a way to making me feel even more vulnerable. I felt I'd wandered along a hierarchy of cartels, starting at the sewers and making it into kingpin territory. I kept my eyes from gazing and my mind alert. I didn't have to think about walking, my legs had sensed danger and were happily doing that at an incredible pace as it was. I crawled ever closer to the light at the end of the tunnel.

Crawled? Maybe the marijuana was getting the better of me.

I managed to get to the end of the street and into the next alley alive and unscathed apart from the niggling feeling clogging my head from all sensible thoughts. Tito would fit right at home in those dark, mysterious bars.

*

I gathered the remaining items needed and those that Tito had left on the list by the money and took a look at the remaining money in my pocket. I was right, the supplies had cost around five-thousand five-hundred peso (two-hundred pounds) leaving me with just under four-thousand five-hundred peso. It was enough to buy a taxi to the airport, I'd likely make it in time to catch Scar and the gang before we boarded our flight. That same money could go a long way to building an incredible Mexican adventure. Maybe I could explore South America, Jasper had always wanted to visit Peru. Maybe I'll keep it easy and go and buy something nice for myself, head to the wealthier areas and buy some slick new clothes, a watch maybe? Then I thought sensibly, head back to England, settle down and make something of yourself. You've got nothing. No future, no work, no lifestyle, no friends, no family. You're a humiliation. Start changing that. Start grinding and working hard like everyone else has to do, what makes you so special?

I was almost set on the idea to leave all these fucking supplies and go my own way, I hardly even knew these people, the same people I was slaving away for. Why put yourself in danger for them? But I went back to the initial question, what makes me so special? The fact I don't spend that money on a flight, I don't spend that money on an adventure. I don't spend that money on fancy clothes or a shiny watch, I don't spend that money on heading back to England. I don't spend that money like so many others. In fact, I don't spend that money at all. So, I made my way back to the safety of the café, huge bags hanging off either arm as I waddled into the dim light sweating and tired. *Is this what travelling around Mexico does to you?* Tito was there waiting for me and I felt an overwhelming guilt that such an idea to abandon this man had been ablaze in my mind just moments earlier.

Though there was slight comfort in the fact I had fought the devil, and won.

Chapter 53

Realisation

I soon came to realise the method behind Tito's unnecessary display of wealth. Test the people around you to understand them. Are they what they say they are? Are they who they say they are? People immerse themselves in friendships that bind from pieces of string. How many followers have you got on social media? And you love and care for all these people? So why embrace their company? You don't know much about them, who's to say they won't leave you on your arse If someone waved a fifty and told them to do that?

Tito in essence did exactly this. Challenged my morale and understood my intentions. I saw it the moment I entered into the dim light and saw his smile, he was just as hopeful of my return as he was my return with the supplies. I guess in that sense I had passed, something he appeared extremely grateful for. Over the week I had known him he had grown fond of me, that was clear, but nevertheless he knew little about my past other than the initial conversation we had when I arrived. Though it may not seem so to a stranger, the decision to return was an easy one stemming from the old-fashioned saying - money can't buy happiness. Happiness comes from the people you share moments with, Tito and Seffe had both given something money can't buy, a place, and for that I was and remain truly grateful. You don't need money, you just need the right people, and I had found that as I returned to the café's warmth, continuing to help out in as many ways as I possibly could.

Chapter 54

Topo Chico Since 1895

It had been near a week since Seffe fell ill and whilst we had seen little steps of improvement, he was still largely incapable of much and spent most his hours still in bed, despite his persistence to get up. I'd turned into a broken record player telling him it was for the best to stay still and comfortable. Easy to do as you watch your friend writhe in pain at the most minute movements. I'm not sure how but news of his illness spread like wildfire and the café was greeted by lots of familiar faces, though I obviously recognised none of them. They all came wishing good health and offering their support to Tito in as many ways as you could possibly imagine. He gratefully denied help from any of the courteous guests, instead insisting God had helped him tremendously already. He was referring to me. I'm not God, that's who sent me. I guess.

*

As you can imagine, I still had not put my finger on Tito's role in the local area, let alone as a café owner in a relatively uninhabitable region of Mexico. How did so many know his name? Why did so many flock to pay their respect? Seffe was ill but not a dying man, why were so many people running through the doors in a state of emergency? I was dumbfounded, at times people queuing outside the café for Tito to come and meet them, like some great liberator thanking his followers. *What the fuck is going on here?*

The street I had strolled down a few days ago never evaded my memory when I spoke or watched him, his cotton shirts and great cigars that rolled around his thumb and index finger a perfect memory of the darkest of bars in that alley. I could imagine him slumped in his wheelchair, being rolled in by some suited bulk. How the lights would flicker as he entered and the customers faces would pale, scared any light would put them in the firing line of the prodigious Messiah. He would have nothing but a newspaper on his lap and that alone made those in his presence quake, as if it were some vintage Obregón pistol. Rumours circled the bars that a pistol lay wrapped up in page five, Tito's finger continuously stroking the trigger with delicacy. Always ready. People no greater than the bugs that darted around the lights told stories of the men he'd shot dead, offering each a cigar before zapping them down with a single bullet through the face of the lucky local who had made the front page news. A smoking hole left in his paper, which left him agitated and acrimonious. The slump of a man who'd tarnished the back wall of the bar had also ruined his paper. How dare he. Of course, since no one ever took a cigar from the great man. Now Tito had an abundance of fine cigars and who was he to share them with? In this dilemma he'd offer them out impulsively with a wry smile, and yet everyone would decline, as politely as if they'd just refused God entry to his own palace. Fear trenched on their faces. In this innocent act, more people began to fear this great lord and his stature became entrenched in the very streets he spread through. The world bending at his feet. Or cigars.

Everytime I consider the great man and reminisce walking down that dingy street, I become more and more adamant I met his eyes in a dark bar lit by nothing but a few candle lights and smoking cigar ends. His bright blue eyes forever piercing through my memory as I once rushed past his hunting ground, paying little attention to anything until I was away from the darkness and had my feet back on safer streets. Whether that's true or a pigment of my imagination, I can't say with certainty. But there is one thing I was sure of during my time at the café - I was in safe hands under the watchful eye of the great Don Tito Garza.

*

I enjoyed the week following my supply run, or at least as much as I could with an ill Seffe in the room next door. I was hands on each day, helping the café with anything and everything, meeting some incredible cappuccino drinkers and early-morning alcohol addicts, a group of people I no longer saw myself apart of. Instead I had pulled myself away from the agony of my past and often found myself prepping cocktails, popping ice cold cerveza's and pouring straight rum regardless of the time of day. It would be safe to assume all Mexican's follow some unreleased thesis that alcohol has health benefits. I hadn't come across such benefits but who am I to deny them a well-earned drink, and it was always well-earned. Something about Mexican work ethic, they work till they sweat and then they sweat till they have nothing left to sweat. They make the pen-pushing of the western world seem remorseful and lethargic. Or maybe just damn right pathetic. I knew there was a reason I never told anyone that I was a journalist when I was in Mexico and I also knew there was a reason I was there.

*

During that week I met Abelino and Boni, a young couple pushing toward their mid-thirties. They were polite and fluent in English which took me relatively by surprise. We sat chatting for hours, both of them fascinated by the English culture and reminiscing their late teens when they travelled round Europe and England. Abelino, which apparently means son of Adam and Eve, was dark haired like most Mexicans but contrary to the common way, wore blond highlights strong at his roots and fading as they neared the hair ends. It made him look odd but fucking wicked and I digged it straight away. His left arm was covered in tattoos though they themselves were also covered by half a dozen rope bands around his wrists – those ones that make you think they have lots of friends and are well travelled, when actually they're not. For all my negative attitude towards the mosaic of colour and patterns, Abe was cool and we got on for many hours.

Boni wasn't Abe's bitch and if anything it looked the other way round as she chatted endlessly for the majority of the time we were engaged in conversation. The name Bonita means pretty or cute in Mexico and I can confirm there was enough truth in that. There's something sexy about the way a girl talks for hours, not needing any cues or support, but the way she flicked her hair around too was game-set-match. I half expected to begin resenting Abe for having her but the feeling didn't come. She had nothing on Scar but fuck, she was fit.

Then there was Leo, he would stop by the café each morning on his way to work. He was a greasy brute and I guessed by his oily, unwashed hair and jumpsuit that he was some sort of mechanic, plumber, one from the trade. His jet-black hair and crooked nose placed him in the same film set as the Great Don Tito in my mind and whilst they were good friends, I guessed it wasn't anything more than Leo helping Tito out with the car, a leaky sink, or silencing a back-stabbing accomplice. It didn't help me wondering how he got those scars across his face. Despite his appearance and a wonky smile, Leo was one of the nicest men I had the luxury of meeting; charming, polite and civilised. He always asked how I, Seffe and Tito were and always blessed us with God. I looked forward to the guy walking into the café and it's safe to say we grew a decent friendship almost instantly. *Is that blood or grease on his overcoat?*

In truth I hadn't expected the café to be as busy as it was. It reminded me of the infamous Bar Italia café tucked away on Frith Street in the heart of Soho. Of course, with all the brilliant people that wander in come the infrequent few. Whilst a young English man trying to learn and adapt to a new culture and language was usually met with a friendly smile, the odd occasion it was not. I was called an English pig and a fat cunt by two young Mexicans who insisted I was ripping them off. I was impressed they knew the word cunt.

An older couple came in and also had a go at biting the foreign guy's head off by moaning that I couldn't speak their language. I was getting better, but I understood their point and took the criticism onboard.

The final incident came within my first few days of working behind the bar, which caused my initial introduction to Leo. A young Mexican came into the café pissed and dressed like a whore. I do my best not to judge based on appearance but however hard I racked my brain this was, unfortunately, the best description I could fit to the woman.

I greeted her with a friendly Mexican welcoming. "Hola."

She saw straight through and began ranting to the few already sat in the café enjoying a peaceful drink. Not anymore. "How the fuck am I to order a drink if the fucking twat can't even speak my language," she pointed at me, and it was only after, from Leo, that I found out this is what she had said. "I'm going to fucking bottle him, go back to your own country you English fuck." She picked up the nearest customers half full/half empty bottle of water (made of glass) and made toward the bar.

I was frozen, unsure how to resist a bottling from a crackhead whore. She continued to scream and shout as she walked over to me, bottle raised above her head. For some fucking reason I continued to stand there, transfixed on the Topo Chico Mineral Water that was arrowing toward my head.

Did you know legend has it that Topo Chico water once saved an Aztecan princess from a horrible disease in the fourteen-hundreds and that a small sip or mere bathe in it can heal you emotionally and physically. The company was founded in eighteen-ninety-five so the princess could have been drinking Evian for all we know?

When it came crashing down the once drinker of the exact bottle I saw coming towards me got up and grabbed the crackheads forearm, stopping it motionless. It was this moment that mine and Leo's relationship went beyond friendly chatter and passing the bill. It was also this moment that he saw my scared face and insisted he take me diving at a local spot he knew, I was wary and sceptical. *Sharks?*

"You'll be fine," he said.

Well that's that then. I'll be fine.

I escaped a bottle to the head but the crackhead wasn't finished and managed to spit a perfectly executed shot of saliva towards my face. It smelt of fags.

"See you on Friday," Leo called coolly as he dragged the bitch out and away from the peace of the café. The other customers turned back to their newspapers and drinks.

Chapter 55

Dive

Coming to La Paz meant coming to one of the best diving destinations in the Americas, with around eight-hundred and fifty species found in the waters of the Gulf. Turns out my earlier scepticism of diving was justified as Leo told me La Paz is the best spot to be able to swim with whale sharks and also mentioned hammerheads, humpback whales, mobula and eagle rays, dolphins, marlins, tuna, Californian sealions, turtles and seahorses to name just a few. In honesty, I struggled to think of anything else that lived in the sea.

Leo, who sounded more American than his native Mexican, rattled on to me in fluent English, barely skipping a beat. "There's so many exciting dives around here. It's like a different world under the surface, bet you've never seen a wreck have you?"

"A shipwreck?"

He took his eyes of the road and looked at me for a moment, smirking as he did so. "It's such a kick."

"Oh wow," I muttered slowly. *Fucking hell.*

He rattled on like a tourist tour guide. "So, there's four main shipwrecks; Salvatierra, Gaviota, Fang Ming and Lapas – each incredibly unique in their own ways. Salvatierra is probably the most exciting, at three-hundred and twenty feet long you see a myriad of creatures and can get lost in the wreck if you're not careful."

I must have looked like stone. "We're. Urr. Going there?"

He laughed, losing the tour guide persona. "I found a new spot recently, if you're keen to try that instead?"

*

I don't remember first impressions too much and it was only when the big figure of Leo fell delicately into the water next to me that I managed to compose myself and gather some confidence. I'd been diving before of course, there was no way I could have done it if I hadn't. But petty diving off the coast of Cornwall and extreme diving in Mexico screamed two mighty different experiences. I tried not to let that comparison overwhelm me.

I looked around. Schools of small, translucent fish swam past undisturbed. Fish I had no idea existed hugged the craggy coral formations below, zipping in and out of sight, playing a giant game of hide and seek with the rest of the ocean. I stalled almost immediately, I couldn't get past the colours and beauty of the world below the surface. That was until I got my first sighting of a mobula ray, not long into the dive, as it stalked effortlessly through the water. Nicknamed the aerial acrobat of the sea, the mobula leaps out of the water during mating season and creates a huge splash in order to attract a mate. Not exactly a turn on is it? We didn't see any such performance, but the spectacle of its fluid movement was as impressive as I hoped. We went deeper, toward the secret wreck Leo had found, the bright colours of the coral reef like a kaleidoscope as I descended past so much life. I suddenly didn't feel nervous or scared, the beauty of nature around me so surreal and clear. We reached the wreck, two old fishing boats stuck together over time after colliding head on to one another. You could see the splintered wood at the bow of each boat cracked and malformed as if to embrace the other, like a ballroom dance frozen in time. Leo gestured we go closer.

It came out of the hull of one of the boats, a large hole smashed through the wood by rocks. The first shark I'd ever seen. Hammerhead. It swam fluently, slowly toward us. Its bulging eyes screaming that I was about to die. I panicked and began shaking my legs wildly in a futile attempt to swim to the surface. Leo stopped me instantly by grabbing me tightly. Any attempt at escape was now pointless, he had certainly killed us both. *Fucking hell, why did I put my life in the hands of a Mexican stranger.* I felt myself go weak, succumbed to the darkness around me, I felt encaptured and saddened that this was how the adventure would end. I'd come so far, yet fell so short too. I would never find the peace I was looking for and I guessed I'd have to live with that. Or not. The shark glided towards us. An almost beautiful killer. I closed my eyes and thought of Scar. How I wanted to be with her, tucked in her arms, protected by her. I was washed of every thought apart from how much I loved that girl. How I loved her and yet still let her slip away. I thought all that in milliseconds as the shark continued to glide closer. It's nose five metres from mine. Closer. Closer. The shark suddenly cut back toward the wreck in a U-turn, swinging its tail millimetres away from us as it did. He wore scars all down his back and across his gills, scars from all the flailing hands and feet of its victims no doubt. He rose toward the surface, positioning himself for a perfect dive at great speeds toward us. He turned back toward us and swung his head round to look me in the eye, his lighter ventral surface (The belly of a shark) now almost directly above me. It posed a sufficient camouflage with the light of the sky coming through the surface of the water, credit to the excellence of this fearsome predator. But no. We were of no interest to it, not victims, not dinner, simply adventurers enjoying his culture. Boy did I enjoy it. He welcomed us politely, offered us a tour of his home then left looking to excite, terrify, or fascinate others.

The shipwreck was insignificant after that, as anything would be.

Chapter 56

The changing world

"You're lucky," he said. "Won't be like that for much longer."

"Why not?" I asked.

"Above, below, on-land, in the sea. Everything. It's all fucked. And you know why?"

I contemplated. "Us."

"Fucking right," He said angrily, the immediate display of emotion taking me by surprise and turning his voice as Mexican as I had heard it. "Selfish, arrogant, deceitful," He spat as he began an insightful rant into the human race that I couldn't help but agree with. "How long has Earth been here, alive and rotating? Over four and a half billion years. How long has life been on Earth? Three and a half billion years, at least. At the beginning of the Paleozoic era, the first fish evolved. Five hundred and thirty million years ago. The Carboniferous period of the same era began around three-hundred and sixty million years ago. The first forests grew."

I think I began to understand where he was taking this as he became more animated. I didn't dare stop an angry Mexican man mid rant. We continued.

"Two hundred million years ago we saw the first mammals. Do you see? The world lived in perfect tandem with all the wonderful spectrums of life that it created for millions of years. Only it had the power to decide when to extinct a species or destroy an environment, it was dominant. Nature controlled everything, a self-sustaining and beautiful equilibrium," he sighed, looking at the dappled sunlight breaking through the trees above, as if the universe was beckoning him to continue. He did so through rage and clenched teeth. "And then came the greatest mistake the world ever made, it gave us the tools for evolution. To grow, enhance and distort the way of life around us. Noah, do you know when we first saw humans? Around three hundred thousand years ago. We've been here on earth for the most minimal time. And yet, we're going through the planet spreading the sickening disease of human nature. The trees, the amazon. The sea, the great barrier reef. It's all decaying, because of us. There's no respect for the life around us, only a consideration that we're better and higher than anything else that grows. We've dethroned the might of nature and the cycle of life, bending it at will. Our planet, ours to create, ours to destroy. Ours ours ours. Us us us. Its greedy and it's wrong. We are nothing," he wiped his now sweaty forehead and took a deep breath. "And there's nothing we can do about it."

Chapter 57

But where?

I continued to work at the café for the weeks to follow my diving adventure and Leo returned each day for his Topo Chico hit and whatever else he was after. We'd sit for hours when it was quiet laughing and chatting and I gathered a friendship I treasure to this day. In those same weeks Seffe improved significantly and was now up and about in the café, often sitting with us as well. He was keen to return to work and had grown bored of the same thing each day, nothing. I guess some people need a routine to keep them from insanity and Seffe was certainly acting like one of them. The weeks had passed quickly and relatively stress free and my mind now began turning its attention toward the future. With Seffe getting better I had no excuse for the hiatus of my adventure, and it meant I'd be moving on within the next few days. I was conscious of outstaying my welcome, not because Tito or Seffe wanted me to leave but I guess I just felt I had been there too long. Though the thought of leaving terrified me, out there on my own. I just hoped Jasper would turn up for company.

*

I flipped the coin round in my hand. It wasn't a two-pound coin, not even close, though it was proving a spark for thought, a flip seemingly decorating my mind with all different ideas and possibilities. I had a lot of time for stuff like that.

I flipped the coin round in my hand as I sunk my feet further into the sand, reaching the cold sand that never saw the light. The early evening sun beat down on me.

I flipped the Nepalese coin round in my hand as I looked at the letter sat on my lap. It was the same letter albeit now creased and torn. It hadn't changed like I had, and I now read it head held high and proud. I didn't cry and I didn't find a dark place to be alone. He said he wanted to travel toward Mexico City, or maybe the southern mountains of Oaxaca - but that was his story? He'd want me to write my own story, so I tried to do just that. But where?

"Soon it will start getting dark you know."

"Made it down here by yourself?"

"Sure, this view is too much, I had to see it."

Seffe came hobbling over like a stiff board and sat down next to me with great difficulty, he rejected my help. The amber sky lit us both.

"What is it you read?"

I gave him the letter and he began reading it for himself. A few minutes passed.

"Did you find this?"

I smirked as Jasper laughed in the background. "My best friend wrote this for me."

Seffe nodded slowly. "Captain Jasper," he deliberated. "This is your friend? Are you catching him up? Was that who you were shouting for when I met you?"

"I've overtaken him," I said.

Seffe laughed. "That is the man, you! When will you see him?"

I shrugged. "One day, perhaps while I'm on the road, perhaps not."

"Well I'm sure jealous of Captain Jasper, you sure are someone I will want to hang out with forever."

I put my arm over my friend, and he did the same as we stared out to the sea. The illness had made him skinnier than he had been the first time he'd saved me, but he was still the same. I'd sure miss him and he would me, but that's just one of the reasons why I had to go and he knew it.

"You'll be leaving then will you?"

"Soon I guess, would love to spend longer here but I have no reason too."

"Why do you need a reason? It's your life."

"Not quite yet," I muttered subconsciously. "There's things I need to find, do and lose before I can go a day readily admitting it's my life."

Seffe looked disappointed. "I'm sure gutted I am ill, wish we could have hung out more," he chuckled. "It's good having a Noah around the place."

We sat in silence for a moment, thinking about our friendship. How far it had travelled in such a short space of time and what it could have been if Seffe hadn't been bed bound for those weeks. I almost grew guilty that I was leaving before it could grow into even more than it had done already.

"Well there is always a place for you here if you ever want to come back. You know, you're the best friend I've never had, and I am sure sad to see you go."

I fell short with what to say, I was letting my friend down. So, we continued to respect the moment our friendship had brought us to, pure appreciation for the people around you.

"Hey, Mexico City is beautiful, you should go there."

I smirked. "Thanks Seffe."

Chapter 58

On the road

I couldn't be running around on an adventure weighed down with shit loads of possessions. So, I packed the bare essentials as I did in London, which meant the hard decision of leaving Cee-Dee behind. Though the memories of it would live on. Anyway, I knew how much Seffe had wanted to learn to board so what better chance to make someone happy.

So began the merry-go round of adios. I'd grown quite fond of many of the locals and they had me, and it brought a tear to my eye to say farewell. That was without even speaking to Tito or Seffe or Leo. Once a man without emotion, a sign of the times. *Is someone getting the best of me?* It's pretty obvious how those conversations went, reluctance to say goodbye and the desperate desire for small talk to put off the inevitable – it never works and it'll always come around as it did. I embraced and spoke to each, Leo then Tito then Seffe. Tito gave me a pendant which instantly lay to rest around my neck and became an emblem of my adventures.

"Keep you safe. It will," he said in a friendly but assertive manner, typical Tito. The man bled wisdom. He sat back down in his wheelchair but remained stood over me, as he has for my whole life since. Guiding me as best he can.

Seffe was near mute and I feared he'd burst if I tried to get words out of him, so I gave him a huge hug patting his back as I did. I felt my shoulder go slightly wet and that almost set me off. I looked him in the eye and gave him a smile. We thought the same thing, friend for life. Then I thanked them all one last time, before slinging my pack over my back, turning, and never looking back.

*

So, I was back on the road. Me, old Mr Lowe Alpine and my, now faded to within an inch of extinction, Forty Niners cap – just how it was coming out of Frisco. I took the La Paz ferry across the gulf to Mazatlán. I watched the beaches I'd sat on so frequently fade into the distance until they were a solitary blip in the vast world before me. I was overwhelmed with excitement, the anticipation to continue my travels and set forth on another new direction and dimension of life. I guess that's why I found it so easy to leave. I was once again free, alone in a place I'd never been, with no plan and no ideas. A feeling of pure euphoria and adrenaline! I sat back on the seat on the top deck, head back, legs crossed. The sun was shining so I closed my eyes, let it seep into my world and let my weariness take me as far through the twelve-hour journey as it could.

*

We got to the Mazatlán ferry port and being a rejunevated, energetic traveller I opted against the line of tooting taxis, and instead walked the hour journey through the town toward the bus port just off the Jose Angel Espinoza Ferrusquilla road. *What a fucked road name. Though I bet Mr Jose is getting a kick out of it.* I had been debating whether to stay in the little coastal town a while but walking through it allowed me come to the conclusion to move on with my journey toward Mexico City and beyond. Mazatlán wasn't boring as such, it just wasn't not. Go see for yourself. The buses came hourly, so thirty-five minutes ish later I was paying for a one-way ticket to the capital, joined on my voyage to the bright metropolitan lights, dazzling streets and wealth of activity and jobs by a number of locals looking to their capital for health and prosperity, in the form of work. I wrapped my head around how fortunate I had been with free education and health care throughout my upbringing. I began to feel dejected over how selfish I was, taking my whole existence for granted. The world doesn't revolve around just me as I once considered. It also made me consider Leo's rant about the west and made me hate the place even more, perhaps I'd live here forever? *We'll get to that one day*. The bus itself was dingy, cramped and lacked the basic air con function, what turns out to be a necessity that few buses actually have in Mexico. My now long hair underneath my cap grew sweaty and I felt it sticking to my forehead as I battled the bright sunlight in my futile attempt to sleep. I gave up in the end and instead sat watching the world go by as we left Mazatlán and began the one-thousand mile drive through Mexican countryside. The rolling hills, thirsty fields of dying crops and the odd market stool thrown onto the side of the road hoping to entice customers off the road with the only Topo Chico water and Modelo lager for miles. Those that were succumbed to the fraudulently high prices of the shops tended to consider the latter a necessity for the long journey along the fifteen D road. I sat back and let my mind wander, the screaming children and worried Mexican families nothing more than gentle background noise to accompany my thoughts.

Chapter 59

Lost In translation

The bus stopped at the small town of Tepic, the capital of the western Nayarit state. We were submitted to the first bit of traffic since being on the road and the driver's patience soon wore thin. He slammed on the horn at the idle vehicles in front. Of course this was futile, there were vehicles in front of them, and vehicles in front of them, and vehicles in front of them and so on. After a mere attempt at surviving the traffic, the driver gave up in getting to the bus stop on the eastern side of town and pulled over at the side of the road, streets away from the Plaza Principal and unconcerned that he was blocking half the road. There were probably people beeping at him, but they were drowned out by the other beeps up and down the road.

He shouted in Mexican and then followed it up with a rash, unenthusiastic attempt at English in which he stumbled at nearly every word. "Stoopin' there (here), stoopin' for three hours."

It seemed everyone took the news we'd be stopping for three hours quite well as they all got off without fuss. I looked at my watch, that would take us till just after five in the evening, meaning we wouldn't get to Mexico City until two in the morning. That wasn't in the price. I began to panic, then realising there was nothing I could do about it, calmed back down. The prospect of sleeping cold on the streets in Mexico City niggling at the back of my head. My wallet would be gone by the morning and so would my life, most probably. I stuffed a wad of cash into my sock in preparation for the inevitable, before slinging Mr Lowe Alpine over my shoulder and stepping off the coach with the remaining travellers and heading for Plaza Principal, the leafy centre of Tepic.

*

Despite the delay in my journey, I was actually quite pleased to have the time to explore the streets of Tepic. The plaza was buzzing with people, some heading for the cathedral, others bustling in and out of the shops that skirted the green square. I strolled through, taking it in and retaining a steady hand on my pocketed wallet. I noticed a wheelchaired elderly man sitting in the centre of the square, right where the centre-spot of a football pitch would be. He sat there with his eyes shut, his fingers tapping away on the arm of his chair, he sat motionless for minutes as people roared past him, some stopping to check he was ok. To which he would beam with delight and wish them well. I looked beyond him to see people laughing and dancing on the grass, beneath the shade of great palms. I noticed a young boy pick up a wallet on the floor and run over to the owner who had dropped it moments earlier, I noticed a young couple help an elderly lady across the road and I saw a man buy a local taco from a taco stool and give it to a homeless man sitting at the side of the plaza. I beamed, the beauty of human nature right in front of me. I took my hand off my pocketed wallet and checked my watch, quick trip to the cathedral before getting back to the bus in plenty of time. No doubt the driver would leave as soon as he was ready.

After seeing the beauty of human nature in the plaza I gave the *Proyecto de restauración de la catedral de Tepic* (Tepic cathedral restoration project) five-hundred Mexican peso, twenty quid, ish.

*

I got back to the bus to see there was in fact no bus, only a banged up Chevrolet Aveo with its boot open, full of Coca Cola. The time was half four. The bus wasn't supposed to leave till after five. I didn't panic, instead taking a seat at a little family run café on the same street. I got a Topo Chico Water in the knowledge it would heal me both emotionally and physically if the worst did happen. If the bus didn't return. I sat patiently and waited. In honesty I'm not sure why I sat there. In my gut I knew the bus was long gone, sailing down the open roads of fifteen D. The bus drivers rusty English had meant I'd got the timings wrong. We weren't stopping for three hours like he said, we were stopping till three. He had stopped for forty-five minutes, I had stopped for three hours and that meant he had left almost two hours ago. *Shit.*

*

I got to the bus stop we should have stopped at, at around six thirty. The café had shut and so had the office leaving me to sprawl across the white benches outside. I guessed with everything shut there were no more buses for the day. My first night sleeping rough. I was awake the entire night, driven by fear yet undisturbed by anything or anyone. Not even Jasper came to visit. I listened to distant cars whine and beep throughout the night until other passengers began arriving and the sound of an old bus came tumbling into the station. I'd made it. The bus driver called out in Mexican and then in English. I sat for another thirty minutes then took a seat on the bus early and went off to sleep.

Chapter 60

Bla la la da da and a bottle of tequila

I woke up at the western City of Guadalajara, the capital of Jalisco, three hours on from Tepic. Guadalajara is considered the home of tequila and mariachi with the birth of both in the Jalisco region. It is also the second largest city in Mexico. A diverse metropolitan of wealth, culture, and people. It is a beautiful place and I was curious to explore but I didn't want any more bus trouble so limited myself to a thirty-minute walk. Back in time for the driver's predictable early departure.

*

As I queued alongside the other travellers to get back on, two Englishmen came running around the corner of the bus. The whole crowd looked their way. Both were sweaty and moving ecstatically, and apparently not noticing the forty odd faces watching with intrigue and disapproval.

"Fucking thank god, we made it. Yeehaaawww, I told you!"

"La laaaa la laaaa."

Both were clearly mental as they began some sort of handshake that turned into a full-blown dance, arms and legs slapping against each other in a flurry of limbs. Everyone continued to stare.

"We are amazing," one said.

"I'm fucking live. This is it!"

I'd never seen two people so excited to be getting on a bus. So excited they didn't see the long queue twisting along the side. They made their way jumping toward the door, stopped a foot away by the big Mexican driver.

"Entradas."

"Ahhh shit we need tickets."

"Well fuckin' ask him how much."

The taller one tried calming himself down, but his arms continued to reverberate around his personal space, and I began to wonder what else was in his body other than the excitement of making a bus. He spoke in almost fluent Spanish as far as I could tell. "Cuánto son dos entradas?"

"Mil pesos." He pointed a chubby finger at the ticket office and then turned his back on the two boys, signalling the end of the conversation.

The two skipped away looking as dejected as they could whilst being wired on something, their eyes darting left and right trying to think of a solution.

"We don't have enough."

"I fucking know that. Fucking fucking da da da da da," went the taller one, as he simultaneously hit his head repeatedly in a futile attempt to rack a solution.

"What are we going to do?" The chubby little one said as he scratched the back of his hands and bit his lip continuously. His eyes were lost to the day and he looked like he belonged in a mental asylum. He sat down in the luggage compartment of the bus. "We'll walk there. How, how far can it be?" His eyes lit up, the first bit of life I'd noticed in them.

"Your fat arse ain't walking there, it's miles away."

The fat boy's eyes faded again.

"I've got an idea," the taller one led the fat one round the corner of the bus in their trademark run, skip, jump, walk, crawl, bounce and I didn't see them again until Mexico City.

*

The bus arrived in Mexico City around seven hours after our departure from Guadalajara. I got off to the early evening heat of the city, stuffy and humid. I looked around. I was at the north bus terminal on the Eje Central Lázaro Cárdenas road. It was the closest Mexico had come to feeling like its hegemonic neighbour of America. Long, wide highways, busy streets, bright lights and huge road signs. I guess the westernisation made me feel slightly comfortable in a city I'd never been too, if nothing else. I begun walking toward the big city lights as I spotted the tall, wired guy stood next to the side of the bus, still shaking and trembling. I couldn't see the fat guy.

"Fucking hurry your fat arse up."

"I'm stuck! Pffhahahaha."

I looked toward the sound coming from the bus to see a podgy leg sticking out of the luggage compartment.

"Give me a hand."

The taller one reluctantly jumped, skipped, rolled over to his friend and pulled him out. The fat one came out wearing a sombrero and holding a bottle of tequila, stolen from someone's luggage. Then they were off, the fat one's legs waddling along to catch his mate up as body parts continued to ricochet off the world in three-hundred and sixty different directions. The tequila bottle was the only constant, going in one direction and one direction only. Cheers. I didn't know what to think of the pair as they went their own way muttering non-existent vocabulary, so I sighed, laughed and scowled at the same time and headed in the opposite direction. *If the English are like that, I intend to stay very clear.*

Chapter 61

The beautiful pair of bollocks

I picked up something unknown to me as I strolled around heading for the big lights and looking for a place to rest my head before dusk. A Mexican delicacy of pure distinction and aromas, the flauta stand pulled me in faster than Scar would have in that moment. What are flautas? I asked myself that exact question and then I asked the Mexican mum who was juggling looking after four children with running the little street stand. She had no idea what I was talking about, responding with a simple shrug and the question.

"You want?"

I nodded. "Gracias."

She began wrapping the flautas up, oval shaped tortillas filled with chicken and then deep-fried in a large pan. Served on a paper plate that would look at home at an eight year old's party. She chucked lettuce and cheese over the top of them then looked at me and pointed to a salsa looking pot and a creamy one. I went for the salsa and cruised along the street in dreamland as I felt the Mexican culture in my mouth, my ears and my eyes. I was alive. Truly immersed.

*

I fell into a hostel for travellers late in the evening, still buzzing from my first experience in this wicked city. The buzz reminded me of the hostel back in San Fran but I was in a far better headspace to tackle that this time around. The young Mexican at the desk seemed flirty and I considered inviting her to my bunk before I saw Scar in the back of my head. Why go for Quorn when you have steak at home? Pathetic comparison. Forget it.

In the end I decided I could always come back and whisk her away if the night went that way. I took the key and made for the room, only to discover the tall and fat wired duo were in the bunk over from mine, lining up a great line of coke on a Lonely Planet book. Pretty sure that's not under the things to do section of Mexico City. They didn't notice me, nor did they remember me, why should they? Neither did they notice my bunk partner staring abhorrently at them, a young Brazilian on her own adventure through the world. I remember wondering how a Brazilian could be so horrified by the sight of cocaine, after all reports suggest Brazil is the leading country for cocaine distribution, above the great Colombia. I said a brief hello to the room more than to anyone in particular and chucked my bag in the locker by the bunk. It was late by this time so I weighed up a quick trip out onto the streets I'd just been strolling but decided it could wait till the morning. I went to sleep laughing at the shit that came out of the wired's mouths, a steady stream of constant diarrhoea.

"La la la la la ey, Sniffy look-"

"Fuckkkk scaaa boom la la-"

"Ouchaaaa tha fuck you doin'?"

"Bonce. Fucked. Cunt."

"Ha ha ha ha."

"Do thaa again 'nd I'll smesh ya fuck'n 'ead n-"

"Know that fckn' horse that we saw earlia?"

The door opened and the conversation began to dwindle slowly as their loud voices eventually began to fade down the corridor.

"Ayupp. Tha' woman?"

"Ay that's a fuckin' ticket. Fancy her I do."

"Ya'll be like a pair of fat bollocks."

"Ha ha ha ha. Oi fuck yaa-"

Chapter 62

The wise man begga'

Mexico City was alive, the days flew by and before I knew it I was heading for the bus stop once more. This time I wasn't alone. Joined by dumb and dumber, the wired duo, known to themselves as Ketty and Sniff. What was I doing? Truth is, I quite enjoyed their company. I didn't think about the sad nature of the world; westernisation or global warming or deforestation or hunting or slavery. I didn't think about myself, suicide, loneliness, emptiness, fatigue, I didn't think about Jasper, or Scar, how much I missed them. When I was with them, I just laughed, a cure for all those things – I guess that's why I agreed to travel into Guatemala with them. We were heading for a moonlight beach party just north of Puerto Barrios, across the Bahia Interna de Santo Tomás at a beach called Punta de Palma on the East coast of Guatemala. I told them they were clutching at straws and it probably didn't exist. The Guatemalan who told them no sooner vanished into thin air.

"Ya petty and pessimistic boring Noah. It'sa gonn' be live. Mark my word."

So we went. Why didn't I just go elsewhere if I thought it was bollocks? Again, I guess I just liked their company.

*

We got to the bus stop.

"Righto' seeyous lata Noah," said the tall one, Sniff.

I was perplexed. "What? What about the moonlight party?"

"What abou' tit?" Fat Ketty grabbed his own as he jumped up and down laughing.

"Well aren't we going?"

"Ay but can t'afford so we're gon' hop in the luggage."

Ketty put his foot in.

"Don't be ridiculous, it's a twenty-two hour journey."

They looked at each other and shrugged simultaneously. It was like they were looking in one of those mirrors that distorts you so you look fat and short or tall and skinny.

"I'll have to pay for you."

They exchanged a look and smirked. Telepathically communicating that maybe this boring fella might actually be useful. I'd never seen Ketty move so fast, must be the drugs. In fact, with these two, it's always the drugs.

"Free coke for you my friend," said Sniff as he put his hand on my shoulder. About the most appreciative gesture the two could conjure.

*

For the first eight or so hours I wished I had let them bounce around in the luggage, better that than them bouncing around while I try and sleep. Out of their chairs, down the aisle, off the walls, on the chair, off the walls, on the ceiling, head out the window, legs out the window. I had fucking spiderman and his fat friend niggling at my head, like two kids who couldn't sit still. I waited for the drugs to wear off, they'd been wired since yesterday, so it was surely a matter of time?

Sniff crashed an hour or so into the journey, his six foot plus skeleton bending and sinking into the chair. He began to snore loudly and I considered waking him up and letting him bounce. Ketty nudged me, his eyes were on the turn as well, drooping and dark but he managed a weak smile which alongside his tired face made him look pissed to fuck.

"Wann' see something' funny?"

Like speaking to a child, I figured a yes would shut him up.

He pulled a picture out of his pocket, it was torn and bent but I made out a student in a library with his middle finger up. He showed me another picture, the same student this time outside what looked like a School of Oxford. "Guess."

"Guess what?"

"Who tis is."

"Gheez I don't know Ketty. Did Zuckerberg go to Oxford?"

He looked at me appalled. "Harvard."

"Shit well I'll be damned. I don't know."

He put the picture to his face and though I saw no resemblance I understood what he was saying.

"You? You. You went to fucking Oxford."

"Life can be full of surprises," he said in a perfect, posh Oxford accent.

"But how? You're dumb as a screwdriver."

"Na, just don't wann' use the big brain," he said knocking on his head.

"But you act like a complete phony."

"That's why I was kicked out."

"You didn't even graduate?" I chuckled. Now it all made sense.

"Best in class I was. Got kicked out for not not being on drugs. Was still top though."

"Why did you do drugs if you were so clever? You had everything set for you."

"Everything? What's everything? Always told to work 'ard and get a gud job, told to speak proper. They weren't sure I could graduate as I wasn' propa' Oxford stereotype even though I was top of my classes. Never told to have fun or smile. The cycle of study, work, die was gonna get the betta' of me. So I said no, where's the livin' an' then fucked off. Now I'm live. N itsa still up 'ere," he knocked on his head again and then popped the picture away. "Funny eh?"

In actual fact I didn't see the funny side at all. It was a mesmerising story, breaking the shackles of society, something I was trying to do. Just as I had broken from my job, he had from the greatest education society can offer. But if that doesn't bring joy then why do it? I guess its fundamentally the same for everything. Only do the things you love.

Why? Well Ketty finished my thoughts off perfectly before the drugs expired and he fell into a deep sleep. "Life isa too short t'do shit you don't wanna do."

Chapter 63

A Sniff of redemption?

I travelled through the remainder of the journey in relative comfort and peace. The odd spontaneous bus stop being the only break in peace on the old bus liner. I got out at each to stretch my legs and examine the little roadside shops. However far I seemed to travel from the first shop I'd visited, the bits on sale never changed. Topo Chico, Modelo and Mamey (a fruit much like an avocado but with a creamy inner flesh). I tried it with a group of Mexican children all surrounding me, interested in whether I'd like their famous fruit. My smiles sent them into a frenzy of dancing which brought me great joy and a memory to cherish. It's the smallest things that can sometimes have the greatest impact. The bus carried on toward Guatemala. We got off at Puerto Barrios and sought a rickety taxi willing to take us round the bay. In reality, it was more of a go-kart given the number of holes in it. MOT failed.

*

I hadn't any idea what to expect when I got to Punta de Palma so as I jumped out of the taxi onto the dilapidated street, I was neither excited nor bemused by what I saw. A continual line of shacks made of the trees that surrounded them. A Catholic church posed as the great monument and architectural feat of the town on the northern end of the winding metropolis of shacks and rural retreats that did everything to bring tourists in. Except there were no tourists to bring in, only three mops that stood hopelessly in the chalk road as their ride wheel spun away back toward Puerto Barrios.

"Yee-fucking-hawww we made't. Trees. Wow the sky. Loud birds, loud. Rickety-clickety shacks. Little kids. Hola niña!" Sniff's hands reverberated around his body like an orchestral conductor as he merged with his surroundings and jumped off the trees. He became it. Lost in the atmosphere and live with the new experiences and adventures. He was living the life, and I was living the western one. Two very different things. Ketty hadn't rewired yet after sleeping all the way through the journey and stumbled around behind me, still finding his bearings.

What a fucking waste of time I thought as I clung to the straps of Mr Lowe Alpine and made for the sea breeze. I was growing infuriated by the lack of path I had, where was I meant to go? How can I become free once and for all? Reset and find peace. Perhaps redemption lay on the beach of Punta de Palma? Where the fuck even is Cunta de fucking Palma? The journey had sent me into a spiralled frenzy of monotony, and sadistic comparisons as my past life filled the void between my ears. It lay a decent base of reasoning behind the unfolding events of Punta de nightmare. *Where the holy prick am I in this fucking world?*

Chapter 64

Tikka and Slurp

Well I'll be damned. The closer we got to the beach the less I believed the world was round. The less I believed that Jasper had died that year, that day, on that plane. And the less I believed I was recovering, rediscovering, and living. I was live. That's how Sniff and Ketty would put it. Damn right, I was fucking thriving. Back to the beach though and I'll be damned. I could hardly believe it. I didn't believe it, was my whole life made up in my tiny head a lie? The renowned Moonlight party was real. Not only real, it was kicking off. We could barely make out the legs and arms that were being flung about when we all mutually agreed the sight before us was material. The long-awaited, long-dreamt reality in the fading hopes of Sniff and Ketty's heads was beating again, like a heartbeat after a flatline. Man, you should have seen their faces.

The beach was lined with cocktails, drugs, and tiki skirts, taking us by surprise. It woke Ketty up and soon he was on Sniff's shoulders with his bag of coke floating around his nose indefinitely. The beach was live, energy resonating through the ground and the people that stood in its company all wired to the back of their eyes and around the world. Hundreds of people, thousands, as far as the eye could see, from all over the world rejoicing in some remote location in the back ass of nowhere. Funny the lengths people travel to let their hair down. The sun was setting a beautiful orange and painted everyone with natural carvings of light, giving everyone the energy of a child having his first beer. Fuck who was I to judge. That's not me anymore.

I weaved in and out of the crowds, trying to find some enjoyment in the mental, underground party lifestyle in the middle of a paradise. It felt like someone had dropped a DnB rave in the great jazz hall of

Ronnie Scott. Someone had thrown a jaguar into SeaWorld. It was out of place and spoilt the beauty of the perfect sandy beaches, curling shorelines, setting sun and mystical blue sky turning darker by the minute. One star, two stars, when I met Scar, when I left Scar. People got in my face as I tried to think of the woman I loved. Mexicans flung themselves about with their favourite Tequilas to hand, the girls violently shaking the feathers of their miniskirts in the general direction of onlooking guys. Americans swapped their favourite lagers for a swipe of Guatemalan coke or a classier Mexican Cerveza. Those very drug dealers, wandered aimlessly through the crowds showing off their great bags that nurtured the weakness of the futile, absent-minded many that lulled around unconditionally lost beyond any reasonable human control. They could be snorting flour for all they knew. The human decay around me was the very thing I had spent the last few months running from.

I became entangled by the dancing bodies, blaring music, and the darkening light. The air grew a fresh aroma of cannabis so strong I felt I was in a small box with nothing but a burning field of the plant. I started to spin. My brain did flips as it worked out intoxication for the first time in months. This wasn't the peace I was looking for; it was no good for me. My self-resolve, discipline and control failed me, something I had promised myself would never happen again. It was fear of failing myself and the paranoia of the consequences that spiralled me into despair, I got drunk, permeating a large blanket of cocktails over the top of my cannabis high with the aim of forgetting the bad decision or maybe simply turning it into a good one? The latter seemed increasingly unlikely as the night was thrown about and I was soon floating around the crowds on my own. Weaving in and out, in and out, with a bird on my arm, no, two. Laughter with a group of lads. *Shit you're English. She's fit. I like your Tiki skirt.*

"I like your Tiki skirt."

"What's your name?" She fluttered her eyes at me and soon I was alone in the world with her. The mass of sweaty crowds and party-goers disappeared. She was beautiful.

“Noah, n these’re Ralph and Alec.” I turned around to introduce my friends to Tiki skirt, pretending Scar wasn’t there, but Ralph and Alec weren’t there anyway. I looked back toward the young brunette spinner. Gone with the wind and I was back floating in the party. Weaving in and out, in out. “I like your Tiki skirt.”

*

“I like you’re Tikkkki skurrt.”

*

“I luck you tikka slurrpp.”

“Shit Noah, you’re live to fuck! Let’s get some man!”

Four Ketty’s skid round my eyes, bouncing into the night sky one by one, higher than the stars above then drilling themselves into the sand below. He had turned into some sort of ghost and I could see through and behind him, more people jumping up and down and swaying side to side, in time with a beat entirely contradictory to the music vibrating along the beach. The music soon fell underwater and became muffled and lost in the background, as did Ketty who spoke releasing no words. I asked him where Sniff was and he looked at me confused and offered me coke instead.

Chapter 65

18

"One of these mornings you will look for me, and I will be gone."

To fuck I thought, who will I be looking for. Sand scratched my face like sandpaper, I tried to wipe it off. My fingers were numb, and I was unable to cut against the skin to get it off. Exhaustion made me forget about it, as it did to the voice that spoke again.

"One of these mornings you will look for me, and I will be gone."

My eyes ached and I opened them to see the sun glaring. Where am I? I began to move my head but didn't lift it from the surface before the gust of anguish washed over my body and plagued me. A hangover. My arms were still twitching and so too were my feet. Tito's pendant lay on my chest like a great weight pushing me into the sand. I pushed against the force and tried looking past my feet toward the direction of the sea breeze torrent that was knocking my face left and right, like I was in a ring with Mike Tyson. In reality it was as subtle as a pair of black chinos and a white tee. My view didn't get further than my cock anyway, in all its show, trousers down hugging my ankles. My head spun, my cock sat shrunk. Hiding something vicious and dark. I looked at the pair of feet to my right, a tiki skirt floating in the wind tied down by one ankle. I jolted away in shock, agony and desolation. I hardly looked at my accomplice, a young blonde. American maybe? Twenty at the oldest. My head blew up into a swollen map of redemption and peace. It was broken and faded. I was lost. I scrambled to my feet and threw myself into the undergrowth that lay feet from the sleeping Americans head.

I felt part of an exorcism as the coke and alcohol ripped at my soul, dragged my brain into water and cracked my heart. Were the last months all just a failure?

*

This was the lowest I had ever been. Lower than my suicidal attempts, how could I be lower than trying to kill myself? Easy really, I now had a place to go, a vision of my future, where I wanted to be, what I wanted to do, who I wanted to be with. I had it all set out, my album of life would get better, brighter. At least that's what I planned. It was a big plan, a brave plan, but a plan nevertheless and that's what made this moment so low, so dark. Having a plan creates a scale. A low and a high. The low is how far from your goal, the high, that you are. The high was my big plan. The low was the furthest from that plan that I could be. When depression struck I had no plan, no direction. So how was I to know I was low? What is low when there is no high? A misconception of depression is that you are fine as soon as ending your life isn't at the forefront of your mind but that's garbage. The hardest part is finding something to live for and then living for that exact thing, no exceptions. The latter was my struggle. Living for that exact thing and eradicating the negative energy of everything and anything negative was like a hike into a Himalayan storm. I'd crumbled at the sight of alcohol and drugs, sinking lower and further from my masterplan. Rock bottom.

*

I fell through the trees and leaves in a frenzy of movement, attempting to stand up but using my hands as support for my uncoordinated body weight. My heavy head led me through the dappled sunlight as it became crushed in a fist of humidity, or humiliation, who could tell? Jasper stood at each tree watching me clasp onto its trunk and propel myself toward the next one, where he would be waiting again. I kept going, getting as far from the beach as I could.

"Give in," he said as I began feeling faint, I threw up over his chest, spray painting the jungle floor with a liquid texture.

"No," I said.

"Give in," he said again as he waited for me at the next tree. "You'll never make it now, sometimes it's better to just face the truth." He looked disappointed and turned away.

"You're wrong. I'll make it," I said through gritted teeth and pierced eyes. Sweat streaked my face, a numbness continued to irritate my body. I couldn't feel a thing, couldn't see a thing. I can't see into the future but in that moment, I wish I could have. Not that it mattered, if you want something so badly, you'll go to the ends of the earth for it, then to the ends of the earth you will go. I knew where I was going. I couldn't see it, but I could hear it. I let go of the trees I'd been grappling to for support and stood myself up. Slowly, unconvinced but it was enough. A small step of determination, every step counts.

Had I been looking or listening I'd have noticed Jasper look back and smirk at my perseverance as he muttered, "That's my fucking boy. One more time."

*

I never made the next tree as I fell halfway, my mind and body collapsing in on me and causing my world to go white. Whilst my body lay sprawled across the floor of a Guatemalan jungle, my mind grabbed the lowest rung of the ladder before me and began pulling myself up toward the disappearing soles of Jaspers Converse for the last time as he called back in a faint echo. "One of these mornings you will look for me, and I will be gone."

Chapter 66

On the road again

The spirit of life visited my sweaty and defeated corpse on the jungle floor as the sun was beginning to descend behind the motionless flats of the Amatique Bay. Sucking the cocaine and alcohol from my body, he dragged me up onto my feet and pushed me toward the road. I followed the road in an agonising journey back to where we had been dropped off just twenty-four hours or so ago. As I walked along the cracked, unfinished tarmac road I dipped into the undergrowth to find Mr Lowe Alpine sat exactly where I had left him prior to embracing myself into the Moonlight party the night before. Boy did I embrace it. The road ran parallel to the beach, separated by a thin slither of exotic, central American jungle. Those great, green leaves, clammy air and hanging vines. The orchestral sounds in the canopy above painted a beautiful picture as I looked through the jungle and out onto the beach. There was a solemn figure dancing away the daytime heat like it was his first day on earth. He blew wildly around a make-believe ballroom he had granted himself on the plains of Punta de Palma with not a care in the world nor a thought in his mind. I watched intensely for a fair while, jealous of how free he was. Alone, but happy and tranquil. It was only when the figure turned round to face my direction that now I understood the picture that was unfolding, burning the beauty of the scene almost instantly. It was Sniff, his eyes were closed, mouth open and jaw gurning. He was still embracing the moonlight party of the night before, still coked up to his eyeballs and pissed up to his nose. I tutted and swore the beauty of the previous picture wasn't just in my imagination. It can become a reality. I turned back toward the road, slightly dejected Sniff was still flying around on Apollo nine. I took one look over my shoulder debating whether to go and say my farewell to him, I'd possibly bump into a slumped Ketty hanging off a tree? Negative, they're Oxford Grads (almost), they'll be just fine. So, I fucked off. Fucked off in search of the Nepalese flags and hillside towns that had lingered in my dreams and mind for so long. Perhaps those flags might just be the motivation to complete my journey of redemption?

*

I turned and left them, two good friends, on the east coast of Guatemala, without an acknowledgement, farewell or even a mere mutual nod. Never to see them again. They were both livewires, exhilarated by the life ahead of them and the experiences they could discover. Never have I seen a greater appreciation for life than the two people I had by chance been brought to. A chance encounter I am truly grateful for. It's my admiration of their positivity and energy that builds my greatest travel regret – leaving without a single good-bye. I don't know why I ran away as I did, for friendship is the greatest tool of human existence and real happiness can only truly be shared. Perhaps people are right when they say some questions just can't be answered but as I soon found out, everything happens for a reason.

"This is your life. Not mine. I'm sorry." I turned and didn't look back.

Chapter 67

London on steroids

My persistence to run from what I had done was both childish and expensive. I hopped on a bus to Guatemala City, where I then grabbed a flight to Kathmandu. I figured if there was anything to pull me out it was Cap'n Jasper and his map. What I would do in Kathmandu I wasn't sure, but I needed to go there, follow the map. Get lost in the mountains, revitalise myself, cleanse the soul. What better place to do that than the birthplace of yoga (There is global debate as to the exact birthplace of Yoga. Whilst some largely consider Nepal as the centre of beginning through the teachings of Lord Shiva from the Mountain Kailās, others refer to the city of Rishikesh in the Northern state of Uttarakhand in India). Though I had never practised yoga, I hoped an area of such teachings would distil a peace and tranquillity that I so lusted, perhaps I could find my meditative zen? *Heck, worth one last shot, right?*

*

I wound up in Nepal's capital surrounded by history; golden pagodas, ancient temples and ceremonial shrines amassing a brief insight into a history dating as far back as anyone could discover. Mini-vans and tuk-tuks rushed past among the hundreds of scooters hurriedly crossing the city. Homelessness struck me like a sword almost immediately, it clearly rife in Kathmandu as the pavements were lined with beggars. Their passers-by represented a different wealth, though closer to their begging nationals than western foreigners. I could sense the distinct climate difference between Asia and the Central America I had been exploring not thirty-six hours earlier. Immediately feeling the claustrophobia of being back in a city, people pushing past you left and right. The pace of the city made it feel like

London rush hour but every hour. Can you imagine? Did I like it? Back in the city? I'm not sure. I was keen to get moving into the mountains, do what I wanted to do. For Jasper. And then I'd move on into Asia and get back on a beach with a view and pretend I was back watching a falling sun over the Pacific Ocean on the top of a cliff with a beautiful girl. At least that's the moment I had dreamed of so many times, struggling to understand if it was the view or the latter that I missed. I think it was my way of telling myself I wasn't completely love struck and heartbroken that the love of my life who saved me from despair and the only person I wanted to complete the rest of my life with, wasn't with me. Wasn't anywhere near me. And wasn't reachable in any way. Would I bump into her? I remember thinking about it, *that's a one in seven billion chance. So no, no I won't.* How could I possibly get that into my head?

*

I did my best to get the thought of Scar out of my head and pushed myself around Kathmandu with my head high and my mind set on throwing Guatemala as far into the distance as I could. I'd cracked, lost sight of what I'd aimed for over the last few months. Had I run before I could walk? The alcohol was ringing in my head and I lost count of the number of times I'd slapped myself over the drugs. I'd never touched drugs and in my futile attempt to pull my life into shape I'd imploded toward the fuckers. I'd danced before I could stand and now I was driven by regret. *You wanker Noah. It's time to redeem yourself.*

I looked around. I was strolling along the Bagmati river. It wasn't much like strolling along the Thames or Seine. It wasn't much like strolling around anywhere really. Strolling sounds as if you're enjoying your surroundings and I wasn't convinced I was doing that. The water was murky brown, flowing inconsistently in between two steep walls of mud and dirt. It was littered with plastics and human faeces, tissues flowing along, slowly being devoured by the monster that lurked under the surface. A solitary figure floated amidst the litter, his eyes shut and his mind at ease. He didn't look at me, he didn't need to. He knew I had seen him, and he knew it would make me sick. I made up my mind. One final push, or I may as well throw myself in. I walked away, not even acknowledging my floating best mate anymore.

I walked over the Sinamangal Pool bridge, taking in the busy life of Nepal. Rushing people, honking vans and a high screeching of tyres on tarmac. The traffic flowed then it was at a standstill then it went again. All the while I walked on slowly, with no idea where I was but an idea of where I was going. I walked past the Ram Mandir temple and felt it a perfect place to pay respects, think and think some more. I had seen improvements, that much was obvious. Once a dark tunnel, this tunnel now had light. It's not as easy as you hope, neither is anything in life. All things that mean something require dedication, hardwork and a strong soul. I had to prove myself. To everyone, and to myself. I thought some more, and then rested my mind and put Guatemala behind me. *It's what I do past this point that really matters now.* I left the temple after a peaceful hour, in search of some local delicacies and ready for a stab at another youth hostel. *I can do this. I will do this.*

"Just fucking watch me," I said under my breath to the figure following me a distance away down the street, and that same figure at the back of my head.

Chapter 68

The game of chance

The next day I queued at the Everest Tours hiking stand, that I had been pointed toward by the youth hostel I had stayed in. It had taken me over an hour to navigate the five-hundred metre journey through the labyrinth of maze-like alleys, which initially wound me up at the beautiful Durbar Square before my directions threw me back into the sweltering carnage of more alleys. I made a promise that I'd come back to Kathmandu to enjoy the spirituality and culture of such an exciting place properly. I felt leaving so soon was cheating it a bit, especially after the beautiful insight I'd gathered exploring just a small part of the city. I was however, drawn toward the visions of colour, peace, and tranquillity within the rural life. The very places both I and Jasper had dreamt of. Other than my fictionalised dreams, I had little idea of what to expect, making the prospect just that bit more exciting.

*

The queue shrunk ever so slowly, and excited chatter reverberated its way through the many people keen to head toward the highest spot on the entire world. Almost all of those waiting were foreigners, and this meant opportunity and money for the locals. Food merchants came to barter whilst excited, albeit less professional hikers proclaimed their tours company consisting of only themselves was the perfect companion and money-saver. One of those locals, Manish, was younger than me and probably younger than twenty. It struck me how different his life would be should he have been born elsewhere on this world; he'd be sat behind a desk revising for his A levels or packing his bags ready for life at university. Life is really just a game of chance. I was lucky and I guess he wasn't. Or perhaps it's the other way around? If he knew this, he didn't show it, a sincere smile plastered on his face which barely changed as I dismissed his bartering. He wished me a good day and left in search of new tourists.

Luck had it for Manish that the hiking stand offered nothing that particularly took my fancy. Besides I didn't want to be walking with a load of obnoxious tourists and their shed loads of cash.

"Hmmm," he said thoughtfully as I approached him regarding walking through the mountains. I found his confusion over the exact thing he had been offering me, a hiking trip, slightly strange, but he composed himself with enthusiasm to do me the best deal in Kathmandu. I was convinced that was the opening sentence of any great Nepalese scam, but sure enough Manish was legit and wanted to help me as much as I could help him.

"Help you with what?" I asked, slightly withdrawn from the idea. The chance of being mugged, raped or killed did cross my mind but I figured I had little to lose so I would ultimately be a cheap blow by the offender, a risk I figured they would be unwilling to take. Sound psychological de-escalation of the threat of death if you ask me.

"I will take you to mountains and good lakes. You will help bring stuff to my mother in mountains. No cost."

I smiled. I liked the kid and figured I'd be safe. "Oh errr, sure thing. How long is the walk?"

"Drive, five hours," he put his hand up with five fingers showing, as clarification to go alongside his unorthodox English, unsure whether he had said the number right. "Walk, four days to there." Peace sign on both hands.

"Alright," I said, cracking a smile despite my nervousness. Did he mean four days there and four days back or? "Lead the way."

We both jumped into the craziness of the street and left the hiking stand and all the tourists behind us. Fuck it, what's eight days at this point? Freedom, that's what it is. I didn't like being around tourists anyway so best to get out when there is a chance. Manish seemed pretty ecstatic at the prospect of going to see his mother and asked questions like it was his last day on earth. I debated putting an arm on his shoulder and telling him we had days of talking to come but instead soaked it up, smiled and danced down the road with the kid. The prospect of freedom and tranquillity was in both our feet as we weaved in and out of the bustling crowds in more of a run than a dance. *What was a kid like him doing on his own in Kathmandu anyway?*

Chapter 69

Metal with wheels. Four not three.

Turns out Manish's running wasn't through his excitement but his parking. He rocked up to his red Nineteen-Ninety Polo, swinging himself round the car to face the windscreen. The wave of anguish that his running had suggested was dispelled and his shoulders dropped with relief. No ticket, no vandalism and the car had not been towed. He resumed his condition of verbal diarrhoea as he had been doing throughout the quick trip to the car. I wasn't listening, instead sussing out the car. It reminded me of the old banger me and Jasper used to drive up to the great Scottish lochs though even ours was better than that which lay in front of me. It reminded me of those cars with three wheels and I considered it outrageous that this actually had four. Which I confirmed after circling the vehicle in disbelief. *I was actually getting in this.*

I still hadn't got in before Manish lit the engine and it coughed and spluttered into life. Well, more brought back to life.

He whistled at me. "Ey, name?"

"Oh erm, Noah. And you?"

"Noah, you drive this, I push."

Strange name I thought as I threw myself into my first Nepalese driving experience, without thinking too much of it, pulling out into a stream of buzzing cars and scooters with few, unrecognisable gaps. I could and probably was beeped as I pulled out from the side of the road but with the orchestra of horns already blaring I had no way to tell if they were directed at me. I preferred it that way.

"Manish," he said as he jumped in whilst I began driving off and pointed to an exit on the far side of the road, the other side of four or five lanes of traffic. "Go."

How the fuck do I get over there I thought as I pulled out, driving myself toward the destiny this kid had chosen for me. *What Nepalese drug lord was I driving my life to?*

Chapter 70

A covetous world

Around twenty-four hours later we were walking through the middle of nowhere. Paradise. The mountains were tranquil, like a holiness blew across them, not a soul in sight. It was these parts of the world where you really see what sapiens have done to the world we live in, nature being the one formidable ruler up there. Wherever there was. We'd driven from Kathmandu to a small town/settlement called Singati on the south side of the Gaurishankar conservation area. I'd have felt both apprehensive and a little intrusive wandering my western bollocks into the small settlements like Singati if it wasn't for Manish. To put it into perspective, the scenery and transportation around us made Manny's Polo feel like a Rolls Royce Phantom. We walked thirty-three kilometres that first day, through the towns of Gurumphi and Marbu and round the mountain peak of Chugima, standing at four thousand five hundred and ninety metres. A relative dwarf in comparison to the big hitters that would fill the landscape in the coming days. Boy it was beautiful. Our journey ended at a bunkhouse cottage-esque shack in the settlement of Naa, by the side of the Tshorolpa lake run by a friendly but shy Nepalese peasant who welcomed us in with open arms, dusted us off, and then was quick to leave us to our own devices. After hiking thirty plus kilometres with bags of shit that Manish chucked in my arms, for his mother, as well as Mr Lowe Alpine, I was happy to be left alone and sat with my feet up looking down at the glacier lake through the window, its surface rippling in the dying light, speaking to the wind that ricocheted off the water before violently shooting up into the night sky as it followed cliff edges and steep mountain sides, howling its freedom as it did so. I soon fell into a deep sleep, like a kid in front of a fire after being outside playing in the winter snow all afternoon. The elements battled whilst I sat tucked away, comatose by the fresh Himalayan air and feeling fucking alive. Thriving. Just thirty ish hours ago I was feeling like a complete fuck up and now I was once again feeling on top of the world. Who ever said life isn't a rollercoaster?

*

I was flying as I dreamt I had been back in London, I was Aquila the eagle. This time I wasn't flowing through the canyon but instead up in the sky, looking down on the busy chaos of the world below. People rushed around, cars intertwined, and people crossed paths with one another, only to never see them again. I couldn't quite make out details, so I swooped down closer to the floor. I saw a scene like I had been in today, cars beeping and pushing their way through traffic and out of the city, it sure looked like Kathmandu but I wasn't there for long enough to be able to figure an aerial view of the place. And then I spotted Manish's Polo, whizzing off toward the Himalayas. It beckoned me to follow and I felt an impulse to do so, almost pulled toward it. I was still trailing as Manish pulled the Phantom to a stop in the town of Singati. I recognised the bridge that spanned thirty-five metres across the deep ravine, linking one mountain side to the next. Manish got out of the car simultaneously to Jasper. My best friend, here again. He got out slowly, the movement of his eyes mimicking the speed of his body's movement, slow, tranquil, blown-away. He stood up and looked around, at the town's stillness and rickety bridge, at the mountains that loomed either side and then up at the blue sky that shimmered with light further above the mountain tops. He closed his eyes, arms stretched and chest out, a symbol of immersion and freedom that I'd seen many times before. I watched as any negativity was squeezed out slowly, calmly. There was no sound, no pain, just an aura. Manish watched with care, breathless, almost in awe of the embodiment in front of him. A peace that I hadn't even seen within Alec. Jasper had everything. Everything and so much more.

I followed their hike as they followed the same route as I had with Manish. Whilst I had found the trek tiring, Jasper kept pace with Manish and I couldn't help but feel Manish was let down by my futile attempts. His patient face looking back at me continuing to jump into my head from earlier that day as I clambered along uneven roads with exhaustion. Jasper constantly had a smile on his face. Nothing would get him down and his laughter resonated across the Himalayan tranquillity. He laughed with Manish, talked to him and consoled him, like a big brother would to their smaller self. I felt aggrieved to have been struck by jealously in that moment, what I'd do for a moment like that with him. Manish was laughing and I could see his character soften toward the upbeat traveller he'd stumbled upon in the midst of Kathmandu chaos; that was Jaspers charm – befriending people almost instantly. The laughter would continue all the way to the bunkhouse I was now dreaming in as they trotted toward the door, arms slung over each other's shoulders and began to knock.

I jolted upright as the house owner waddled over and let them in, my eyes transfixed to the space in front of the door.

Chapter 71

The imaginative realms of reality

Manish woke me whilst it was still dark, though it had that feel of air just before sunrise, you know the magical sort of excitement about the rise of a new day.

He whispered softly. "Come with me."

I obliged, packing up my stuff still blurry eyed but keen to head into the mountains with a new sense of motivation and freedom after watching Jasper hike the route I was on. The dream made sense I guess; it was his vision first. I couldn't help but be confused by the situation of being here, alone, without him. I knew what I was doing of course, I had come here to do this for him, to be with him, and to have that bit of him that was right. He would hike through Nepal after all. But something had changed, like a tug-of-war in my head. I wasn't convinced I was doing this for him in spite of everything.

You know that ladder I said I was to start climbing once and for all as I sat there butt-naked on the beach of Guatemala? This was the ladder I was talking about. This was the first time I realised I was doing this for myself, and that was ok. More importantly, that was what Jasper had wanted all along. Or didn't want. Who's to care? *It's my life so it's up to me to enjoy myself, which means forcing nothing and doing everything that I desire.* That's truly what Jasper wanted me to find and that was what I was beginning to find. I was there because I wanted to be there. Not because Jasper wanted to be there, or Jasper wanted me to be there. As selfish as it sounds, it wasn't about Jasper. I think that is what he had been trying to tell me the whole time. I had to faze him out, as much as I didn't like it, that was the only way I could look forward and not back.

Manish took me to Dudhkunda, a second, smaller glacier lake north of Tshorolpa. The sun hadn't risen yet, though the first beams of life were reaching round the top of the distant rocks and mountains. It made the rocky stumble in the early morning breeze difficult but exhilarating. An adventure through a distant, mysterious land. We reached the sacred lake just as the first sunshine began to fall on the cloudy water, like a spirit from above waking up and diving in to immerse itself and cleanse the soul. There they were, the coloured flags that rippled through the Nepalese streets in my dreams, strewn from one side of the lake to the other in a zig zag formation from length to width. A lake of colour and holiness. It was as if the Hindus were celebrating something, the way the little rectangular flags jumped up and down in the morning breeze, singing with the wind and filling my world. I took a step onto a great bolder that looked down on the lake and closed my eyes, my face was rushed with a sudden gush of the morning, my hair being propelled behind me and my body nervously balancing on the boulder. The freshest of air entered my lungs, its coldness making me shiver but cleansed. It was revitalising and magnificent. I remember thinking I could stay there forever and hardly a day goes by where I don't think of it.

*

Those great flags in my dreams, that flew across the lake are actually prayer flags laid by Sherpa's. They are found all across trails and paths within the Himalayas with the attempt to promote peace, compassion, strength, and wisdom. The prayers and mantras written upon the cloth flags are hung in the wind to spread good will and bless the surrounding countryside. Each colour flag represents different elements; blue – sky, white – wind, red – fire, green – water, yellow – earth. The flags are all incredibly sacred and according to legend must be hung in the specific order stated.

There was no doubt the energy these inscriptions brought to me and I felt there was a reason my path had led me to the sacred place where peace, compassion, strength, and wisdom are spread naturally, as intended.

*

Manish was equally taken aback by its beauty, on his knees by the side of the lake as if in prayer. There was no doubting this was the place to thank Him for anything, and everything. It was powerful to see the impact such a natural place has on someone who has visited so many times, undoubtedly a feeling irreplaceable to anything. We could have been there at the lake for hours, but it would still not have been long enough. I wished time would just stand still, the buzzing horns, bustling markets and desperate beggar's miles and miles away. How I liked it, I had decided.

"Liberation can come from immersion into these waters, it is believed," said Manish softly some while later, breaking the divine glaze across my face but doing no such thing to the tranquillity of the environment that continued to resonate around us.

"Liberation?" I asked intriguingly, whispering to respect the world as best I knew.

He nodded without breaking his gaze across the lake. "For fulfilment, atonement or just a desire."

I wondered if it could help me? Soothe my life into a path I could rediscover? I almost began taking off my shoes but was stopped by my own thoughts that had stayed so silent since discovering this great enclosure of wonder, *if you are strong enough to get here on your own, you are strong enough to go the rest of the way.* That was me speaking, not Jasper, so I got up having paid my respects and left. I looked back to watch the colours flutter in the air one last time, a pigment of my imagination that had seen the realms of reality. Perhaps my imagination of peace and tranquillity at the end of the long dark road wasn't just the conclusive make-believe we all desire?

*

I hiked the rest of the day like some great Nepalese warrior, lost in the ambience of the scenery and the world I lived in. Oh, what people were missing. I was the Queen and the world was a chess board, I was striving across great distances effortlessly. Thrive – To be your best self. Was I thriving yet? I began to discover the sheer height of some of the mountains that surrounded me from all sides. I felt like a kid looking up at the big kids that surrounded you at lunch time, threatening you and pushing you around, and whilst I was all too aware of nature's ability to play the bully, at that moment it was like heaven. We hiked through the valley between the mountains of Kongde Ri and Tengi Ragi Tau, standing at six thousand and eleven metres, and six thousand, nine hundred and thirty-eight metres approximately. I was so incomprehensibly small in this landscape, and it was exhilarating. I had an urge to climb despite being out of breath from eight hours of relatively flat walking.

"Have you ever climbed any of these Manish?" I said to break the holy silence that had resonated as we pushed through the beautiful canvas that lay in front of us. It was like breaking through a picture only to be in front of another beautiful picture, breaking through that one in the same vein to be greeted by yet another beautiful picture. I guess that summed up the next six or so days to be fair.

Chapter 72

Valley of light

On day three we made it to Manish's house, where his mother stayed, often alone in ambience. Turns out they owned a Sherpa lodge resting on the mountainside in the settlement of Lunden, so when she was alone, she was occupied by many hikers from across the world. She was an incredibly reserved woman who I likened a lot to Tito, respectful and wise. Her love of her son was arguably her greatest asset, and it warmed my heart being a part of their reunion. It was clear Manish was the whole reason for his Mum's existence and I could tell she would be lost if she hadn't had her dear, and only son. It did get me wondering, *why was Manish living in Kathmandu and why has she stayed in solitude?* I guess certain mysteries are taken to the grave.

The lodge had the company of a number of hikers, twelve to be exact, mostly from Germany it seemed, with the exception of their two native tour guides. It meant space was tight, but Manish had his own room tucked away just past the kitchen which meant I could sleep on the floor in there, away from the hustle and bustle. I sat in there for quite a while after arriving and greeting his mother warmly. There was a little circular window that looked out toward the valley, so I stared with my arms folded and chin resting on my forearm, for what felt like hours, into the abyss. I thought about my journey, where I had started, where I had been, where I was. More importantly I thought about what I had left behind and what I had managed to pick up, like a snake shedding its skin. I'd begun to lose the darkness, anger, and pain, replacing it with joy, love, and excitement. Excitement of the present and future. I figured one day I could also look back and look there with joy, something I haven't been able to do the past years. The thought alone filled me with more excitement. It's fair to say I was live, thriving. What a time to be alive!

There was only one cloud in the vast future. I had found grains of love and let them fall through my fingers, onto the grains of sand on the beach – impossible to find however hard you look. It filled me with sadness, and I did my best to push it toward the back of my mind, knowing it would always come creeping back in when I'd least expect it. *What could I do?* I had no way of finding her and despite our conversations and love for weeks on end, I knew very little about her. Though this thought loomed over the Lunden valley, it proved a place that I reflect greatly on, the place I finally realised how far I had come and I guess once at the top of Gokyo Ri the next day, the first sight of the light at the end of the long, dark, winding tunnel.

Chapter 73

Decision to do the beautiful sister

Being young and enthusiastic, Manish soon became bored of the lodge's four walls.

"Tomorrow, we will climb, my friend," he said with joy.

I struggled to contain my excitement, for though I was nervous, the thought of climbing that which I had been immersed within for days was incredible. "Really?"

"We go for Gokyo Ri in the morning," he roared whilst hanging off a dilapidated and bent pole that lay rooted in the ground outside the lodge, at a forty-five degree angle, Long John style.

We laughed like kids in our excitement and I imagined how amazing a feeling it must be if someone who has grown up climbing still reacts like this. I figured it would be one hell of an experience, and that, that it was.

*

Gokyo Ri is a mountain that provides unimaginably enigmatic views, of its intimidating sisters, Everest, Lhotse, Makalu, Cho-Oyu and others. In addition, the trek beholds incredible strings of turquoise lakes and glaciers. At five thousand, three hundred and fifty-seven metres, it was higher than I'd ever been (without flying) and despite Manish's enthusiasm when it was decided we'd be ascending, he approached me seriously and for a moment the sun was shaded by the single grey cloud that eclipsed my view. This was a serious deal. He told me, in his best English, about the dangers and difficulties on the body, specifically hypoxia (a deprivation of oxygen). He was stern as a teacher for a good hour, talking me through everything. I'll spare the details. If you struggle, stop, was the ultimate teaching I got.

*

We set off on our long journey toward the summit in the early hours of the next morning, fortunately because Lunden valley was already four thousand five hundred metres above sea level, we could accomplish summiting within a day (just). Sources suggest climbing over a thousand metres in a single day isn't accomplishable when you consider acclimatisation, but Manish insisted if we took it slow, all would be fine. We did exactly that. I'd also been acclimatising the past week or so since setting off from the car in Singati so my body was already incredibly comfortable with lower levels of oxygen (although of course it would get lower). I won't bore you with the minute details of the ascent, for the seriousness of the task cannot be undermined and thus even the smallest things were considered and accomplished with great care. Emergency supplies, rescue kits, and certain nutritional tablets were all stuffed into Manish's backpack. I'll be honest, I didn't have the slightest clue what half of it was.

The pace was slow, significantly slower than we'd been hiking through the last few days and at times I was itching to break into a greater stride. My body was consumed by frustration, a desire to sprint through the mountains and over the great boulders with my head up and my arms out wide. Manish continued to ring through my mind though, as I maintained the reserved pace he had set. I guess it allowed us to appreciate the beauty of the world for longer and by all accounts I'd wish to be back there now.

We were to ascend and descend via the alternative trekking route of Renjo La pass, a pass that cut between Gokyo Ri and the Lunden valley and welcomed very few tourists. The sun was out, and the journey was an open valley of rocks and distant mountains for the most part. The air was crisp and rippled to the bottom of the lungs after every breath. The Renjo La pass itself held a beautiful panorama of the great stairways to heaven that engrossed us, and we sat for over half an hour at the peak, for I did not want to move, while watching the sunrise beyond the tallest of peaks, glistening the incredible landscape a warm golden glow. Eventually we moved toward Gokyo Ri, whose views surpassed even those I had just seen. I didn't believe it for a second but it would later prove true.

Chapter 74

Wolf

From within I could feel it rising, clearing everything, emptying. Purifying my soul. The plague was magnetised by the wave of euphoria that rushed over me, the same wave that tried striking me to my knees but while they wobbled, I kept alive, burning. It continued to rise, like a beacon in the sky, screaming its warmth across the lands. The power of the fire stoked by the beauty that was around it and pushed forth by its past. It spluttered at the top but continued to crack, pop, fizz, doing anything and everything a fire does to light even larger. The demons within continued to be attacked until they were mere mortals. Some were thrown from the great mountain into the abyss below, where they lay dead. Forever. Others evaporated like smoke, leaving a cloud that faded into non-existence. Meanwhile, the flame continued to burn. It would grow in size, that was obvious, like a wind fanning it bigger. Sometimes it was almost doused, emptied of all its might, but the little fire could never die and soon it grew, larger and larger, further, and wider, until it once again had no more. Until it was barely a flicker. Its appearance seemed to die, but it was still there, warming the land and melting the ice caps. A sphere of warmth around it, like a sun in its own universe. I discovered it had left a trail in its wake, spreading over the world like a mystical quest, to tie the world together and harmonise all who met it. It had done so to great success. It continued to pass through unknown lands, unaware of the beauty it was leaving behind it, the joy it had created for so many.

I stood there at the summit, as the wind battered me from all sides, screaming, as loud as I could, as defiant as my soul could muster. It made me shake, like an evil was leaving me. The Himalayan Sherpas singing me into an exorcism, protecting me from the evil that haunted my mind. I felt it leave me, in a vicious wind through my body, a boulder off my shoulders and a darkness removed from my sight. I screamed louder. It wasn't a scream of agony like the first, it was a scream of relief and emotion. I felt it all there and then, a freedom and a liberation. Most importantly I felt a love for the world, a love for the life I was living and a grasp I had attained for the first time in years. I was almost there.

I finally looked out. I'd been at the summit for five minutes before I took note of the landscape before me. The giants of Nuptse, Lhotse and Everest rose like archangels over the comparatively small cliff that lingered elsewhere in the panorama. The sight was magnificient, and my eyes remained transfixed on the highest point of the world, like a trophy the Earth had given to itself to appreciate its beauty. It seemed so tranquil, the white snow- capped craggy edges, standing still and solitary, a false façade to the reality of the conditions that actually existed up there, in a world of its own. I never once felt like climbing it, there is a reason it is that high and a reason humans aren't supposed to go there. I thought of Leo then, how he would consider it nature's playground, where humans aren't meant to go. If they do then any injuries are of their own doing, they had been warned. Jasper was the same. But hell, it was beautiful, like nothing you can ever imagine. The rest of the Himalayas seemingly fell at its feet and I found myself seeing for miles, beauty everywhere. At the base of Gokyo Ri was the Gokyo village on the shores of the turquoise lake. There were two more lakes surrounding Gokyo Ri, the largest of the three on the Northern side of the mountain and the smallest beyond the village further south. Like their surrounding nature, they seemed so tranquil, moving at the same speeds people travelled through the Himalayas. Tentative and respectful.

*

You're thinking the portrayal of summitting Gokyo Ri is written in a barely understandable way? You'd be right, but why? Because what happened up there doesn't have an explanation, nor does it have an acceptable way of writing about such experiences. A feeling of ambiguity and yet absolute clearness. I wasn't out of the tunnel or at the top of the ladder just yet, but I was very close, there was just one thing to relinquish now. I screamed one last time at the thought of my final hurdle, one I would reluctantly let go. It was a scream that trembled with emotion and fluctuated as my emotions tackled me off the mountain and back down to the bottom. I was ready to begin my final ascent, to a place where I would never look back. Have you understood yet?

*

Manish sat and ate some sort of Nepalese sandwich whilst watching me drink it in. He wasn't alone of course, and you can guess who was sat next to him, watching his best friend's negativity be thrown across an endless, unreturnable void. I guess what had happened to me up there was greater than the view, watching the eradication of such deeply rooted problems paints a perhaps impossible solution to humanities problems. If I could find redemption in life, why can't you? I struggled to accept why Manish and Jasper watched me instead of looking out into the beautiful world they shared with me, I guess you just want the people around you to be happy. After all, happiness can only truly be shared.

Chapter 75

Plains of everything

I decided where my final destination had to be long before we got back to the warmth of Manish's lodge. I felt rejuvenated by our crusade and was ready to set forth on the final instalment of my treacherous journey to salvation. I would have gone without setting foot in the lodge but for the darkness and bitter chill that hallowed down the Lunden valley. It would have to wait till tomorrow.

*

By noon the next day we were hiking back toward the car in Singati and a few days later, after descending terrain we had ascended and ascending that which we had descended, we made it back to the Phantom. What was my plan? I knew I had to get to the coast, there was something about the ocean that made everything go away and I knew there was something to find there, my final answer. I pondered Cap'n Jaspers own quest and after deliberating with the knowledge Manish had, I was set. He dropped me at Kodari, I was reluctant to accept his travel, but he insisted and like so many others I had met on my journey, I concluded he just enjoyed my company. Sad to see me go, he gave me a farewell hug at the Nepalese-Tibet border and then the little Polo was off, churning up the chalky road heading for the lights of Kathmandu. Another person who had entered and left my life. Another soul I would never forget.

Kodari and its neighbouring Zhangmu, where the bus would arrive, were rather desolate towns, hugely affected by the twenty-fifteen earthquake in the area. The bus rocked up only an hour later and I jumped on, heading for Lhasa, and leaving the rubble gladly behind me.

The journey took twelve long, reflective hours as I travelled along the three-one-eight national highway, the longest highway in all of China. It started at the friendship bridge in Zhangmu and travelled through to Shanghai, a whole three thousand four hundred miles. The journey was long, but it was in relative, unexpected comfort and though it trailed the comfort of the greyhound bus from Cisco, it sure beat the bus to Guatemala. I guess I didn't have Ketty bouncing off the walls or rolling across the floor this time. The thought of leaving them on the beach with no idea what had come of me was sad and niggled at my head for the first few hours of the journey. I watched Sniff dancing away in the late morning sun like it was his last moments on this world. I watched Ketty hold up his portrait and for a split second he resonated the collective, perfect Oxford grad he was expected to become. Of course, Ketty didn't become the graduate he was destined to be, nor was Sniff dancing away his last moments, but they were nice memories nevertheless and I was grateful that they'd come into my life. I fell asleep at around midnight local time as the bus continued to whistle along roads with little sights, curving with the land and across vast plains of nothing. I filled the plains with beautiful fireworks, great locomotives, and Sherpas that travelled spreading their prodigious flags. There were buses whizzing across the world in front of my eyes like a picture of how far I had travelled. I noticed the London bus being chased by a Greyhound and that also being chased by central American remakes, all varying in durability and height. In the midst of bus frenzy, I noticed a little red polo and a hand painted campervan sending it through heaven and hell in search of something. Whatever that something was. They began swerving as a bear began slamming his paws down from above but this bear was no scary bear, he had Mr Lowe Alpine on his back and Jaspers map in his hands, he was laughing and everyone in the picture began laughing with him. It was a unison of liberation and freedom and I laughed myself at the sight, however ridiculous it was. There were surf boards gracing the waves of a great tsunami that had sprung from the backdrop but this tsunami was peaceful and it rolled over the expanse lifting everything up like a dad lifting his little boy as they enjoy a day out at the seaside town of Studland, all those miles away. It made me smile as I nestled my face into the window and closed my eyes, my imagination shutting off everything across the plain simultaneously.

There was one picture left before me in my mind that I had grown quite fond of sleeping with, a picture of beauty. My best friend and me.

Chapter 76

World of zen

Through my experiences, I had grown quite use to sleeping on a bus and the journey to Lhasa flashed by so fast I found myself being shaken viciously by a perplexed native, the driver I assumed. He muttered in Chinese and though I hadn't brushed up my knowledge of the ancient tongue, the language barrier didn't prove too indecipherable. I grabbed Mr Lowe Alpine, battered and bruised as ever, and was quickly swept off the bus into the morning air of Lhasa.

The bus stop lay precariously on the side of the highway and at first the centre of Tibet's Buddhist faith was unrecognisable. The name Lhasa comes from the word Lāsà, meaning 'Place of the Gods', so I should have expected what I would find in this holy place, but it was only when I strolled unwarily into the Norbulingka that I began to see the world I was wandering and the wonders it hid. Norbulingka Palace was built in seventeen-fifty-five as the summer home of the Dalai Lama and stretches over hundreds of thousands of square metres. The Buddhist aura made the palace and gardens peaceful and zen, and painted a pretty picture of what else the winding alleys and fascinating backstreets of Lhasa had to offer. I made my fifteen-minute cameo in the garden as respectful as I could, wandering aimlessly through beauty and harmony. I wished I could stay longer and if I had perhaps, I would have found the prostrating pilgrims in Jokhang or the wafting incense leading up to the mighty Potala Palace. It remains on my list of places to visit (revisit) and I'll make sure we do so one day. But my journey demanded I carry on, even when I wished I could get lost in this different world. I could of course, but there was much time for that, and I relished the moment I could do so.

For now, onwards.

*

I jumped on my first sleeper train at around four that afternoon, I had a mere five hours to discover a place that had a history that probably couldn't be learnt in five years. I was heading for the city of Chengdu, capital of the southwestern Sichuan province. It was a mere thirty-five hours away. I had booked a hard sleeper for the journey, a smaller bed, with communal facilities. I wanted to behave the way the locals would and indulge in their way of life. I sounded like Jasper, but I failed to grasp why, because I grew up in the West so I should have better treatment and privilege myself on better travel? I suffered the curiosity and interest of the locals at an English man in the middle of nowhere and did my best to engage with a smile. It was a new me and embracing everything life has to offer was one of my plans.

Only a few days till I was where I wanted to be.

Chapter 77

Wanderingly Aimlessing

For the days to follow, I drove myself in and out of cities before I could even say their names. The train to Chengdu had been followed by an almost immediate six-hour train to Kumming. Even in the late evening air, Kumming had an unexplained ambience of liveliness and modernity and though I'd never heard of the Southern capital of the Yunnan province, again I had found a place I wished to return to. The list was ever-growing and with that thought I had no sooner taken residence on a fourteen-hour bus toward the capital city of Laos, Vientane. I'd lost concept of time at this point as the driver began churning the same bus forward out of the capital and back on the road, this time further south across the Thai border.

*

Don't get me wrong, many of the journeys I took were exhilarating, as we crossed the lands past forests and over rivers. Great temples stood shimmering in the backdrop and local palaces, extinct and unknown to Google, wriggled in and out of view of the dwindling highways and unpaved roads that we travelled. It was an experience few natives took concern over but I often found myself speechless. These holy places were unfamiliar to strangers and the worlds of Google Maps and Facebook, and it was this that gave these places a beauty, a power over the modern world. They say we've discovered near everything about our world on land, but I'd imagine places like these stray far from that line of thought. Perhaps the indulgent, self-absorbed human race aren't quite as knowledgeable as we all think? Are we just small fish in a big pond, living our lives believing we are the big fish in small ponds?

*

I scrambled south from Laos for a final twelve hours, making it down through Thailand to the booming Bangkok. The capital, I found, held a vibrant night life as I once again rolled into a new city in the dark. I wandered aimlessly for hours, trekking what I anticipated was south from the Mo Chi bus depot. Coincidence or not, I strayed far enough to kamikaze myself into the blinding lights and smoke guns of Khao San road. I instantly smelt the booze and dope and heard music blaring from little pubs that sprawled people out into the street, creating an almost uncrossable dancefloor. Backpackers from across the globe rejoiced in an epitome of love and peace, laughing with their friends from across the pond that they'd met only days ago but felt they'd known for years. There is a spell that all travellers fall under: everyone is your friend. That's how everyone is so happy, it's like a bizarre social experiment taken from the realms of Aldous Huxley. I looked briefly down the road. I could once have seen myself falling into a cumulation of hundred baht pints (around two pound fifty), but that me was long gone. In a display of moral strength and redemption, I decided to walk through the road, diving in and out of oncoming backpackers and evading the thrusts of bar menus and special offer vouchers. The humidity was suffocating, and I couldn't help but laud the brilliant marketing of ice-cold beers and perfectly placed cocktails just close enough to the crowds, to help the dehydrating prey from the depths of exhaustion, heatstroke, or suffocation. Like all modern cities, Bangkok was a clear hub of commerciality with the bright pill boards that flashed above the streets, drawing tourists in from far and wide. The vibrant life made quite a contrast to the temples and mountains I'd been surrounded by over the last week and I had little struggle determining my preference as I was forced deeper into the street.

I continued to wander for what felt like hours, and almost began enjoying the Asian carnival approach to a Saturday night. Intoxicated backpackers stumbled from one bar to another before me, as I inspected the market stalls of food where the sellers were making as much noise as possible to drown out their rivals. Delicacies that ranged from tourist approved western foods to unfamiliar Asian delicacies that were best left unknown.

I strolled further through the crowds, allowing myself a peek into the various bars that continued down the street. I found myself staring toward the back of a bar at a head I knew all too well, Scar. Her blonde hair flowing just past her shoulders and her tanned neck beaming under the strobe lights, she had a white floral crop top on that ran round her numerous times before being tied at the back. It exposed the lower part of her back, which was tanned just how I remembered it. My heart sank and I felt for all my disbelief that I had found the needle in the haystack. I began to make a move toward the figure who resembled the woman I loved but I was hit by a passer-by and soon found myself being knocked back and forth in the on-rushing partygoers. I weathered the storm, pushing through the traffic and past the bar staff who were chucking coupons into the uninterested crowds. I rushed through the sweaty bar and put an arm on the shoulder I had held so many times.

“Scar,” I said, almost sobbing.

“Get your hands off me!” She shrieked, falling backward as she turned to face me.

My heart sank again, and I allowed myself a moment of hesitation before turning my back on the stranger and sinking into the floor without even muttering a word of apology. I re-entered the crowds and headed for the nearest hostel as quick as I could.

I should have known better. Scar loved that shell necklace, she’d never have taken it off.

*

I tossed and turned that night. I was kicking myself for rushing the past few days and not enjoying the ambient life that prospered around me as I had always tried to do. But it was different now, I was focused, fuelled, and found myself almost rushing toward my final destination, wherever that was to be. I was on the finishing straight and just as an Olympian would, I was accelerating round the final bend and tearing up the final one hundred metre track at a speed I hadn't shown before. I promised myself that it was almost over, and I could live in harmony with all that I had seen around me, all that I had gained, and those that I had lost.

Chapter 78

How far South?

I left Bangkok early the next morning, heading south toward the Gulf, at this point wondering where exactly I was heading. I had no idea what to look for or where to go, I just knew I needed to get to the Gulf and all would be well. I hoped.

I headed South on highway three, following the coastal route that weaved in and out with the lie of the land. It was nothing more than tarmac in places, in other places potholes were almost filled in but left unfinished and further away from Bangkok there where potholes that had never been considered worthy enough for a filling in. In an extreme thought process, I considered the journey might have been what it was like driving a thirty-two seater across the moon but I didn't mind, it was getting me toward my goal and for that I was grateful.

I jumped off the bus at Pattaya City. What was once a small fishing village, Pattaya now took the form of Bangkok's little brother. The streets were lined with resorts, clubs and shimmering cocktail bars that spilled out onto the sandy beaches. The beaches themselves were beautiful, albeit ruined by the countless deckchairs, blaring sound systems and designated swimming areas. It wasn't here I would find anything, so I walked further south until I was out of the town and away from the blaring music. I continued south to the bay of Dongtan beach which led out to a scatter of equally beautiful islands, or so I imagined. I contemplated jumping on a local crossing boat and running around these islands indefinitely but instead continued along highway three. And as if God himself (or Jasper) had praised me for continuing along the highway, a mile or so past my contemplation, I stumbled across a bicycle being sold. In a significant effort to maintain my positive spirit, and drive away the thought that I hadn't the slightest idea what I was looking for or why I had traipsed halfway across the globe for it, I made my way to the door of the little bungalow.

The house itself was actually considerably better off than the street it fell on judging by the patioed steps toward the red door and the water feature that had been placed on the middle of the lawn. I knocked and waited. After a few seconds and just prior to a second knock, the door swung cautiously open. At first I wondered who, if anyone, had opened the door, then upon looking down, I discovered a Thai youngster in just a pair of white Y fronts. It made me smile as he partially hid behind the door, frizzy haired and bleary eyed as he preceded to yawn at my presence. I was just about to begin a conversation into how much he wanted for the bike when his mother came rushing to the door screaming in the native tongue. In a violent thrust he had been ripped from behind the door and away back into the house. The mother took his place, standing her ground slightly more than the child had by filling the doorway. She was clearly taken back to see a white face at her door.

"The bike?" I said unconvincingly. My Thai was non-existent.

She returned a face that suggested this could be a long conversation, so I began miming the action of riding a bike. I then preceded it with a point toward the chained beast that hung off the tree by the road. I was pleasantly surprised by the speed at which dialogue had been passed and soon she began shooting numbers at me in a rustic English.

"One hundred – zero, two hundred – zero, one hundred – zero, half?" (One thousand, two thousand, five-hundred, I think.)

"Baht?" I replied inquisitively.

She nodded, looking behind her at the youngster who had reappeared with a t-shirt on over his head but his arms not yet following the decision to put the t-shirt on entirely. It lay limp around his neck as they both looked back at me, their eyes egging the money out of my pocket like two sets of magnets. I handed over one-thousand baht (around twenty-four pound) and the woman hastily slid me a key and shut the door in my face. Negotiations with a smile.

I fondled the key in my hand as I made my way back to the bike and slid the rusty metal into more rusty metal. The lock fell to the floor with a crash and I turned the bike toward the road. With a second thought I decided to slide the lock into Mr Lowe Alpine, perhaps it would come in handy.

Impressed with my new wheels, I was soon tearing up highway three, a buzz that I was flying. Racing towards wherever again. I was live, exuberated, free! Like Aquila, I was once again soaring, painting my own future. I flew through thirty minutes of out of the seat action and a plethora of woops and yeehaw's, not to mention an uncountable number of waves to locals (who I may add, seemed incredibly excited to see me). It soon left me exhausted, slumped over the handlebars and sweating indefinitely. In a bid for respite I jumped off the mile killer and walked it down a rickety road that cut through the Thai jungle. *Too rocky to be able to cycle here* I said in a futile attempt to convince myself that I wasn't unfit. Must've been the climate.

The path crawled left and right, up and down for the best part of fifteen minutes before the rocks and earthy path gave way to sand that soon got lost in a beautiful turquoise ocean. As I made to leave the dark canopies behind and feed my skin with the light of the world, the sun faded and was replaced by dark, menacing clouds. It all happened so quickly, like a comic book extract or flipping a coin. I went from picturesque beauty to unfathomable misfortune.

So, I found myself standing on a beautiful beach in the pissing rain, as a roaring wind and unprompted claps of thunder echoed around my world. In that moment I wondered – *what the fuck am I doing?*

Chapter 79

End of the chase

The rain continued to pour for hours and despite my hope, the secluded beach between the provinces of Rayong and Chanthaburi had failed me. The world had turned from a beautiful mistress to a terrifying alien. In despair I left without looking back, the shattering wind almost pushing me away. My mind had become clouded and I was confused and vulnerable once more. I felt there was nothing to achieve and wondered for my sanity. I wished to be back in my London flat, or in the Frisco hostel, smashing my head again and again till the flow of blood opened my eyes to reality. The world we live in – is it all just a fabricated fantasy of lies and apathy? I stumbled back toward the highway, why? I didn't know. Would I ever know? I didn't think so. I was once again consumed by the idea that perhaps there was nothing for me. *Is there actually a way out? Is a dream just a false façade of what you desire but can't have?*

The path of roots and boulders became the devil in me and sucked the despair out, replacing it with anger and frustration. Both of which I'd hardly felt since leaving the Mayfair Journal or my petty little flat. In an instant, I had jumped back on my bike and was pedalling as hard and as fast as I possibly could. This time I pedalled for hours, feeling exhausted but never stopping. I pedalled through the night, the cars that passed becoming few and far between. The jungle came alive around me as human civilisation diminished and I was left to my own devices. In a land I'd never explored, on a road I'd never travelled. I screamed. As I had done on the top of Gokyo Ri, but this time it was painful, a plea of help. I can't to this day decipher how far I actually got, my adrenaline and frustration pumping me further and further until I began passing signs toward Cambodia and Namtok Phlio National Park, the latter which was significantly closer. I pressed on further and further, looking into the darkness through squinted eyes. My jaw was clenched with exasperation until I collapsed with exhaustion. I'd ran into the hands of those I had met and those I had loved and it was with that thought that I knew; if all future hopes and desires fail, if I can't find the final chapter, the journey was still a beautiful success.

*

I woke to the sound of passing cars once more. The light was still dark, but the morning was close to breaking and the cars passed without bothering with lights or beams. The bicycle remained stuck between both my legs, my right pressed firmly into the ground against its will. I had collapsed whilst on it and brought it down into the shrubbery with me but now I brought the life back into it as it did to me and deflecting the scampering looks of local passer-by's, I scrambled to my feet with a resurgence. Onwards we go.

I soon reached Thailand's south-eastern province of Trat and uninspired at the prospect of crossing yet another border in search of redemption, I found myself at the pier of Laem Sok. The first boat didn't leave for the island of Koh Kood for another hour, so I found myself hungry for the first time in a day. I walked my bike along the four-zero-zero-eight road in the knowledge I had time to kill. The sun was shining again, and the trees blew delicately in the cool morning breeze. I felt hope in the idea that the world had woken up to boost my mood of the night before and in return I did my best to remain uplifted but for the negative light flickering at the back of my mind. Though those same questions floated around my head, I skipped in and out of the dappled tree light in various attempts to elevate myself. Despite my surroundings I feel ashamed to say I remained apprehensive and far from relaxed. *Perhaps it just wasn't to be? Would my whole existence be plagued with questions like these?* I pushed on and even began humming to myself to change my train of thought. A placebo at best.

I soon made it to Loma's Coffee House which stood braising in the sunlight. It reminded me of Seffe's coffee house, albeit more modern and significantly busier. Laughter ricocheted around the sheltered tables and for a moment I forgot all about my worries and questions. It reminded me of the quirky independent coffee houses you find in backstreet London, where the staff laugh and greet you like lifelong friends, offering vast selections of syrups, vegan milks, and cupcakes to go alongside your coffee. It was equally as westernised as those places. I delicately placed my bike against a tree, just metres from where I would eventually sit.

Approaching the counter, I was greeted by a beautiful Thai.

"Good morning, my name is Karnchana. How are you?"

I found myself stuck between an equilibrium of wondering why her name tag said Kara and answering her question. "Well, thank you. How are you?" I replied after deciding, like the café, her name had been westernised for customer approval. I wasn't sure whether I approved of that reasoning, but it wasn't my worry. "Karnchana is a beautiful name," I said after much deliberation of the topic.

"Thank you, Sir," she responded softly. "Can I get you anything?" She asked again after I had failed to hear or reply the first time, too deep into the westernisation of Thailand.

"Oh sorry, erm." We both looked at the lengthening queue behind me, which caused my decision to be taken in haste and with little deliberation. Mango smoothie it was. (After all, Thailand is the third largest producer of mangoes in the world, with over three and a half million tonnes of the fruit being produced per year – impressive, huh?)

The smoothie itself went a way to perking me up as did Kara with her wonderful smile. I sat in one of the chairs overlooking a flowing field or plantation of some kind and took a deep breath. *Calm. Calm.* I forced myself to breath slowly. To take it all in and appreciate where I was and how far I had come. Alec had said it himself, it would come - perhaps it will be a moment, somewhere special where you're tranquil and undisturbed. It made me think of Alec and Ralph and once again of Scar. How incredible I had felt with them, like I was flying in the sky, in Alec's city, embracing every moment and forever happy. Then I thought once more of my adventures after, the countless embraces of interaction and beauty. I decided in that moment to forever live with a smile on my face and forget about chasing the happy ending. If it wanted to, it would come to me. I slurped up the remaining mango smoothie and laid a healthy tip on the table. *You make my day, I'll make yours Kara.*

*

I was soon back at the pier and feeling the full force of my decision to stop seeking and start living, I found myself wrapped up in a debate with some other English travellers whether the east was better than the west. I was voting in favour of the east and threw the debate in our favour, four to two.

We jumped on the Koh Kood Express, a ninety minute boat ride.

"But I wouldn't want to live out here you know," one said.

"Look around you man, of course you would," another said.

The first turned up his nose. "Wouldn't the beauty fade if you constantly surrounded yourself with it?" The idea was met with some quizzing faces. He had a point, didn't he?

"You have a point," I chipped in with my traveller confidence. "But the westernised world of big jobs, fame and influences is such a burden on our own dreams. Don't you think as you grow older you change because of other people? Sometimes against our will. Look at consumerism," I listened to myself, I sounded just as Jasper would. *Hell, where is Jasp?* I continued. "You need new shoes, go to the shop and see the worst pair you've ever seen. A week later you go back and that's all they sell because that's what all the famous people are wearing. The shoes on my feet now have holes in so I need to buy a new pair. I have to buy these ones that I hate. Eventually I force myself to like them and now I'm changed. But not the way I necessarily wanted."

They nodded.

"Here you can be yourself," I muttered, more of a thought than a conversation. We all stood deliberating for a moment.

The one that had initially sparked the debate became lively again. "Right, how about forever in the mountains or forever by the sea."

He seemed pleased with himself as the divide this time became unrecognisable and the debate continued until the boat touched down on Koh Kood.

*

I was once more travelling on my own and a refreshing chat with other likeminded people had got me to Koh Kood in prodigious spirits. The island itself was the fourth largest Thai island, twenty-five kilometres from top to bottom, so I made the subconscious decision to head west, as far from the port as I could.

I followed the Pho Cho Trat road for the most part, choosing to deviate at my own will. I threw myself into the plunge pool at Klong Yai Ki, to the amazement of the locals, before standing insignificantly underneath the great Sai Yai Chai tree. It reminded me of standing underneath the great redwoods of California and again I was reminded of how far I had come as the dappled sunlight beamed into my eyes and vibrated a wave of life all across the jungle. The nature reserve itself was a land of untouched beauty, vines hung from trees and great sounds reverberated across the jungle floor. I wandered aimlessly through the jungle, getting lost in its charm and eventually came to find myself upstream from the popular Huang Thap Kwang waterfall, hidden by the jungle that enclosed in around the pool. Another piece of paradise.

Before I knew it, the day was again escaping me and the darkness began to loom over the trees. I made my way back to my bicycle, that I had locked to a road sign earlier, and paved my way south once more, eager to wake the next day in solitude. It was gone ten o'clock by the time I stopped pedalling and that meant another night sleeping wild. I'd become quite use to it by now and the prospect no longer fazed me. I scrambled through the jungle in the dark and found my way onto the beach of Ban Ao Jak. The sand was light under my feet and because of the darkness, it hadn't retained any of the heat that it had soaked up during the day so was cool and pleasant. The water crashed softly to my left and though I couldn't see it, I imagined it to be only a few metres away. The moon lit up the ocean afar in a beautiful canvas of darkness and light that merged with the starry sky above. I stumbled forward with my hands out in front hoping to find some sort of hammock to rest in.

After some while of mimicking an old man waddling forward with caution and a bent back, I kicked my foot into something hard. It fuzzed and shot a sharp pain.

"Fuck," I whispered, as if scared to wake the fish. I grunted a few times before the pain subdued and I began inquisitively feeling that in front of me.

It didn't take me long to feel it to be a boat, a wooden rowing boat maybe. Without second thought, my weary eyes and knackered legs threw me into the boat, and I lay to rest with my head tucked into the bow. My eyes shut heavy and absolute as I fell into a deep sleep to the sound of the rolling waves.

*

I dreamt dreams of crusades, adventures, beauty. I dreamt I was a pirate sailing off with a map in hand, leading my valiant men to eternal glory and fighting off mutineers with terrifying menace. Of course, the compass read south, and it is there that all great things lay. The piles of gold, glistening like a city above us, the gallant sculpted ship that lay empty and marooned on the desert island. It was all perfect and I was the greatest captain to ever sail the seas.

I turned my head and entered a new world. Carving my way through a jungle, slashing at that in my way with a great sabre that shone under the dappled light above. Dragons roared around me, hiding from the eye of the sword that devastated anything that stood in its way, I was the great saviour of the modern world and the hordes of people that I had saved from the wrath of a violent dictator flung themselves at my feet. I maintained the equilibrium of the world, and while the beasts that hid feared me, they were safe. Safe in a world of prosperity and freedom. The people's world. The everyone's world. Everyone and everything. The population sang behind me as I carved civilisation through the difficulties that we endured, *Cap'n No—aahh, No—aahh*. They shrieked in time to the melodic beat of the drums. *Boom-Boom-Bo-Boom.*

Boom-Boom-Bo-Boom.

Chapter 80

Liberation

I woke bleary eyed and sat transfixed, with my eyes shut, listening to the crashing of the waves. It sounded further away than it did the night before but was equally calm. Harmoniously breaking against the sand. I listened to each part of the waves progress, how it grew in sound as it rose and then crashing as it fell with gravity against the floor. The warping sound as it slunk back into the ocean, falling away from the beach until it was lost in the next wave. Rise, fall, retreat, repeat. I sat silent listening for some time until my world opened up to the sound of the jungle past my feet. This time I opened my eyes, my sight was immediately met with trees that bent overhead, their leaves spanning wider than you can reach and fruits hanging delicately, fruits larger than you can ever imagine. It was still early morning and the sun was only just beginning to rise, producing a dappled light coming through the trees. I sat up in the boat and immediately felt refreshed from the cool morning breeze that gently pushed against the side of my face. I took a deep breath, inhaling from the bottom of my lungs the smells of the salty sea that lingered just metres away, with my back to the sea I could hear it fizzing, as the bubbles from the waves disappeared into the sand below. Despite all my travels I had hardly paid attention to the sounds of the sea, an orchestra of nature and relaxation.

I stood up and stretched before stepping out of the boat onto the crisp white sand, my imprints from the night before had now become faint and the new ones I began creating dominated them with an air of supremacy. It was only now after walking five strides away from the boat that I allowed myself a glimpse of the sea before me. The Gulf of Thailand, spreading out across the island's panorama in a hypnotic illusion of a never-ending plain. The water remained unmoved but for the rolling waves metres from my feet and I found myself in a surround sound of developing waves and early morning jungle tones, three minutes past six to be exact. I continued to stroll delicately down the beach, approaching each step like it was my last, in an attempt to maintain the beauty of everything that was around me. I reached about halfway between the boat and the jungle path I had clambered through the night before and stood there. Still, silent, watching, listening, dreaming.

I stood there with my eyes shut for five minutes before slowly peeling off my t-shirt and wandering slowly into the water. I again found myself taking extreme care to avoid ruining the scene and each footstep was quaint and delicate, minute ripples running away from the area that my feet pierced the water. The water level against my body rose as I waded fluidly further into the sea. It eventually reached my waist, no more than twenty metres from shore and I stood still, letting the ripples around me fade into non-existence. With the sun beating against my back I put my hands in the air, a V shape like Jasper had done so many times. This time it felt perfect and I let my head roll back, my face engrossed in the light of the day. I soaked it up like a beacon of light, it warming my soul and pushing everything negative far, far away. Cast far enough away for me to never worry about a thing again, all things bad hanging to the edge of my universe in a futile attempt to reinfest my brain. It was worthless, I was free. Away from the darkness and in the light. I was the light. I closed my eyes and breathed a deep breath once more. This was it. I had done it.

I felt a wave of liberation rush my soul, it made me feel complete. The last piece of the puzzle. I was free, ready to embrace life for what it is. Ready to prove to myself that Jasper didn't die in vain and ready to live life to the fullest. That's all you can ever do really, and I had found over the past year how amazing you can feel in doing so. I thought again of where I'd been, who I'd met, how far I'd gone to breaking, and how far I'd come back. I'd dip once, and then again, getting dragged left and right, but I always found a way back. This was my life and I wasn't going to let another moment pass me by. Life is holy, and unfortunately life isn't given to everyone. *Make the most of what you have.*

Jasper waded through the water equally carefully as I had and stood next to me gorging off the suns power. He began to play his guitar, as he had done so many times on our adventures together, when we'd sing, dance, and embrace the energy of each other and all that was around us. It was a familiar tune I knew all too well and I began singing softly as I always had in his company. It fitted the scene perfectly, creating something sacred. The sound skipped off the water's surface, cleansing the ocean we stood in, pushing an aura far and wide across the Gulf. I sang for a few minutes, my eyes closed and my mind bewildered with the magical place I had found myself in. I was grateful to everything. Everyone. My music eventually faded as did Jaspers guitar and he put his arm over my shoulder and without speaking a word, we laughed, together forever, his head resting on my shoulder as we stared out toward the light at the end of the tunnel, the great sparkle of the ocean. We laughed contagiously, one that grew and grew until he disappeared and left me laughing alone. My laugh became wobbly as his arm was replaced by a gentle sea breeze. How I would look for him in the future and he wouldn't be there, never to be seen again. I waited for the loneliness. Only, it never came. He would be with me forever, and I would never be alone.

*

It was ten past six when I stepped outside, escaping the stuffy room that I'd been forced to share with Alec and Ralph. I slipped on my flip flops and tied my blonde hair into a ponytail, before walking quietly away from the little cabin in the woods. It was an idyllic spot, but it still hadn't helped me sleep. Riddled with nightmares and thoughts since the day we were separated. I figured I would forever have restless nights and it was something that I would have to live with - in my idiocy of leaving, I would have to live with. I brushed the loose strands of hair that had resisted the grasp of my hairband from my face and retied them behind me as I began down the path toward the beach. I enjoyed these morning strolls away from the boys. I only felt free when I was alone, alone to think. Reminiscing what was and dreaming what could have been. I wish I could be with him now. Know where he was or at least have a way to find him. I'd do so in an instant; he had my heart and I knew there would be no one else like him. I had travelled back to Seffe's two weeks after leaving only for him to tell me Noah had left a few days before. It broke my heart and not even a sincere Tito could settle me down. We'd travelled across the world chasing after him always a few steps behind. We'd spoken to people that had seen a lone Englishman and others that thought we were mental. Maybe we were. We had reached the Laem Sok pier and despite hopeful news from the friendly Koh Kood Express ticket seller, the trail had gone cold. Our luck had finally run out. We were out of ideas. I looked up from the ground where I'd been staring in contemplation. My hands folded over my chest. I'd felt insecure since. Why? I had no idea, but I guess it's something about that niche saying of, they're my rock. I understood it.

Deep in my imagination and fantasies of being back with the one I love so dearly, I didn't see the beautiful sunshine that had begun to rise for the day ahead, nor did I see the bike thrown onto the forest floor with its handlebars twisted and its thick rusted lock draped around the frame. I didn't hear the beautifully soft singing in the distance, toward the ocean, only just louder than the mesmerising waves that crashed forever meticulously in this world. I was lost in my imagination. A world I would much rather be walking in – until it became reality.

It was only as I stepped out of the narrow jungle pathway and onto the beach that I noticed a figure looking out to sea, standing fifteen metres or so to my left. Who? I addressed his appearance with an attentive air, but I hadn't got far in my assumptions as he turned and looked straight at me, as if he was expecting me to come out onto the beach at that exact moment. He smiled softly, nothing more and nothing less. I was sure I heard him say - *you made it*, but his mouth hadn't moved from that precious yet unconvincing smile, so I figured it was all in my head. I smiled back at him and soon began wondering what he had been staring at as he returned to what had initially caught his attention and produced a beaming smile that would last for all eternity. I began following his sight but was stopped as he began falling backward and I went to scream only for nothing to come out. Instead, I stood in shock. Shocked as he disappeared, gone. Poof. I looked left and right, puzzled, but damn sure he'd gone. I wiped my bleary eyes and shook my head in disgust of my sanity. I wanted to cry but I'd lost it all, even the ability to do that.

Out to sea I saw a person. He was laughing and now I knew what the disappearing figure had been looking at. Why was he staring at this person in the water? I walked closer to the shore. And with that, a laugh I'd reminisced over, a laugh that had filled my world since the day I had heard it. It was a laugh that I had learnt to love and a love I had wanted to never live without. My body froze in shock and my face became flustered. Imagination becoming reality. My eyes watered as I stabilised myself, my body felt suddenly weak and dreary. As the tears began to flow steady down my face, I made a scream, a dying scream, but a scream of life and compassion. A scream of never let me go, and a scream of – *is it you?*

He turned round, his red eyes looking softly back at me as tears streamed down his face and an alluding, unforgettable smile filled my world. His face told the story of a thousand of my dreams. Freedom. Liberation. Redemption. Peace. Immersion. I didn't know whether to collapse to the floor or run through the water, so I did both.

I never looked back.

Printed in Great Britain
by Amazon